TULIPS IN THE SNOW

Tulips in the Snow

Cay Towner

Dear Anissa

Merry Christmas 2013!

Enjoy the sultry hottie....

Cay.

First published using CreateSpace in 2013

ISBN 978-1484190906

In memory of Anne Elizabeth Harwood
(aka Smiley)
1969 – 2009
Much loved, much missed

Prologue

1830

'I often think there is an almost primeval pleasure to be gained from the simple act of chopping an onion. So many meals begin with such a humble task, it's as if it creates inside us a very pure link to all the mothers, who for thousands of years, have begun to provide a meal for their families, by chopping a lowly onion, on a plain wooden board.'

Elizabeth looked down at her own hands as her knife slice-crunched down and wondered at the capacity of her mother's calm voice to steady her in moments of difficulty.

'Grandma!' cried Freddie, Elizabeth's youngest, as his elm chair scraped backwards across the brick kitchen floor and he ran over to greet her joyfully.

'Well, if you wouldn't mind helping with such a simple act,' said Elizabeth, kissing her mother on each cheek, 'I'd be humbly grateful. I'm just behind with everything today.'

'A pleasure, my dear,' she said, unwrapping herself and shaking off the snow. 'Freddie, you're to fetch a stool here to keep me company while I work, if you please.'

Then Elise herself looked down at the dappled, undulating, walnut terrain of her own skin, stretched now as it was over bone, as she took up the next brown-papered orb and started to unwrap its goodness.

'Grandma,' said Freddie, organising himself on a high stool beside her, 'didn't you used to live in our house, when you were a little girl?'

'A little girl and beyond; I grew up here.'

'So, you might be able to answer my question?'

'If you give me a hint of it, I suspect I might, Freddie.'

'Why, Grandma, do we live in one house with two front doors? I mean, there's the front door that everybody uses, that lands you straight into the sitting room and then there's this front door, that you've just come through, which brings you into Mother's kitchen.'

'Why, this isn't the front door, Freddie,' said his mother, carefully cutting a handful of thyme tips from one of the herb pots that stood on the windowsill, 'this is just the kitchen door.'

'But kitchen doors are at the side or on the back, Mother. Ours is at the front and if you walk over to the other side of the lane and look back at them, both of the doors are exactly the same, the same size and the same decoration, the beautiful leaves entwined with roses, both of them along the top: two front doors.'

'Roses?' queried his grandmother.

'Oh, Freddie, with everything that's gone on today!' said Elizabeth, good naturedly enough, slamming a sizable wedge of stewing steak down onto a board and taking up a broad blade.

'The events of today have nothing to do with Freddie, do they?' said his grandmother.

'No, not exactly,' he whispered back, 'but we must be kind to Mother; she and Father seem terribly cross about Susannah.'

His grandmother smiled back her approval to Freddie and winked.

'You'll be pleased to hear, Freddie, that I can tell you exactly why you live in a single house with two front doors. I must, however, make you aware,' and she lifted her forefinger to him, just before finishing the last chopped onion and readying to take them over to the range to soften, 'that the tale is a long and complicated one, which might be too much for a boy of your years to take in and listen to for such a length of time.'

Freddie jumped down and followed his grandmother with his stool noisily hobble-bobbling behind him. He climbed back up, a sensible distance from the frying pan his grandmother was sliding butter into and leant sideways onto the brick surround.

'I suppose you'll never know, Grandma,' he said, shaking his head but then smiling coyly, fingering the warm bricks, 'unless you try me.'

His grandmother looked in his direction and arched her eyebrows.

'Well then,' she said, 'the question is,' and she searched for a moment with her wizened forehead furrowed, 'where to begin?'

Chapter One

Freddie's grandmother watched the soft yellow butter melt as she travelled back through the waving cornfields of time to the vibrant green pastures of her childhood. Tableaux from the early rural tales of her life in Heartbourne presented themselves to her, but no, she thought, I need to travel back further than that, if I'm to explain where the seed of the difficulty was sown and took root.

'There was once a priest of this village,' she began.

'What, like Father?'

'Just like your father, Freddie, and even more like you.'

'How can that be, Grandma?' a self-assured girl of fourteen sauntered into the room and slid her arm around her grandmother's waist, 'He's not Christ-like, he's just like any other seven year old brother; a trial *beyond* belief.'

The onions sizzled into the hot butter as Freddie pulled a face at his supercilious sister.

'Simmer down, the pair of you,' their mother intervened, 'Catherine, come and help with the carrots, please.'

Catherine joined her mother beside the table and the three women worked; one diced, one peeled, one softened. There was a brief hiatus in the conversation, during which a stair board creaked loudly. Elizabeth's eyes met her mother's but neither woman stopped what she was about.

'There was once a priest of this village named Thomas Porter. Both in his heart and his actions, he was a devout and kind man, in line with the two most important, over and above The Ten. He had a wife, called Anna and finally, after many years of patience, a daughter of the same name. All, however, did not fare well. Anna's mother cradled her infant child in candlelit starlight for a mere half hour before slipping into a sleep of eternal peace.'

'That does sometimes happen, doesn't it, Grandma?'

'It does, my son, and the sadness of the experience for Thomas Porter, who had so tenderly loved his wife, led him not to trust but to be afraid.

'The priest raised his daughter Anna himself, allowing kindly matrons of the parish to help with the practical matters of life, in addition to the two maidservants, which was all the paid help his stipend would allow. Anna's spiritual life and her awareness of her fellow man were guided and directed closely by her father. She grew up to be a beautiful and caring child, who was well known and well-loved within the community. Some matrons, however, well-meaningly I'm sure, began to use the word 'sheltered' as they watched Anna visiting the sick, while her contemporaries had begun to walk out, holding hands.

"Protected', was the word Mr Porter preferred, when village opinion politely but inevitably reached the reverend's ears.

'The voice of the Heartbourne matrons, however, obliged him to contemplate that which he'd been postponing for two or more years by this time: Anna's womanhood. As he looked at her using a hoe to weed the vegetable patch, or shaking out the sheets to lend a hand with this week's laundry, it was no longer a little girl that he saw before him and he grew afraid, afraid of what might be.

'Out of what he believed to be kindness and protection, he began to make enquiries about the possibility of Anna joining the nearby convent of St Olivia, situated just half a day's ride away. He wrote letters to the bishop and the abbess, outlining the depth and the breadth of Anna's theological knowledge and understanding, but was rather surprised when they both wrote back expressing their concern that Anna was simply too young, at the age of sixteen, for such a path to be considered.'

'Six-teen?' Catherine mouthed to her mother but Elizabeth simply raised a finger to her lips.

'The priest comforted himself for a while with the thought that he couldn't ever have borne for Anna to be so far removed from where he himself ministered and dwelled. As he listened to her reading to him in the evenings, he regarded her and contented himself with the notion that she was not a woman, yet.

'It was but a standing-tide of time; there was a precious, languorous summer, when Anna and her father could often be

11

seen walking arm in arm and laughing, delighting in each other's company, around the lanes and fields of the village.

'Then there were the uncharacteristically thunderous sermons in church, where he preached at great length about the sins of the flesh. Common folks remarked that he might be having a mildly beneficial effect on one or two of the more down-at-the-heel Heartbourne milkmaids; Retty Browne and Penny Barlow had looked particularly horrified the Sunday after Harvest Festival but then again their ruddy complexions might simply have been the result of too much dancing the night before.'

'Hmm, 'dancing' and maybe in just the ways Mr Porter –'

Elizabeth halted Catherine's interruption with her elbow, gesticulating in Freddie's direction.

'Others noticed that he might almost have been speaking to his daughter alone, so directed was his gaze, while her eyes remained upon her prayer book and her cheeks, the purest pale.'

Their grandmother removed the pan from the hot plate and added the onions to the dish of deep, dark stock, which sat waiting on the warming plate next to Freddie's stool. She then walked across to the kitchen table, to receive the beef for browning, which just happened to give her the opportunity to lean in closely to Elizabeth and Catherine's hearing.

'And, or so it was told, there was an occasion when Billy Smithers had a quart pot more than he ought to've at the Gun Inn and shot his mouth off declaring roundly, 'There's no sin of incontinence in that girl, the dance has not yet begun with her, the only person wetting themselves around here, is the priest himself!'

'Mother!' whispered Elizabeth, trying to muster a disapproving scowl, while Catherine's somewhat feebly suppressed merriment leaked out, destroying Elizabeth's composure briefly, before she waved her hand above Catherine's head and glared at her mother in an imitation of serious censure.

'Grandma?' said Freddie.

'Mind the fat doesn't spit on you now, Freddie, and pay heed.

'Mr Porter then fell into serious contemplation regarding Anna's future. He took it upon himself to observe more closely, the, shall we say, less spiritual and more earthly goings on among the adolescent population of his parish. He undertook two somewhat innocent-minded forays, which could only be described as naive, both of which ended in his rushing back to the vicarage with an extremely flushed face, suffering from hyper-ventilation and needing at least half an hour's worth of relief in close communication with a brown paper bag.

'As a result, his thoughts of preserving Anna safely from the physical dangers of womanhood and childbirth became overwhelmed with the far more potent fear of her immortal soul being led astray and corrupted forever. In short, he decided, she was to be married.'

'A brown paper bag, Grandma?' said Freddie, trying not to look as if this was all beyond him.

'At six-teen?' Catherine's incredulous voice rang out, 'To be married at sixteen? Why, Susannah's eighteen, Mama, and –'

'Anna was seventeen by this time, wasn't she, Mother?' asked Elizabeth quickly.

'She was, but only just. But you're all missing the point, I'm sure. Does it matter what age she was? Or, is the point that the dance, as Billy Smithers had so adeptly put it, had not yet begun with her?'

'Who was Billy Smithers, Grandma? And what's he got to do with our story?'

'Is the point that, what was operating here, was fear and fear alone, not love? Might this be a point, which parents who mean so well, can so often miss?'

'Mother,' Elizabeth looked at her calmly, 'perhaps you'd best not interfere.'

'Interfere? My dear, nothing would be further out of character, as I'm sure you'd agree; I'm simply telling my grandchildren a story about their home.'

Chapter Two

1754

"Anna, Anna, where's my thick-lined jerkin? The mornings might be bright enough but it still turns chill by four and we'll have to work all the light hours God gives, if I'm to be home on Saturday for Theo's birthday.'

'It's where you left it, William Godstone, when you came home last Friday, on the peg in the rear lobby above your father's old adze.'

'Ah, so it is.' He leant for a moment, with his head on the wooden doorway, 'Now, will you stop stirring that porridge and come and wish your husband a safe journey and return?'

Anna moved away from the inglenook and scooped up her younger son Samuel from the flagstone floor, on her way over to her very endearing but ever so tardy husband.

'Kiss your baby son, will you ever get going? Jed'll be damning his eternal soul with cursing you, if the others move off before you've gained your pace.'

'Oh, Anna, a stonemason's life is a curious thing, always travelling and so often away from one's wife and children.' Will stroked Sam's cheek gently.

'You'll be home for Theo's birthday, that's what counts. There are worse ways to keep one's family warm and vital, I'm sure.' Anna spoke softly, as she allowed her husband to peck her on each cheek. 'Now will you ever –'

'I'm gone, I'm gone,' and finally, with due speed, Will departed from the house and deposited his tool bag in the cart outside. The cart had already been carefully laden with provisions prepared by Anna and a habitually patient pony had been hitched up, waiting for his master to board, for some half hour or more besides.

Now, Will whistled softly to the pony, winked at his waving wife and they were off to pick up Jed and head away for another week's labour.

Anna was left on her own during the week. She was by now twenty-seven and had borne her husband two sons: Theo, who was about to turn seven and Samuel, who was still a babe of seven months. As the daughter of a priest, she'd been brought up to be tolerant and patient and she was genuinely and intensely fond of her husband, despite the lack of discipline in his timekeeping and his inability to remember where he'd put down his book or his scarf or his elder child's shoe (or indeed, whether the unfindable shoe, was one he'd yet polished or not). She was aware that he was a little younger than her in his soul but she chose not to condemn him for youthfulness, preferring to believe that her own rather serious-minded nature was perhaps a little premature, brought on by her motherless childhood and the sacred bent of her father's mind, with his thoughts so constantly and righteously focused on his vocation.

As she stood there waving, Anna felt herself to be blessed; she had two healthy sons and a caring husband who rose out of bed and earned a stable living for them all each week. She felt she was more blessed than Retty Gables, who'd had three babes all born still and who, they were saying, had begun to take to drinking before noon as a consequence. Anna didn't quite like to believe it. She had Retty on her mind though and made a mental note to slip in on her later, after finishing the pew end posies for Bert Pickens' funeral.

She felt she was blessed by God, as her father had always told her she would be, if she maintained an honest and thankful heart. As she gazed at the April beauty of the spring fields beyond the lane her husband had just vacated, she felt a pulling on her skirt. It was Theo.

'Mother, don't worry, I'll look after you, when Papa's gone.'

As Anna crouched down to level with him, Theo slipped his arms about her neck.

'Of course you will, my son and heir, of course you will.'

'And may I have my breakfast now?' he asked, with a beaming smile upon his sun-warmed face.

'You may indeed, my valiant protector, you may indeed,' said Anna, as she scooped him up into her arms and hugged him.

Chapter Three

'Now, upon Anna's marriage, Thomas Porter had procured for her and William a reduced rental rate upon a small cottage in Heartbourne. It belonged to a parishioner who'd become an admiring friend of Anna's father, over the passage of his many years of ministry. The cottage was not large but its position at the edge of the village, down a very short lane, with only two other attached cottages, was idyllic. The cottage was placed at the end in the terrace and, being a preferred tenant, upon hearing of Anna's love of cottage gardening and growing all manner of plants, her landlord promptly carved up the neighbouring field declaring roundly it had, 'Always been ungainly large.' This produced a very sizable garden for Anna. Over the seasons, Anna had filled her garden, dividing it, on each side of a neat lawn, into a series of avenues: those which bore vegetables in the sun; those which produced sweet peas or lavender to fragrance her home throughout the height of summer and those which were laden with berries, by the time the autumn mists began to rise. Near the kitchen, there was a smaller, sheltered section, marked off into squares, divided by bricks laid in herring bone fashion by Anna's own hand. This housed her herb garden, producing among other delights, rosemary which would later in the year be very essential to the suet pudding which would surround the Christmas beef and sage and thyme to flavour her family's dishes throughout the long, long winter-tide. All in all, Anna's garden considerably enriched their family home and table. William's life as a stonemason could be hard and although his gang were well known and respected, there were often breaks between contracts when life might have become austere, had it not been for Anna's industry in her garden. Herbs, onions, chutney and jam were always in plenty, even on the odd occasion when the meat ration was a little slenderer than usual.

On the morning that our story begins, Anna was supposed to be arranging the flowers in church for the funeral of poor Bert Pickens, which was to be officiated over by her father later that

day. Anna was in the kitchen, clearing away Theo's breakfast
things while talking to Sam, who was babbling in his wooden
high chair. The vastly more mature Theo, having consumed his
very own favourite (hot, creamy porridge oats graced with a
spoonful of honey) was now on his way out of the door to join
with a neighbour's son for the short walk to their day's toil and
play at school.

'Yoo-hoo!' called a familiar voice around the door and
without waiting for an invitation in strolled Anna's neighbour,
Millie Price. 'And how are my favourite eastward neighbours
today?'

'Just off to school, Millie Price,' called Theo backwards.
'Good-bye, Mother!'

'Why does he always do that, d'you think?' asked Millie, with
her head on one side like a thoughtful sparrow, as the open
door let in the sounds of Anna's clucking chickens.

'Do what?'

'Call me, 'Millie Price', instead of just plain, Millie. It makes
me feel like some kind of an oddity, which I'm sure you'll agree
I'm not, but then again, that's probably just because you're just
too polite to say any different.'

'Would you like a cup of tea, Millie?'

'And now you're trying not to smirk.'

'I'm not!'

'No, of course not, ever the clergyman's daughter, never to
tell a lie, you're not trying not to smirk, you're just failing
completely.'

'Too true, *Millie Price*,' said Anna nudging her good friend.
'Now, will you stop your fretting and fetch yourself a cup and
saucer from the dresser, that I might pour.'

'Oh, I thought you'd never ask,' said Millie and the two
young women organised and settled down to their second cup
of tea, as if this were to be any other day.

An hour later, Anna had tidied her kitchen, while hearing
how Penny and Ed Mires had been overheard rowing over the
price Penny had paid for a piece of beef brisket. She'd tidied
the bedrooms upstairs, while learning how old Mrs Smithers
had taken a tumble down the stairs and Billy and his wife were

trying to persuade her to come and live in a little more comfort and security with them but the stubborn old toad wasn't having a bar of it so far, insisting on maintaining her own independence, no matter how impractical this was becoming. She'd handed Millie her own set of secateurs, as she heard of how Rob Pickens had sucked on his pipe by the fire at the Gun Inn, with a glistening tear creeping down his ruddied cheek, telling of his father's last moments, as she cut dark crimson camellias from the bushes in her garden and laid them in a waiting trug, with twelve sombre strips of jet black ribbon within it.

Without warning, Millie's reverie on the moment was broken by the sound of another familiar voice, that of Judith, the third mistress of the cottages in their row of three. Judith was expecting her first child and although her voice was familiar, her urgent tone was not.

'Anna, Millie, come quickly, you must!' Judith called from the back doorway, holding the underside of her belly.

'Why, Judith, whatever's the matter?' asked Anna, hurrying to her.

'Is it the baby? Oh no, heavens forbid!' shrieked Millie.

'Millie, will you hush now,' said Anna, with uncharacteristic impatience. 'Judith, it's not the baby is it?'

Judith shook her head, still panting for breath.

'My word, what've you been doing?' Millie was off again, 'Running about the village, with a baby bouncing along in your belly!'

'Millie!' Anna interrupted her sharply and looked once more to Judith, who'd just about managed to compose herself.

'Oh, don't fall out; you've both got to help. You see, Mrs Gables has been put up at the Gun Inn overnight, '*the* Mrs Gables', as everybody calls her, without Retty knowing aught about it. Rumour has, apparently, reached her ear about, you know, Retty's 'little weakness', shall we say and she's arrived for her brother's funeral today, without so much as a word to her daughter-in-law, actually saying that she couldn't come at all.'

Judith was a relative newcomer to the village and hadn't crossed paths with *the* Mrs Gables before.

'Well, I'm sure it'll all be fine, I mean, even if the rumours about Retty have any truth about them at all, which I'm sure they don't, it's her uncle-in-law's funeral this afternoon, she surely possesses the sense,' Anna faltered at the contortion of Judith's lips, running from left to right on her face, 'to stay standing up straight?' Judith's lips formed a contorted rose bud and Anna just ventured, 'On this day?' before giving up any expectations whatsoever.

'Her husband Henry's been out of Heartbourne these two days, fetching relatives for Bert's funeral. Never mind just this morning, nobody's at all sure that Retty's been upright since he's been gone but we didn't think it'd be of any great consequence until her mother-in-law showed up.'

'Oh, Anna, whatever'll happen to Retty now?' squeaked Millie, before whispering as if confidentially, 'Don't you remember, before Mrs Gables moved away, when we were younger; we used to say she'd got attitudes out of the ark.'

'Out of the ark?' asked Judith.

'Oh no,' said Anna, leaning against the pink wall, her mind spinning back to her childhood, 'I remember Mrs Gables, I remember her well, how could anyone forget? She was a formidable force in an argument, I can tell you.'

'And, does she have opinions out of the ark?' asked Judith.

'Worse,' whispered Anna. 'She's got attitudes out of Leviticus.'

They all drew back.

'We need to act with haste or Retty'll be all undone, with a house at sixes and sevens, no doubt, with *the* Mrs Gables banging on her door.' Anna's thoughts moved quickly, 'Judith, can you mind Sam while I take Millie with me?'

'Of course, but what are you going to do?'

'I have a plan, I have a plan,' repeated Anna, running as she grabbed Millie by the arm, who squealed loudly before being bodily ejected from the garden into the lane.

'We need to run, but discreetly,' said Anna.

'Oh, do we now?' said Millie, before being jerked into action, being tugged along by Anna. 'And when exactly did I agree to all this malarkey?'

'When you became my friend, Millie Price.'

'Well, I'm sure that happened more by habit than by choice.'

'As do many marriages, but if people are good inside, it all works out just fine, in the main.'

Anna drew Millie discreetly to a trot as they were now approaching the bend into the long village lane. They looked southward towards the hub of the village, where the usual bustle of the day carried on. In addition to the sounds of chatting shoppers and beer barrels being hauled into the Gun Inn's cellar, a delivery vehicle was narrowing the highway on the curve of the lane, while a merchant was unloading a tray of cheeses for the village shop. A stable hand attempting to pass in the opposite direction with a cart of hay, was throwing ill looks and comments in the merchant's direction, for not pulling over to the wayside more fully, 'Making everybody's life a deal more difficult than 'ad to be.'

Suddenly, Anna stopped still, holding Millie's hand tightly. There, on the corner of the bend, stood The Gun Inn; in front of the same, stood Mrs Gables herself.

Mrs Gables was standing plumb square in the middle of the forecourt of the Gun Inn, dressed from head to toe in black silk, as to be expected, on such a solemn occasion. Anna couldn't help but think, what a peculiar beauty was to be held, watching the smooth, glistening ribbons from her bonnet streaming in the spring breeze. By nature somewhat portly of stature, she held onto a long, black walking stick, leaning upon it with both hands in a most determined fashion. With her chin locked in a forward position, she looked about herself from left to right and back again, as if, Anna thought, almightily dissatisfied not to find the merest thing with which to discover the most serious quarrel immediately.

'Porter, Porter!' her voice rang back the many memories of times, when the likes of Anna and Millie had fled from the very sound. They held on tightly to each other's hands, falling in instinctively with that particular phenomenon in human nature; reverting back to childhood patterns of behaviour, when faced with a terrifying relic from the past.

'Porter, oh, it's you, George Jenner, and how's your mother doing these days? Not still giving your father more and more mouths to feed, I presume?'

'No, Ma'am, she's a given up that some time since now, on account of not really being of child bearing years no more.'

'Oh good, I'm glad to hear of it. What number did she stop at in the end? Quick now, tell me.'

'Ten, Ma'am, of which I am proud to be...'

'The fifth, half way, tell me I'm right, for I know I'm not wrong, George Jenner, I remember holding your slight body in my arms the day you were born, sixteen years since now.'

'Shall I send her your regards, Ma'am?'

'You will most certainly not, I wouldn't dream of being so impersonal; I shall visit her tomorrow in person after the solemnities of today have been put to rest. That much, you might convey. Now, enough of this tittle-tattle, follow me with my trunks, if you please, George Jenner.'

'But, I can't fit three great trunks on one trolley, Mrs Gables,' said George, scratching behind his head with his bent elbow in the air. 'Nobody ever comes to Heartbourne with three trunks.'

'Blessed with your father's intellect, I see,' commented Mrs Gables to herself, approaching the lad, who was now nervously backing away. 'What, pray may I ask, is to stop you coming and going from my son's house, which is after all no more than five minutes' walk away, to fetch, each, trunk?' as she spoke, she banged on the lid of each one, as she uttered the last three words.

'But, what'll protect 'em from thieves and robbers, while I'm walking to and fro, Mrs Gables?'

'What, in Heartbourne, boy, this well-known den of squalor, thievery and general immorality?'

He looked at her blankly and she deduced that her irony was lost.

Maybe thinking of his mother, of whom she was very fond, she became a little more reserved in the harshness of her tone and tapping this time, on the lid of the first trunk, she asked, 'What, George, do you see written here?'

'Emmaline Gables, Ma'am, your name.'

'That's right, my boy, Emmaline Gables, writ large upon all three and in Heartbourne,' she leant in closely as she spoke, 'that is all the protection they will need.'

George jumped backwards in fright, with his back straight and his legs bent outwards like a frog's.

'Now, follow me!'

'Millie,' whispered Anna, 'she's going straight to Retty's! You'll have to waylay her while I nip round the back way and see what I can do.'

'Waylay her? Me? And how the dickens do you expect little Millie Price to waylay that contemptuous old goose? It'd be like a daisy trying to hold back an oak tree.'

'Ask her if she wants to view the arrangements in the church and then try to take her back home to enquire as to why the flowers aren't finished yet.'

'But, but,' Millie flapped her hands ineffectually.

'Millie, go, now.' Anna's voice softened, 'Please, just try, for Retty's sake?'

'Oh, all right, as I live and breathe, the things – I'm going I'm gone.'

Anna watched for just a moment, as Millie approached the imperious figure in black silk, before darting off at speed down Mill Lane, to the little track that ran alongside the farm, which would buy her a few minutes over Millie's tenuous efforts and George Jenner's slender pushing arms. Decorum thrown over in favour of friendship, she prayed that the Lord might make it possible for there not to be any of the senior village matrons within eyeshot of the spectacle of the priest's daughter, a married mother of two, tearing hurly-burly down the mud packed path.

Retty's cottage was positioned side on to the farm at the end of Buttsfield Lane and Anna was able to slip in through the side gate without being waylaid. She hurried across the unweeded path to the kitchen door, choosing not to look in through the windows before she crossed the threshold. She rapped anxiously on the door and called Retty's name twice, without much hope of being answered but, a little like closing the kitchen door when in the bath tub, even if you're the only soul in the house, it wouldn't have felt quite right not to adhere to usual manners.

Usual standards, however, were not what met Anna's eyes as the door swung open and she surveyed the chaos before her; washing up not done, old vegetable peelings on the table and laundry piles of ironing that must have been wanting a press for two or more weeks beside, judging by the volume of it. She picked up a half-eaten piece of toast, whose blackberry jam had stuck it to a grey and grubby tea towel and dropped it again, having disturbed a busy bluebottle. She ushered out a chicken, who had thought to set up nest in a pile of clothes on the dresser.

'Retty! Where are you?' she called, as she hurried through to the hall and stuck her head into the living room. Empty, untidy, more laundry and unwashed crockery and another chicken. She withdrew and strode up the stairs.

'Retty, where are you?' She burst into the main bedroom to find Retty propped up on one arm, pulling herself out of slumber.

'Anna, my dear friend Anna, what can you mean by disturbing me rest?'

'Retty! It's nearly midday! Your uncle's funeral day and your mother-in-law's three minutes from your door! Have you seen the state of downstairs?'

'Seen it, got used to it, got over it – but Ma Gables on her way?'

'Yes, this minute!'

'Not good,' she ruffled her muzzy hair and flopped backwards, 'I give up.'

Meanwhile, Millie Price, poor soul, was doing her humble best but as she herself had predicted, of all the conversational partners you could pick; this was not an equal competition. She'd enquired, rather unconvincingly, about the state of Mrs Gables' health, only to be accused of wishing her in a similar direction to her much beloved brother. This she'd resisted most firmly, only to be quizzed as to whether or not Mrs Gables looked to be in robust health or 'a little on the peaky side', which she'd been obliged to admit, didn't really appear to be the case. She'd found herself apologising for asking such frivolous and irrelevant questions on such a sober day, attempting to justify herself by pointing out that she'd only been trying to be polite and perhaps pushing it a little, by feigning indignation and declaring that on another occasion, however solemn or otherwise, maybe she wouldn't bother.

Mrs Gables raised herself to her full five foot two and leaning forward firmly on her stick, pinning Millie down with a piercing stare announced, 'Young lady, if that is what you are, I am unaccustomed to being spoken to in such a fashion and am not about to familiarise myself with the experience.'

Upon this, she ordered a rather confused looking George Jenner to follow her and set off down the High Street, as if bound on a mission.

Millie stood in George's way turning her head between Mill Lane and Mrs Gables, uncertain which path to follow. Promptly deciding that her mouth would probably only do more harm than good, she plumped for the less arduous route of following Anna's footsteps.

'George, go slow would you and pretend you can't keep up?'

'I won't have to do no pretending; have you felt the weight of these here trunks? Anyone would think she were staying...'

He stopped, aware that his audience had fled off down Mill Lane and that Mrs Gables had halted and was calling him sharply.

Millie arrived at Retty's in time to meet Anna descending back down the stairs.

'She's in bed, I've told her to keep quiet and said that I'll tell Mrs Gables she's not well, which she isn't. The living room, I'll take the living room, we'll usher her in there and try and keep her from the kitchen but do what you can with it, will you?'

Millie held her hands out flat, palms upwards and exclaimed, only to have Anna return to the hall and place a chicken in her hands, 'And try to keep these out, would you?'

25

Anna returned to the lounge and opened the rear window, before hastily storing what laundry she could in the alcove cupboard, setting straight the cushions on the chairs, righting an upturned lamp and collecting up all manner of plates and cups and cutlery. Hurrying through to the kitchen, she set her pile down in the bare ceramic sink as Millie came back in.

'Where's the washing up gone, Millie?'

'In the shrubbery, she'll not go out there, she said as she picked up a garter belt dangling from the plate rack on the dresser and tossed it into a hanging pot.

'Millie!'

'What? She's shorter than we are, she'll not see it up there. I'm doing my best to help, you know.'

Before Anna could protest, three loud raps came from the front door, undoubtedly made by a stick rather than a knocker.

'Here,' she threw Millie a dish cloth, 'at least wipe down the table and hide some of these clothes, would you?'

'Gratitude gone out of fashion, has it?'

Anna headed for the door, attempting to smooth down her gown and her composure at the same time.

'Mrs Gables, as I live and breathe, I'd heard you were in the village but I don't believe Retty was aware of the fact until - only this morning.'

'First, the ridiculous Millie Osborne and now, you, Anna Porter, but not yet Henrietta, I observe.'

'I'm sure she would've been along to wait on you, Mrs Gables, but you see I'm afraid she's not quite well and finds herself obliged to keep to her chamber, more's the pity, as I'm sure she'll be - mortified - for missing today.' Anna's speech faltered as she tried to find her way through without breaking the commandment on not bearing false witness. 'Oh, where are my manners?' said Anna. 'Why, won't you come in?'

Mrs Gables sucked in her cheeks and chewed on the left hand side for a moment. She dismissed George, sending him for the next trunk and assented to being ushered into the living room by Anna.

As they entered, a shriek and a crash came from the direction of the kitchen but Mrs Gables didn't acknowledge it.

As Mrs Gables looked around the room, Anna felt her eyes surveying the scene. Perhaps she hadn't heard Millie's cry and maybe she wouldn't notice the three warm eggs Anna had missed, sitting in the midst of a cardigan, in the corner of the deep window sill. Perhaps the pile of discarded socks, now poking out from behind a cushion, would escape her attention and maybe she wouldn't notice the slight but distinctive air of a chicken coop, now that the window was open. Maybe, even the layers of dust and the tea cup growing mould on the side table, might, Anna weakly hoped, be overlooked.

Mrs Gables observed the room but uttered not a word. The brooding chicken returned through the open window to the sill and resumed her matronly position on the cardigan. This drew Mrs Gables to the window, to look out over – quite possibly the shrubbery, feared Anna. She descended onto a chair, squarely upon some socks and condescended to ask after the health of Anna's father and, recalling now that Anna herself was married, her own husband and offspring. Anna in return enquired as to life in Frampton, whence Mrs Gables had been obliged to remove, 'As a trailing spouse!' so she'd bewailed at the time, owing to an improvement in her husband's business affairs, some nine or so years ago.

'Yes, one of my very last days in Heartbourne was your wedding day and I remember it most particularly,' she spoke thoughtfully. 'Now, the Holy Week preceding it and Easter Day had been so glorious, we were all bedecked with a touch of sun upon our cheeks and yet, not a week later, on the day that you were wed, the young spring tulips...'

'...were stacked high with snow.'

'And your arms, exposed by your short sleeved wedding gown, designed for a more mature spring day, were covered in little raised goose bumps, like a school girl's arms in a short white blouse.'

The door banged open and hit a chair behind it as Millie kicked it open before her, bearing a laden tray.

'Tea. Tea. A nice cup of tea...' she stopped mid-sentence, aware of some incongruity somewhere. 'Oh, don't tell me I'm wrong again, when I've been trying so hard, Anna!'

Both Anna and Mrs Gables turned aside in an attempt to hide their pursed lips from the genuinely well-meaning Millie.

Mrs Gables was the first to recover, 'I would be delighted to take a cup of tea with you, Millie – Price, I believe it is now?'

'In name, yes,' Millie confirmed Mrs Gables' enquiry, as she set down the tea tray with an awkward bump, in her amazement at the grace with which she was being received.

'And would like to assure you both of how grateful I am that Henrietta is in possession of two such good and loyal friends.'

They drank tea, politely and formally talking of anything but the state of the house or Retty, after which Mrs Gables took it upon herself to show Anna and Millie to the door, where they came across George Jenner taking a lie down on the lawn.

He jumped up, surprised, 'Three great trunks all delivered, Mrs Gables.'

'Why, however long are you planning to stay?' said Millie, without thinking.

'Quite some time, by the looks of it but if the exact extent to which my stay is a necessity could remain a private matter, between ourselves?' Her rising intonation, coupled with the grandness of her presence, instantly drew out an understanding, understated nod from Anna.

Even Millie's perception led her to remark, 'I should say so –' before an elbow in the ribs from Anna corrected her manners and tone, 'of course, Mrs Gables, anything you say, Ma'am.'

As they walked back to their own lane, arm in arm along the back path, Millie kept giggling and squeezing Anna's arm as another funny recollection passed through her mind. As Anna mused, she had the most peculiar sensation that two things had happened both quite unrelated to Retty. First, as she looked at Millie's smiling face, she felt that, however odd bed fellows they might appear to others, her friendship with Millie had been reconfirmed. Secondly, and most unexpectedly, she suspected that a whole new and quite different relationship had just begun; however inept their efforts had been, the value of friendship was what Mrs Gables had recognised.

28

Chapter Four

'Anna was in church when it happened. She'd finally got as far as the pew end posies, when he walked into the archway of the porch and called her.

'May I steal your attention, Ma'am?'

She was struck by his height and his broad shoulders as he stood silhouetted, with the light streaming into the nave from behind him. As she approached him, she noticed his sun-kissed skin and youthful, untidy shock of black, curly hair. Then there was the directness of his gaze, emanating from those marbled blue eyes as he touched her elbow, just for a second, without even meaning to. Pensively, he looked into her amber-brown eyes. Neither one of them spoke or moved.

'Ah, Anna, there you are,' her father came hurrying up the path, 'I was just starting to worry. Have you met young Raphael? He's here to measure up that rotten joist in the vestry, from where the roof was leaking last year. I've left it as long as possible so as not to incur any pain for the poor Pickens family but needs must and as Raphael moved into the rooms above Bert's old carpentry last night, I thought we just ought to get on with it. Still, it wouldn't really do to have him here during the funeral of his predecessor, so I suppose we'd best press on. Follow me, young man, if you please.'

With that, Anna's father strode off down the nave completely oblivious to the tender and poignant scene he'd just interrupted.

When she looked back from her father's departure, to Anna's surprise, Raphael had bent down on one knee. He rose back up again with a crimson camellia in his hand. As she accepted it back into her hand, their fingers couldn't help but touch, transferring a fleeting awareness of the warmth each other's skin. Their eyes met again but this time only for a moment, as a confusion of emotion on both sides led each one to turn away. Raphael walked away up the aisle, while Anna was left looking after his impressive form departing for the first time.

She walked into the porch, sank down onto the bench and leant her head on the smooth stone of the wall. She looked at the crimson camellia in full bloom. What her father had feared all too early, had come all too late. Now, she didn't know what to do. Thoughts were cascading through her head as she found herself trying to think of an excuse to follow him and engage him in conversation, but she knew she shouldn't. She knew she could never be so bold, so impulsive. She rose up distractedly and stood at the threshold of the church looking out. The impulse was causing her mind to picture the scene where she'd found a perfectly good topic of conversation to engage Raphael in and was standing before him once more dwelling in his eyes, not stumbling and stuttering for words but eloquently conversing with the soft, gentle voice she'd heard utter only one sentence, so far.

'Ma'am,' before she even turned, she knew her guilty wish had been fulfilled. The pair of them stood in the intimacy of the small porch for a moment before he spoke again, 'Ma'am, I must pass by.'

'Oh, I'm sorry,' Anna blushed and felt awkward at her own stupidity as she stepped aside from the porch way.

'Do you grow the flowers yourself?' he asked softly, as he stepped forward to pass through, touching the velvet of a petal.

'I do,' she replied monosyllabically, meeting his eyes but with none of the longed for eloquence springing to her lips.

'Seeing their beauty, seems almost a shame to put them to such a solemn use.'

'It's a mark of respect, like stating a very deep kind of love. After all, flowers from the very same bush may celebrate a wedding another season, who's to say?'

'But not your own?' he ventured to ask.

'No, no,' Anna's blush challenged the depth of the camellia's colour, 'that day has come and gone a long while since.'

'For me also,' he looked at her quite directly with a steady, serious gaze.

'I see,' said Anna, almost shocked to hear the boldness of her own words. Nevertheless, she heard herself saying, 'It lies the same way with both of us, then.'

Just then, the sound of her father humming a resounding, funereal tune reached their ears and both of them at first started and then laughed.

'It mocks us with our own assumed solemnity!' said Raphael, smiling and fingering the rim of his hat.

'Indeed, how foolish we are. I must get back to my arrangements.'

'And I, to my trade. Good day to you, Anna.'

With that, they nodded their mutual respects and parted company, retreating back into their own, separate lives.

Bert Pickens' funeral went off with all family members present and mercifully without incident. Anna started to wonder how Mrs Gables had managed it and then chose not to dwell on the matter, as she noted Retty's upright posture in her pew being tightly supported by her husband Henry's steady arm. She noted that Retty appeared not to be present at the wake, held as it traditionally was in the village, at The Gun Inn.

By the end of the day, Bert had been laid to rest respectably, Mrs Gables and her three trunks were installed with her son and daughter-in-law and Raphael De Vine was Heartbourne's new resident carpenter.

Chapter Five

'At home, Anna escorted her two sons to bed. It was late and Sam was already sleeping peacefully as she lowered him gently into his cot. When she turned to Theo, he accepted a kiss with the air of a young man with thoughts upon his head. She smiled down at him and gently tapped his thigh for him to shift over so that she might sit before replying to his tentative enquiries regarding, as it turned out, his birthday celebrations.

'I have counted correctly, Mother, I think?'

'Why counted what, Theo?'

'Mother, don't tease,' he said, 'my birthday, of course!'

'Oh that, to be sure, with everything that's happened, I haven't had much of a chance to give it my attention fully, as of yet.'

She attempted to look out of the window but as it was now dark and there was nothing to see, she failed quite utterly, to suppress a smirk. In short; she was found out.

Theo giggled, 'I do love you, Mother, and you must tell me everything; I want to understand it all.'

Anna looked at him and with a sufficiently enigmatic tone and style to keep him in suspense, whilst implicitly telling him that the day was not to pass without due excitement and celebration, she quelled his fears to sleep.

That night, as was usual, Anna lay alone. As a spring thunderstorm raged its way around Heartbourne, pelting and beating her beautiful camellias, she struggled to overcome the turmoil in her mind. In the daylight there were duties and cares, plenty to distract her heart; the flowers, the mourners, the giving of gloves, the wake, Retty's conduct, Millie's discretion, Mrs Gables' temperament and of course, her boys. Now, she lay in bed, between fresh, stiff cotton sheets, unable to find sleep no matter how she searched. Her own words and his echoed over through her mind, as his face and his eyes and his curly black hair reappeared each time she tried to close her mind. It lies the same...It lies the same...It mocks us with our own solemnity... Of course, that's it, she tried to pacify herself, nothing so very grand or solemn has happened here, nothing akin to the seriousness of Theo's brown eyes contemplating his birthday. I must mock myself, at my age, a head turned by a pretty face? And a sturdy stride and a handsome voice? 'Tis all, that's all, 'tis nothing of great import. I must think of Theo's birthday, there's still so much to do and do I invite Mrs Gables at the risk of offending Retty? Or not invite her at the risk of offending Herself? There's so much, so pleasuresome, what need have I of marbled blue eyes? And that voice? And curly black hair? It's nothing, next to God's wishes and sons and motherhood, nothing to become uncalm about at all. All will pass, away.

Less than half a mile distant, above the village carpentry, its new incumbent couldn't sleep either. His more travelled soul couldn't so easily be dissuaded from the magnitude of the day's meeting. His soul also, however, was coupled firmly with the will of God and he was (and had been for five years) a married man. What a marriage it was, he couldn't describe to himself, let alone another. His wife was called Violet and she hadn't, apparently by her absence, yet managed to finish the task of packing her personal belongings from their previous residence in order to follow her husband and their furniture and utensils to their new destination in Heartbourne. Quite where Violet was, he didn't know. Quite shocking though this would be, had they known, to the many husbands and matrons of Heartbourne, he was aware; but they needn't know, yet. It was by no means of late the first time she'd absconded from their marriage without warning or explanation. It wasn't a sensation he'd ever expected to become accustomed to. Accustomed though, he was becoming, as he stared at the vacant other side of his bed. What he'd experienced today, however, that, he wasn't used to. That, most certainly hadn't been expected. He closed his eyes and dwelt, just for one moment, on the memory of Anna.

Chapter Six

'As Anna awoke, she felt a slight breeze blowing across her arms and chest. It was still spring and although not cold, she sought to retrieve the warm comfort of the quilt by searching for it with her hand and drawing it back up but her effort met resistance. Instead of movement, a small but distinct giggle emitted itself from the floral covering. Of course, she thought; Theo's birthday. She opened her eyes and they met Will's, smiling back. They both looked at the suspicious looking bump under the quilt which was inching slowly up the bed. Will pretended to yawn and casually landed his arm across the quilt, which giggled again. Will and Anna both shut their eyes tightly but couldn't help but take frequent peeks at the bump's progress.

All of a sudden (or so he believed) Theo burst from the bedcovers shouting a surprise but the surprise was to be his; his waiting father sprang into action and bundled him up, quilt and all with a bear-like roar and stood up on the bed with him shouting, 'Ahh! Quick, Anna, quick, thieves!' He jumped off the bed and roared again with the now hysterically laughing bundle in his arms. 'Robbery and treason, ahh! Open the window that I might throw it out!'

A shriek came from the quilt and an arm fought its way free, 'No don't, Mother, don't, you know it's me really, Papa!'

Will unwrapped the bundle and with theatrical surprise, grasped Theo by his shoulders, 'Well, what a blessing it is to have a son with a sturdy pair of lungs, who might otherwise have landed himself in the garden, on his head, on the morning of his birthday!' Upon which they both promptly collapsed upon Anna, laughing as she kissed them.

It was the most glorious spring morning you could pray for as the preparations for Theo's birthday party got underway. Anna's kitchen was the hub of activity as she, Judith, Millie and Mrs Emmaline Gables, yes, *the* Mrs Gables (who'd spared Anna the worry by simply presuming that she'd been invited) chopped and stirred and whisked and baked, at times working in tandem, at times as a production team and sometimes independently, to get all the necessary tasks completed to Anna's satisfaction. From time to time one or another of them, Millie in particular, would concoct a task which Retty would be able to manage, wrapped as she was in her own mother's favourite shawl, sitting at the kitchen table drinking tea.

'Oh, Retty, Retty, now the birthday cake's still sitting here waiting but I just have to start on the refreshments for the grown-ups, if I leave you with this marzipan,' she walloped it down in true Millie Price style, 'on a board with some flour,' which she then haphazardly dispensed, 'and a rolling pin,' another Millie wallop, 'I'm sure you'll cope while I just...'

While Millie bustled out of the room, wiping her hands on her apron, her imagination having been exhausted for the moment, Mrs Gables stopped what she was about and turned and looked at Henrietta, with her head on one side. Retty, although not smiling, sighed, looked back, roused herself and began very slowly to sprinkle the flour across the wooden board. Mrs Gables gave her an understated nod and the chatter of the kitchen resumed as Millie re-entered with more food and yet another frivolous topic on her tongue.

Soon after noon, guests began to arrive in dribs and drabs both before and after the appointed time of one o'clock. Will was in his element with children's party games in the garden. Theo's face was alight with laughter and delight and by three o'clock Anna was standing with her arms almost akimbo, holding up her rib cage from the aching of her laughter.

By half past three, the 'Pin the Tail on the Donkey' winner had been announced and it was time for tea. Anna's kitchen table, arrayed in a starched white table cloth, was laden with all the most scrumptious delights a seven year old child and his friends could have imagined, as they lay in their beds waiting the night before. Cheese straws, savoury tarts, pigs in blankets, stuffed eggs, cobnuts and dried mulberries were promptly replenished and later replaced with fruit jellies, meringues and cream, apple tarts, iced biscuits and of course, the pinnacle piece of the party; Theo's birthday cake.

With all the attending children and parents squashed together for the moment in Anna's kitchen, Anna gratefully noticed her father's late arrival at the front door.

'Will, would you mind letting Papa in while I light the candles?'

'Of course not, but don't start singing without me, now!' he said, winking at Theo as he left the crowded room.

Anna had just finished lighting the seventh slim candle as she heard the kitchen door re-open.

'Is that you, Will?' she asked, starting to carry the cake over to Theo's place without turning around.

Will answered by starting to sing and Anna placed the cake down by her beaming elder son as the last birthday greeting faded. Theo blew out the candles and squeezed his eyes shut. As Anna turned to Will, hoping that they both knew what the wish was for, she caught a glimpse of a slightly portly figure of a man dressed in a gentleman's black cape. She smiled. Theo opened his eyes and looked thoughtful.

'What is it, Theo?' asked Anna.

'Well, I was just thinking,' he said, fingering the pattern on the damask table cloth, 'it doesn't make sense, Mother.'

'What doesn't, Theo?'

'Well, if you're not allowed to tell your mother or your father what you wish for, then how can it ever come true?'

'Ah, well maybe, just maybe,' came a booming voice from the back of the crowded assembly, 'that's where a magical uncle comes in!'

Sweeping out of obscurity to the table came the dark cloaked figure, who raised his arms and hands as he announced himself like a conjurer, 'Tah daah!'

'Uncle Christopher!' Theo's surprise and joy were evident in his voice, 'Why, however did you get here?'

'What? Did you think I didn't know what day it was? And did you think, that I didn't know,' he lowered his voice as he leant a little over the kitchen table, drawing in the whole assembled company, 'what your birthday wish was for?' And as he spoke, he raised from a pocket in his cloak, very slowly and very tenderly, a small, jet black puppy. Everyone sighed with delight.

'Uncle Christopher! Mother, Papa, may we?'

Without needing to look at each other, both smiled and nodded at Theo, who yelped with delight as he unfettered himself from his place at the table and went round to greet his much longed for new friend.

As he held the puppy and it licked his face, Theo announced, 'You really are the most truly magical uncle in the world, Uncle Christopher!'

'Not to mention not being averse, perhaps,' Mrs Gables' eyebrows were raised, 'to taking a little more of the credit than is due, Christopher Coates.'

'Ah, Emmaline! And what a delight it is to see you too again, old girl!' he said, holding his nephew and with an emphasis which created a small a ripple of amusement, as just a few of the assembled grown-ups dared to express themselves in Her presence.

There was a brief pause, which would have been followed nearly twenty years earlier by an outburst regarding being referred to as, 'old girl', as if she was, 'some piece of baggage'. Although the expression still passed through her mind, Emmaline had noticed across her daughter-in-law's countenance the first, albeit suppressed smile, that she'd seen since her return to Heartbourne. Instead, she chose to look at Christopher Coates with an air of disdain and content herself with a half amused, 'Humph.'

That evening by the fireside as Anna sat sewing, she surveyed her life. Will was still nursing Samuel in his arms, doting, quite unnecessarily, hours after he'd fallen asleep but she didn't see fit to bring an end to the scene as she watched Will stroking his son's cheek and rocking him in comfort, when he so frequently had to be away from home.

She watched and listened as her much loved Uncle Christopher, her dear mother's brother, the enigmatic traveller, forever in pursuit of far reaching trade, sat with Theo and the playing puppy on his lap, telling tales gathered on his journeys both at home and afar. Sometimes, Theo was listening to tales he'd heard long and often before, which he nevertheless liked to listen to again, as he turned the puppy round and round about by tracing his finger in a circle above his head. Sometimes, he'd allow the puppy to catch his fingertip and then he would squawk out loud and roll the puppy over to rub his soft belly, so the catch turned into not chewing but licking and stroking and tendering care. For a long time, there seemed no end to the puppy's energy and then suddenly, without warning, he lay out flat with his head on Theo's leg and fell asleep. Then, Theo laid his head against the warmth of Uncle Christopher's chest and before very long his uncle's mellow voice had entered his dreams.

In communal silence, Sam was passed from Will to Anna and Theo, from Christopher to Will and the two were peacefully installed in their beds for the night.

When Anna returned downstairs, she caught sight of an unguarded expression upon Uncle Christopher's face as he stoked the fire idly with the poker. She sat down and watched him.

'You're my closest living relative, my dear Anna,' he said, without turning his gaze from the fire.

'As you are mine, bar my father,' she replied.

Although their silent congregation was a comfortable one, Anna was aware of some discomfort in the thoughts of her uncle as he returned the poker to its hook and sat back facing his niece.

'Penny for them?' she asked.

'Aha, my dear, you remind me of your former self, enquiring as to the possibility of my conjuring a lollipop from my cape.'

'That reminds me,' said Anna, catching Will's outstretched hand as he re-entered the room, 'we haven't thanked for you bringing the puppy on time.'

'Yes, thank you, Christopher, I was a great deal disappointed not to be able to fetch him myself and the look on Theo's face...'

'Was a little moment of magic in my own life, well worth the small amount of trouble the errand caused me, I promise you.'

'I'm glad,' said Will, 'and now, I'm ready for my bed.'

Anna's eyes glanced at her uncle's.

'My dear nephew, would you be terribly offended if I kept the company of your good wife here for just a short while longer, by the light of a fire called, 'home', not 'hostelry' or 'inn' or worse still, 'boarding house'?' The loud, mock-stern sonority of his last utterance made his niece and nephew smile.

'Not, if you'll not be offended by my absence, Uncle? For being a scary bear got out from the woods all afternoon has quite worn me through.'

The matter agreed and Will departed, Uncle Christopher returned to tending the fire.

'I wonder if Theo will ever tire of hearing of 'The Boy Who Lay Abed' or 'The Folly of the Fox'..?'

'Or 'The Tale of Proud Chauntecleer', my girl, don't forget that one!' her uncle chuckled and sat back. 'Hmmm, but the matter on my mind is not a wise or a cheery one, I'm afraid, my dear, but one which requires a grace and a wisdom I'm unsure I have yet acquired, even at my age, which is why I seek your ear, my child.'

'My ear, Uncle Christopher? Why, I'm sure you flatter me, how could a head like mine be of use next to a wise mind such as yours?'

'Because, my dear niece, you remind me very much of your mother, who was always a great deal more generous and long sighted than I ever managed in my youth. Hmm, now then, how to explain.'

Chapter Seven

"I have been for many years, as you well know, a traveller on the road of trade, bringing wool where they have need of it and taking away other requirements for far off counties, from cotton cloth for round frocks, to fine silk for top hats. The livelihood is a good one but the life is at times, somewhat lonesome. As a natural consequence, among those of us who plough the travelling furrow, a certain amount of camaraderie can at times be found. Not so much as you would call us a community or anything so wholesome or so grand but across the years,' he searched for the right words, 'acquaintanceships are formed and company kept on evenings when the distance in the eyes of the locals holds you asunder from any hearthside warmth.'

'But Uncle, the stories you've regaled us with, of the evenings you've told tales and kept whole inns consumed in the latest news and your lively company...'

'Among many of the villages, particularly here about 'tis so, 'twas always so and one hopes, will always be but further afield where the distances between are longer and the name of Coates means naught at all, most notably in towns and fine cities where the rarer commodities I'm requested to procure are sometimes to be obtained; I am but a stranger, a mere merchant at that and only above a common pedlar by the cut of my coat and the size of my vehicle, as my voice is but that of country Hodge to such folk.'

'Uncle, your tones are nothing akin and you know it!'

'To you and me, maybe, but to them what gives themselves airs and graces,' he gesticulated and Anna giggled. 'But I become unchristian, I know my place in God's scheme of things, Anna; somewhere in the middle and there I'm fit and happy to be. I am neither the richest nor the poorest, the greatest nor the least blessed, the wisest nor most foolish of men placed upon this earth. My matter, however, concerns one, who quite possibly is.

'My tale is a sad one, Anna. Picture a girl, such as yourself, in the full bloom of youth. Such a girl there was called Maria, who grew to a suitable age, fell in love with an entertaining and handsome young chap and married him. Her husband, Nathan Lunsford, was a travelling tradesman and often away from home which saddened her, however God blessed them with a child who filled her heart and her daylight hours with joy. The child, a daughter, grew but Maria began to notice that Nathan's absences had become longer and seemingly more persistent. She became fearful, her waking thoughts haunted and her dreams filled with the spectre of what might be. She began to feel that her life was blighted with shadows of suspicion.

'At length, tormented by her own lack of grasp on where reality lay, in a pastoral landscape with a sky ripped only by the bine-stems of her own mind, or in a brambled copse, a prickled sham, too awful surely, to be deserved or borne, she determined that for all three of them, it was best she knew the truth. Her mother, after counselling her calmly that only those who were ready to see what they thought they wanted to know, should go looking, agreed to take the grandchild for a while, that her daughter might seek reality.

'Maria made preparations and on the next occasion when her husband left, after a stay of only a week, she set out to follow him with a heavy-weighted heart. The practicalities of following without being found out, however, she hadn't thought through. With inferior transportation and inferior funds it's to be presumed that Nathan's path was lost to Maria quite quickly, but exactly what happened, is still not known to this day.'

'Why, what happened to her, poor soul?'

'She was found a fortnight later, bloodied and face down in a ditch.'

Anna gasped.

'Her purse had been taken and presumably her boots, for she was barefoot and had been beaten about the head. The authorities determined that she'd fallen foul of common thievery. Her husband, it was ascertained, from establishments along his trade route, had gone out of the county completely some time before. Where? It wasn't easy to say. It appeared that up to a point, all of his acquaintances and the staff who served at inns and hosts themselves could speak freely as to his comings and goings over the course of many months but beyond a distance of some forty miles, his tracks went cold,' Uncle Christopher snapped his fingers, 'just like that.'

'Just as cold as his poor wife's feet,' said Anna.

'Indeed, poor girl, indeed.' Uncle Christopher placed another log on the fire and Anna sat back, as she deduced that the story was not yet nearing its conclusion.

'The burial took place in Nathan's absence and Maria was laid to rest. Rest, however, her mother, Ruth, could not; would not. With the image of her daughter before her, in her young grandchild, she determined to know for herself why her daughter had died. In short; had Maria been right or had she been wrong? Was she responsible for placing herself in a position of vulnerability at the hands of robbers and thieves, or had her husband's betrayal led her into a path of perilous danger previously unknown to her and simply not navigable to one of such innocence and inexperience? Her mother simply had to know.

'Letters had been dispatched to various towns and places to Nathan Lunsford trying to reach him to inform him of the sad news of his wife's death. One of these missives bore fruit and a letter came through to Ruth. The letter spoke of grief and great distress and not wishing to return to such a place of unhappiness. To Ruth it reeked of betrayal. It also bore a postmark.

'Unencumbered by the necessity of youth to protect herself from unwanted attention and with the addition of a moulded wart and a sallow complexion applied with her own hand, Ruth's pathway through unchartered territories was more straightforward than maybe her daughter's had been. She had the foresight to don a thick, brown, three-quarter length cape with a full hood and carry a basket of, 'Lucky Heather, Dear?' to ensure that first, no-one unwanted would choose to come near her and secondly, that she had a plausible reason for approaching any stranger she chose to, to get a closer look at 'em, without the bother of them desiring her better acquaintance.'

'A shrewd woman.'

'A determined woman, driven by grief and love, both powerful forces in their own right. And what did she discover? That her advice to her own child was sound; only those who are ready to face the truth should seek it out. She found her son-in-law, not alone, but not in the arms of some common hussy or another man's wife. These eventualities, she'd fore-guessed and prepared for. The truth, she hadn't foreseen and the evening of the day she discovered it, she spent pacing, to and fro, up and down the flimsy floorboards of her shabby accommodation. For what she'd discovered wasn't a fallen woman but a second dishonoured maid: nothing short of a second wife, a second home, a second kitchen hearth where she'd sat drinking a cup of weak, warm soup, watching the innocent wife tend her own beloved infant of much the same age as a babe three counties distant from the place.

'She paced the floorboards back and forth with what to think and what to do. At last, she sat down on the bed. She was decided: the young wife wasn't to be troubled with any traumatic revelations. Her own daughter was past repair and damaging another of God's purer souls wasn't the work she'd set forth to achieve. The husband, however, she truly desired his repentance that he mightn't simply repeat his treachery and carry on a further duplicitous, deceitful and damnable life. She decided to be brave and take perhaps a circuitous route which *might*, she only hoped, bring about the change she desired, that Maria's life mightn't have been sacrificed only for the service of future sins. Quite beyond her own surprise: she decided to haunt Nathan.

'The next morning, at some considerable personal cost, Ruth ordered a dress to be made of the self-same fabric last chosen by her daughter and in the self-same cut and style as she'd last seen her in. Ruth's brown cape would have to suffice but she sat down at the small, cracked, hinged mirror in her lodgings and took out a modestly decorated box. Inside the box, her eyes travelled across the carefully stowed objects she'd brought with her; they fell on a long and distinctively patterned red, cream and black ribbon, which had formerly adorned her daughter's hair. She blinked away her sorrow and selected it, closing the lid on the other mementoes of her love.

'While Ruth was waiting for the dress to be made she used her time profitably. The guise she'd brought with her continued to serve well as she watched and followed and noted her son-in-law's movements each day.

'Four days later, she collected her purchase and began, very slowly, to torment the young man. At the hour at which he left the house and headed for the High Street, she was careful to be walking in front of him by a distance of three or four pedestrians with her hood down, the ribbon on display.

'As he came down the steps of the hardware store, putting some coins away, the hem of her skirt all but brushed his toes but as he lifted his head, her cloaked form disappeared around the corner. She noticed him hasten after her but she slipped away easily and went home. Enough for today, she thought.

'The next day, she was careful to wait until the afternoon. As he came out of the bank, she was looking into the window of the milliner's straight opposite. She watched his reflection as he stopped, started, and began to cross over to her. At that point she went into the milliner's, not a place he could easily follow. From the darker corner of the bow window, she watched him remove his hat and shuffle it around through his fingers, his gaze fixed on the threshold she'd just crossed.

'In the throng on the way to church with his wife and child, he caught glimpses of his first wife's hair, her ribbon, her dress, her gait but he could hardly break free with any sensible explanation from the company he was in and in church? Homeward bound? From a vantage point, Ruth watched Nathan's turning head and searching eyes as they roved in vain.

'She continued in this way for four days, after which she turned to haunting him late at night. His favourite tap was in a hollow where the mist lay low on chilly nights. As he came out, befuddled by drink, he seemed almost relieved to see her dim outline before him. He stretched out his arms and fell to his knees in silence. She began to walk and he followed her cloaked form, calling her daughter's name, 'Maria, Maria, forgive me, forgive me!'

'The next night she waited for him again, outside the public house, and then led him to the churchyard before disappearing into the mist. Watching from a distance, she saw him sink to his knees at the church door and sob, banging his head against it violently.

'The following morning, she watched once again. To her surprise and satisfaction, the young man left the house dressed not in his work clothes, but his Sunday suit. He walked, not to the High Street, but the church. He hesitated at the lych gate, but then entered. Dressed as a traveller, she followed and watched as he walked straight in, up to the altar and knelt in prayer. She sat down in the back pew and prayed herself. She thanked God for Nathan's repentance, prayed for his young wife Annette and for the soul of her beloved Maria.

'After half an hour, Nathan arose and went home to his wife and child. Ruth watched him playing with his daughter for a while and then returned to her own county and the village where she lived.'

'A curious tale indeed, Uncle Christopher, however did you hear of it?'

'Ruth is a widow, a respectable Christian woman, who often stays at one of the better appointed boarding houses I frequent from time to time, called Brambleberry Hall. You see, being a shrewd woman, as you observed, she recognised the stratagems employed and the profits to be made from a little travel and a little trade. At this time, she found herself husbandless, not young and with a child to provide for. So, she took to the road on a part time basis, relying on the support of village friends to provide stability for the child. She met some resistance to her new role initially but she found that shopkeepers and tradesmen soon become blind to the tenderer, in the face of a jolly good deal. Moreover, being a wise and not greedy person, she knew how to establish sufficient habitual partners to succeed in trade. I have known

Ruth and occasionally enjoyed her fireside company for over a score of years but she only revealed this history to me five days ago. Imagine that, Anna, to have known a person for over twenty years without knowing such a tragic tale.'

'It must bear weight on her heart daily, Uncle.'

'And yet never to tell a soul, for she assured me keenly I was the first one outside of those involved to know the truth of it, bar the good Lord himself. Until now, that is and that, my dear Anna, is where you come in. My reason for troubling your idyllic and blessed existence here in Heartbourne, with your pretty sons and playful husband is this: there's been a troubling development in this tale, all these years later and Ruth has sought my advice as to the same.' He leant forward and stoked the fire thoughtfully.

'Upon her travels, Ruth has made it her business to keep a weather eye on Nathan Lunsford and his wife. She does no business in Frampton for fear of being spotted and recognised by Mr Lunsford but will sometimes stay a night at 'The Greene Man' where she first lodged, often in the very same room where she paced those twenty odd years ago. Initially she suffered from gross tremors and trepidation each time she stepped across the threshold, for although this was not an observed drinking place of Nathan's, his presence was not an impossibility.

'Over the years, however, she is aware that her resemblance to her former self has faded; her figure is more robust, her hair is grey and her complexion is, well, that of a long travelled sixty year old woman. Although she still sups in her room to avoid unwanted curiosity, she now walks into the public house with her hood down and passes the time of day with a landlord similar in years to herself. If her room isn't ready, she's content to sit in a booth with a small measure of weak ale, which she makes last until she may retire to her privacy upstairs.

'Well, Anna, imagine her surprise, anxiety and distress when the last time she was seated with a jar of beer before her in the public lounge, she found herself out of sight but within earshot of a conversation centred plumb on the topic of her son-in-law and his wife.

'I'm telling you straight, Nathan Lunsford's been arrested and taken in for the murder of his wife Annette, this very afternoon.'

'But they took him up once already, on account of her fall and grievous injuries, only to decide it wasn't possible at all he did it.'

'I know, but that was a different case altogether; suspicion was raised on account of a terrible argument between the two but such things we know do happen between a husband and wife, especially with one so fond of the ale house as Nathan.'

'Indeed,' a third voice entered the conversation, which Ruth recognised as the landlord himself, 'it was partly on account of his being so incapacitated with drink, that he couldn't rightly remember what the rowing was all about, that excused him. If you ask me, he was in no fit state to go tramping about over two or three fields besides, never mind controlling a distraught wife to manoeuvre her to a steep edge. In my experience, a man in that state can't lift his head above the gravel in the roadway he's fallen into, let alone lift a grown woman over a ridge, to throw her to her near death.'

'Opinion about the town is much divided; did he push her over Devil's Ravine or did she simply fall? I myself would say one goes on past experience. Has this man ever rowed with his wife after an evening at the tap? Why, yes, for many a moon he has but unlike a certain other breed of man, he's never been known to lay a finger on a woman, no matter what his state of mind. You can't hang a man for being a drunkard, you know, however undesirable a state of going on it may be.'

'Far more likely,' the landlord resumed, 'she simply felt as though she'd had enough of his ill-tempered tongue for one week and was headed to their daughter's house for a little sanity and respite for a while.'

'Her daughter's new home is in that direction; she would only have had to have been a few hundred yards off where she thought she was, to have fallen.'

Assent was murmured and pipes drawn upon in thought before the talk continued.

'This time, however, who's to know what to think?'

'The fact they've taken him up must mean they've some evidence.'

'What, like they did last time, only to have to let him go?'

'There was the opportunity this time; he was there, she was there, she was dead in the morning.'

'Yes,' said the landlord, 'she went to sleep three days after a mighty blow to the head from falling down a ravine and simply didn't wake up. What you make of it rather depends on your view of the first event. Did he push her over the ridge and then finish her off, once she'd started talking again? Or did she, rather understandably fed up of him, take a very unwise journey, where she fell foul of mischance, survived, but only to die of a tragic haemorrhage to the brain, a bit later on?'

'Had she started to talk again, recognisable like?'

'That'd be significant to discovering the truth of the first event, which might account for its covering up by the second; motive, you see.'

Again, the assent of possibility rippled around the room, while much puffing on pipe ends was producing a fathomable fug.

'What'd she said, do we know?'

'Did it make any sense?'

'Not much,' the landlord assumed the air of an authority being consulted. 'Some nonsense to do with her childhood, I believe, 'tis well known people often go back in their minds to their childhood, after such a blow to the head.'

This brought much assent and murmurings as to its truth.

'She was an orphan brought up at St Olivia's Convent, four mile from here, you see. Her parents both died of the scarlet fever, when she was a babe of three.'

'But what did she say, sir? Had it any significance on what we assembled here are attempting to ascertain?'

'Only two words, as according to what the daughter has told the authorities, each one repeated over and over three times

48

and only when the daughter was in the room alone with her. Nathan declares he'd not heard her utter a word since the fall.'

'But what were the two words? Are you ever to tell us, my good man?'

'Oh, I see, sorry, begging your pardon, the first was, 'Sister, Sister, Sister,' presumably as if, in her mind, she was back in the convent of her youth, calling for help or attention or what not.'

'Well, that's of no significance to the virtue or damnable condition of Nathan Lunsford's soul then, is it?'

'Ahh, but you haven't heard the second word.'

'Why, what was it? Give us your evidence truly, man!'

'It was, 'Secret, secret, secret.' Aha, so what do you make to that, my fine jury?'

There were some sharp intakes of breath, more puffing on pipes and much decided rumination of the cheeks and lips. In the smoke filled room, no one had noticed Ruth's approach to the bar but they noticed as her hand flailed about before her as she tried to reach the sanctity of the world outside and fresh air. Her shock, however, was too great. Her eyes swam and her knees gave way beneath her, as she sank into a dead faint.

'Ruth spent the night in a feverish condition, which, knowing no better, the locals put down to a physical infirmity. She herself was painfully aware that her condition was due to severe mental anguish. She allowed herself to be nursed back to some form of stability before heading back to Brambleberry Hall, not wishing to be seen just yet in Wessex, for fear of their recognising her altered state. It was there that the kindly landlady, having recognised Ruth as being quite unwell, lit a small fire for her in her room and bid me eat my supper with her, hoping that she might rally with the stimulation and comfort of a little polite company.'

'And that, I gather, is when she told you this tale.'

'Indeed, but the question is...' Uncle Christopher's voice trailed off as he turned over the last log, unleashing the intense heat of white and bright orange embers.

Anna sighed deeply, surrounded by huge shadows.

'What should she do?' Uncle Christopher shook his head slowly. 'What should she do?'

As Anna's thoughts fell to deep cogitation, it fleeted through her mind that a brief moment of giddy attraction to a stranger might not be as momentous as it'd at first felt, not at least, in comparison to Ruth's unenviable dilemma. What to think and what to do; difficult questions whirled about her mind like curious glowing puppets, each holding out a deceptive looking, darkened pitfall.

'So much centres on, 'What if?'' she looked at her uncle.

'I know and she knows; if you start going to the authorities speaking of bigamy, why you ruin a man and unlike God, society won't forgive you.'

'You could, quite possibly, in trying to do the right thing, condemn a totally innocent man, who repented more than twenty years ago, to the gallows! For I wouldn't fancy his chances of an unbiased hearing if word of his past was out.'

'So what, then? Do you counsel a woman like Ruth to do nothing for fear of doing mortal harm?'

Anna looked, with her eyebrows raised to him in a sceptical fashion and her chin tucked in.

'Ha, Anna, aha, what a thing it is to have a blood relative! I know exactly what you mean. A woman like Ruth, do nothing? The woman who had to know? Go to her grave not knowing? You'd more easily push her over the ridge of the Devil's Ravine yourself!'

'Oh, Uncle Christopher, don't! But you're right, therein lies a part of the dilemma: Ruth is faced with the Ghost of Possibility, of seeing herself as, in part possibly responsible, for a recent murder. She must also be hourly banishing the spectre that she may be responsible for the irretrievable loss of the, I know, doll-comfort Justice, for the stealing of her own daughter's life. If she says nothing, a double murderer will walk as a phantom through her thoughts, for the rest of her hours.'

The white-orange embers threw an unwanted heat upon Christopher Coates and Anna Godstone, in the dark shadowed room.

'There is also, of course, the salient point of Annette's dying wish.'

'Secret sister, secret sister,' Anna whispered into the night. 'Of course, a dying woman, orphaned as an infant, leaving her child with just a father, who at the very least she must've now known had betrayed her all those years ago and at worst she must've thought her daughter to be in the deepest danger with...'

'Her dying wish, maybe no matter how dark a danger it placed her in, maybe just a dying wish, was for her daughter to know she has a sister in this world.'

'I think that point, however, although we mustn't forget it, is a knot too far for us to untie in one night, Uncle.'

'You are right, my dear Viola. Well then, let us stick to the main: we cannot advise Ruth to do nothing and leave justice to the Lord, as we know it would leave her mind leprosied, however much she might pray. We know we cannot advise her to tell all to the authorities as the justice of men, being so woefully inferior to the Lord's, would most likely condemn the man, wherever the truth may lie and leave Ruth with worse uncertain fears as to her own culpability in the matter. What options does that leave her? We can hardly arrive at the truth by arranging for a dead woman we don't know to haunt him this time, can we?'

'No, I think that this time we have to work on probabilities Uncle; what is most probably going to bring Ruth closest to the truth, although I scarcely dare suggest it, is a confrontation with Nathan.'

'What, Anna? When the last woman who came to know more than he wished her to, is now lying in her grave?' He tapped the poker on the hearth surround as he spoke.

'Ruth will need protection, I grant you, she cannot go alone, Uncle Christopher, but I believe her desire to know the true situation is most likely to be satisfied if she confronts him swiftly, before his own thoughts and feelings over recent events become fixed and settled and most probably, as she worked before, when he is most vulnerable.'

'Namely, when he's in his cup?'

'Indeed, in drink: no matter how much of a charlatan he may be, his innocence or otherwise is almost certain to be written across his countenance, however briefly, if she shocks him unawares after an evening, as you say, 'at the tap'.'

'I'm more than prepared to accompany Ruth, you see I have come a certain way ahead of you in thinking, what I need is people with whom I may place letters, Anna.'

'Letters?'

'Yes. I can see no other way of guarding my own and her safety. Remember that much of our view of the story is as yet unknown to Nathan. Remember that he's not set eyes on Ruth these twenty years and more. Remember that, to use your phrase, it is 'most probable' he committed bigamy but no more as a young man and then repented of his sin in grief. The probability attached to this latest tragedy; that, we cannot be certain about. If Ruth and I are to ask Nathan for his account of events, he needs to know that we've lodged letters, here and about, detailing his history, which are only to be opened in the event of Ruth or me coming a cropper, under any mysterious circumstances whatsoever.'

'Being shrewd rubs off on a man, I should say, Uncle.'

'I only hope it will be sufficient, Anna. I mean, I hope truly in my heart he turns out to be merely a fool and a drunkard, that Ruth may go home in peace and keep her own counsel over the affair. The granddaughters' acquaintance could then be quietly managed in private, if Nathan could be prevailed upon to see his way clear to such an event. If, however, he proves not just to be the most foolish of men but a villain to boot, he will dissemble in his story. Being a complex tale, it is most likely that Ruth and I will come away with a feeling of veracity or vagary about his account. The former will lead us to peace, the latter to the Justice of the Peace. Either way, the matter will be placed in the hands of a higher authority than ourselves and I, for one, will be glad of it.'

'Well, it seems you have your plan, although whether I helped you to it, I'm sure I don't know.'

'Maybe it's more that I meant to ensure that there was no easier path I was missing, my dear Anna, for this road I would've avoided, had there been a simpler lane.'

'Isaiah, Eight, Twelve, Uncle, 'Fear not what other men fear'.'

'Remember that I, the Lord, am Holy.'

'Take God with you in prayer, Uncle, each step on your way.'

'What a comfort you are, Anna, with Him, all things are possible, indeed.'

Chapter Eight

'The next time Anna found herself alone was on the following Monday morning. Theo had just left for school and Samuel, having had considerably less sleep than usual, with a booming Uncle Christopher in the house all weekend, had fallen asleep over his porridge. Anna had just taken pity on the poor little mite and lifted him into his crib for an early nap, when Millie popped her head around the kitchen doorway.

'Yoo-hoo!' she cried and then stopped, when she caught a glimpse of the look on Anna's weary face as she raised her head up from her crossed arms on the table. 'Oh, silly me, house full all weekend and all of that, I should've thought.'

'No, Millie, come back, I've been so patient with so many folk all weekend and the last person on God's earth I'd ever wish to upset would be you!'

Millie stuck just her head back around the door frame, 'The last person? Me? Do you really mean that?'

'Yes, Millie Price,' Anna smiled broadly, 'in God's name, I do.'

Millie just giggled, 'I don't think anybody's ever said anything that nice to me before. I won't keep you though, Anna, if I were you, I'd take Samuel's lead and go and put my head down for an hour, you know, the world won't come to an end and even if it did, the good Lord wouldn't condemn you anyway. I mean, there's few enough of us folk down here as good-hearted as you, if he's going to be more choosy than that, who's he going to have up there to talk to? Anyway, as I said, I won't keep you but may I just ask you a quick question?'

'Of course you may, Millie, what's on your mind?'

'Would you think I was mad, I mean, completely 'off my rocking chair' as they say, if I...'

'If you what, Millie?'

'Well, if you're tired, which you plainly are, if I spent my morning visiting Ret –, well, Mrs –, well, the pair of them really, would I be welcome, do you think? I mean,' she giggled again, 'even I might be upset to get knocked back twice in one morning.' She paused. 'Am I mad to even think they might want my company?'

Anna sat up with her back straight and considered her friend who, she remembered, had taken such particular care of Retty in her own seemingly haphazard way, when they were all so busy with Theo's party preparations.

'No, Millie, indeed I don't think you're mad at all. In fact, as I think about it, you might even find that a third in the company might make it a less burdensome morning for them both.'

'Do you think? Only I wouldn't want to get ahead of myself only to go falling on my face, you see, I've never been very good at these things in the past and I usually end up feeling as if people just wish, I would, go away...'

'Not Emmaline Gables, not after last Monday and Saturday, Millie.'

'And Retty?'

'Retty's not daft, Millie, nor is she a real drunk, she's just in a bad place right now and one she probably wants to get out of, at bottom.'

'All right, I'll go. The things you talk me into as I live and breathe, Anna.'

The two women met eyes and smiled at each other, before Millie departed with a giggle.

Anna went upstairs to tidy, as was her habit, after Will and Theo had breakfasted and left. This morning, however, there was a third bed to be attended to. She walked into Uncle Christopher's room to change the sheets and immediately noticed three crisp, cream coloured envelopes on the mantelshelf. She walked over to them and ran her finger along beneath them. The first had a small neat number one written in the top right hand corner and was addressed, in Uncle Christopher's distinctive hand and dark green ink, to her, Anna Godstone. The second, with its neat number two, was also addressed to her. These two she could guess at the contents of, for although she'd been mightily exhausted going to bed as she had in the small hours of Sunday morning, she remembered every word of the history recounted to her. The third envelope was more of a surprise; it had a neat number three, where a stamp might otherwise have been pressed and was addressed to her father, the Reverend Thomas Porter.

Anna carefully took the two envelopes addressed to her and sat down on the bed with them. Turning over the first, she saw the instruction on the reverse: 'To be opened immediately'. She followed the instruction, presuming rightly, that all she needed to know about the other two envelopes would be enclosed.

My dearest Anna,

Following your kind, patient and thoughtful attention to my demands upon your time and conscience this weekend, I know that these envelopes will not come as a surprise to you. I hereby humbly request that you destroy this message and its envelope and keep in a secret and safe place its following numbered companions.

My second letter, addressed to your good self, you will find to be quite bulky, containing as it does, the various histories and details conveyed to you on Saturday by fire light. I would not have a certain gentleman, if he may be called so, have any inkling whatsoever as to your knowledge of these affairs; he need only know of them having been deposited with friends here and about in secret, as a safeguard against foul play to those (namely R – and myself) who are about to accost him as to the condition of his immortal soul before his Maker.

The third letter, my dear Anna, addressed to your father, merely contains my solicitor's details as to my newly made will. I do not see the need to trouble your father with matters which, knowing his 'other worldly' disposition, would only disturb him without giving him the pleasure of any of the influence he is accustomed to, in changing or altering events for the better, as a result of his intervention through the words of the Good Book. I would therefore bid you to keep it safe until, we hope, a day I do not care to mention some while distant, when you will see fit to destroy its companion and convey my wishes as to my estate to the world, after I have departed from it at a ripe and proper time, for a better life with Him within whose power it is to dictate such things.

My dear Anna, I cannot tell you what, not a comfort (for sadly it is not yet a time for such) but a robust bolstering it was to me, to speak with you and hear your thoughts on such a strange and troubled history. It is in the nature of man to seek the easiest and least troublesome way forward in life and often there is wisdom in such a philosophy. In this case, however, we are agreed; a difficult path must be travelled with wisdom, care and prayer.

I shall speak no more, my child. I travel, I know, with your thoughts and prayers and with those for my much tested companion, that we might seek her much needed peace.

Everlastingly yours in love, gratitude and affection,

Christopher Coates Esq

Anna lay back upon the bolstered pillow, which had so recently comforted the author of this letter. She prayed for his safe carriage and that of his acquaintance. She prayed for Nathan Lunsford and the souls of his departed wives, remembering the words of Jesus, that dutiful women are not to be encumbered with the worry of who they were or were not married to after this life. She prayed for her own immortal soul, as she dared not compare her own difficulty to that of Ruth's. As she pulled her hand across her forehead, however, she could not help but remember that it was a week to the day since she'd first met him: Raphael. His image drifted across her mind and he smiled at her. Then, before her, appeared the comforting vision of her Uncle Christopher sitting by the fire, talking of her, 'idyllic and blessed existence' in Heartbourne. In her mind, his voice drifted on, 'with your pretty sons and playful husband'. Then, in a moment, she blushed right up to her closed eye lashes at the recollection of her reaction to Raphael. The delights of such a splendid family weekend celebrating Theo's birthday. The goodness and youthfulness of Will as he played in the garden. The warning of Retty's disordered, chaotic life.

Anna sighed and turned fitfully as Raphael's image arose in her mind; only as he turned to her it was not Raphael under the black curled locks but the face of a menacing stranger like a living gargoyle, leering and jeering at her with not one but two wives, one under each arm with just their heads protruding through, both pale and grotesque with indignity, 'So, you'd like to join me, 'eh? So, you do want more than one? So, you think it might be fun?' The monstrous gargoyle began gyrating his hips in a lewd fashion around and about, swirling each bent over woman about with him, as they banged with their arms on the wooden panels of a dark, narrow corridor, calling for him to stop.

Anna jolted into consciousness and sat bolt upright on the bed. Darkness and small beams of light descended from the top of her vision downwards obscuring the room before her. The nightmare had vanished but the knocking still continued. She heard the front door open and remembered that Samuel was downstairs, asleep and alone.

She panicked, as a rip tide swept through her veins, 'Who is it?' she called out, stumbling onto the landing only to see her father's 'off collar' straw hat down in the hallway. She sank downwards in relief and lost consciousness, this time completely.

Chapter Nine

'As Anna slowly came to, she gradually became aware that she was lying on her own bed, fully clothed and that it was daylight outside. This seemed peculiar, as she'd never taken to lying down during the day, not even when she'd been expecting each of the boys. The daylight disturbed her vision and she found that even squinting, she couldn't focus, so she closed her eyes again and tried to recall what day it was and how she came to be lying there. As she lay with her cheek against the soft, downy warmth of the pillow, covered as it was in crisp, cotton linen, she almost felt she'd be content to remember nothing much beyond her own name. Such a simple existence, she soon started to recall, was beyond all possibility.

Her jumbled musings were interrupted by the creaking of the door. Slowly, steadily, the door crept open revealing not the familiar sight of Will, but none other than Raphael. In her stupefied state, rather than feeling panic, Anna remained calm as Raphael entered carrying Samuel on his right hip, with a tea cup outstretched in his left hand. It looked most awkward an arrangement, but as the child appeared more securely held than the cup of tea, Anna chose not to worry or interfere but rather to enjoy the spectacle.

Raphael's voice, his softly spoken words addressed to the placidly gazing Samuel, made Anna smile involuntarily.

'Now, if we just put this down here, next your mother, we can sit you down with me here, young chap,' Raphael lowered himself onto a bedroom chair and adjusted Samuel's position onto his lap. 'You're back with us then?' he addressed Anna but continued without wanting a response, 'I do hope the tea's not gone cold, the pot on the table still felt warm, only I'm afraid I banged about a bit fetching it to revive you and accidentally woke your young man here up in the process.'

Raphael looked at her directly and smiled, 'You still look dazed, Anna, maybe prop yourself up and try some tea?'

Anna's vision had restored itself but she feared her senses couldn't have, 'How did you? How did I?'

'You don't recall? You came to the top of the stairs, called out and then dropped like a dead man, squarely banging your head on the stair rail and attempting to plummet your entire self to an early grave, down the whole case in one, like a child on a loosed sledge in the snow. I'm afraid it happened so all of a sudden, I moved as swiftly as I could but I fear you may find yourself a little tender here and there about. I lifted you as gently as a shepherd could a new-born lamb and laid you where you are, with no compromise to your dignity or honour, I do promise you, Anna.'

Raphael blushed at the memory, as he omitted to convey to her the tender feelings it'd aroused in him, carrying her thus, so close to his chest, with the weight of her against him, the warm skin of their arms touching and her head resting beneath his chin. Nor did he describe to her the tumult of feelings coursing through his natural blood, as he lay her slender body on the bed and without forestalling the inclination in time, stroked her perfect, pale cheek just once with his finger tip and removed a lock of hair from across her face, where it had fallen out of place. He didn't trouble her either, with the strength of will it'd taken him, once he'd assured himself that her breathing was still regular and no great damage was to be feared, to remove his gaze from the rise and fall of her chest and the calm serenity of her face and withdraw from the room before his venial sin, by being dwelt upon in mind alone, became more potently mortal. He didn't tell her, that he was by nature a careful and not a clumsy man and that the din that he'd produced, searching about for some sugar for the tea, as required under such circumstances, was a direct result of his utterly discombobulated state of mind, after experiencing such physical proximity to her softness. That he was glad of the distraction of Samuel's awakening, to wrench himself away from the overwhelming feeling, that he was hopelessly and passionately absorbed by a woman, who was a near stranger now, but whose company would undoubtedly, unavoidably, be present in his days and weeks to come.

Anna propped herself up on her elbows and looked into his eyes.

'You've done me a great service and no dishonour by the sound of it. I should apologise for disrupting your life in such a manner...' Anna broke off and their look turned into a mutual gaze.

Samuel saved them by interrupting with a loud cry, as he could now see his mother but not reach her from his vantage point on Raphael's lap. Raphael lifted the outstretched babe to his rightful place but couldn't help notice how Anna closed her eyes, as she kissed Sam's head, as if she were troubled at heart. If he'd been stood before his Maker at that very moment, he could not have told truly whether the emotion he felt was fear, amazement, anguish or gladness or maybe all of these at once. He was so very close to speaking out of place, that he knew he must leave immediately.

'Shall I go and fetch a friend to watch over you, Anna? Is it Millie? Your neighbour?'

Anna tried to control her emotions and composure as she raised her eyes to meet his once more.

'Of course, you must, we wouldn't want...any upset.' Anna broke off as a tear rolled down her cheek.

Every element in Raphael's being yearned to rush to her side, to hold her and to comfort her but he knew he couldn't; to do so would be betrayal indeed. Instead, he stood transfixed, unable to do what was wrong and approach Anna but humanly unequal to the task of doing what was right and leaving.

Anna was distraught: the nightmare, the fall, the blow to the head and then Raphael's near presence; her usual exterior shell and tranquil demeanour were in pieces, shattered, her thoughts, she found to be in disarray. She dared not even look in his direction as she felt the warm, tell-tale tear descend her cheek.

Without prior warning, before either party had gathered themselves, there came three loud raps at the door. The sound of them assaulted Raphael's and Anna's senses like blows beating down from a villain's bat. Suddenly, the state of affairs between them took on a whole new perspective, assembled as they were in Anna's marital bedroom in the middle of the day, with no other adult present on the premises.

61

'Mrs Gables!' Anna whispered in panic.

'How do you know?' asked Raphael.

'She bangs with her stick like a beadle. Did anybody see you come in?'

'No, but your father sent me and besides, I dropped my hat as I lifted you up the stairs.'

'Anna Godstone!' A familiar voice raised itself up to them resonating through to the rafters beyond. 'Raphael De Vine! Come down this instant and explain yourselves!'

'There's no need, my dear good woman,' Mr Porter's tones chimed in, 'for any kind of confrontation, I'm sure.'

There was silence. Millie, Retty, Mrs Gables and the Reverend Thomas Porter stood crowded at the foot of the stairs, while Anna and Raphael looked at each other above, horrified at the implications of the unfolding scene.

'Look, I've known Anna Porter since we were babes in white cotton dresses, Ma.' Retty took control of the morality posse downstairs, 'You go and seat yourselves and I'll go up, I'm sure there's a perfectly honourable explanation.'

Meanwhile, Raphael regained his chivalrous nature upstairs, 'Lie down Anna, you're in no fit state, if I go out quickly it'll look better than this delay.'

Before anyone had moved, Raphael stepped out. He looked down and saw his hat, identical to the one on the priest's head, resting three quarters of the way up the stairs. He walked down the stairs, picking up the offending article on his way. He stood before the company bearing a calm and dignified mien.

'Millie, you need to go upstairs and attend to your friend. Pastor, I'm afraid your daughter's suffered a fall, I believe she'll recover but it was fortuitous,' he placed emphasis on the word, 'and not anything else,' he said looking at Emmaline Gables directly, 'that I was here to break her fall and carry her to her chamber to rest.'

'Where's the baby?' asked Millie, glancing anxiously into the kitchen.

'I was just placing him in her arms in order to descend to you, hence my slight delay,' Raphael blushed at the untruth, 'but I'm not sure if she's sufficiently stable...'

'For it to be safe for her to hold him, come on Retty, we're needed.'

With that, Millie pulled Retty up the stairs behind her, as everyone breathed a moral sigh of relief and began instead to fret about Anna's state of health and the baby not falling off the bed.

It transpired, through endless discussions throughout the parlours of the village, over too many tea cups to list and many a piece of fine sponge cake, that Anna's father, presuming that Millie would be with Anna in the morning, as was her habit, had sent young Raphael around to fix a hanging high trellis, that, he'd noticed at Theo's party, Will had still not quite yet got around to attending to. The trellis was beginning to be used by a runaway bramble in a ramshackle fashion and Mr Porter wished to see it restored for Anna, back in its regular place to support her fine roses, which would soon require its strength to keep their blooms ordered and beautiful, as in any well-tended garden they should be. Little had he known, as he called upon Emmaline Gables, naturally, after her first attendance at church following her return to his parish, the consternation that imparting information regarding this small task would create, with Millie Price sitting there in the parlour with him and not at poor Anna's at all. The fact that the speed of Mrs Gables' response had undoubtedly averted a moral shadow being cast over the reputations of two, as it turned out, still very upright members of the community, was put to her credit, as were the gentlemanly, indeed maybe heroic actions of Raphael, to his.

At this point in the narrative, many a sigh was issued and tea cup placed back down in a saucer, while a wistful air circulated the room. For it had not been missed by the many matrons and maidens of the village alike, that although their deeply dashing new carpenter did sport a wedding ring, no female companion had yet joined him in the rooms above the carpentry, where he retired at night. Despite numerous, suitably subtle enquiries on the matter, an explanation had not been drawn from Raphael himself. He had, however, stated quite clearly to

Bessie Piper (when she was on her way up to Whyly on Wednesday) upon her casual comment about the vexation of unruly children – didn't he think? – that he had no knowledge of the same, having never yet had any of his own.

Anna, meanwhile, was universally declared to be expecting once more, for why ever else would she be fainting in the middle of the day? And so soon after Samuel (the poor dear) that it was decided there could be nothing amiss in her marriage to be wondered about, for sure.

So rife was the village with talk of undoubtedly the most interesting event to happen in Heartbourne all week, that word of it reached Will's ears just before the end of his homeward journey on Friday, as he stopped off at the Gun Inn for what he thought was to be a quiet pint of his favourite, Honey Bee Ale.

A quiet pint it was not. As he drove his cart homeward, Will reflected. He was quite shocked; his Anna, the centre of gossip. He was, it had to be said, quite amused also, for the tale undoubtedly, surely, was very much ado about nothing very much. Wasn't it? Village life, the Reverend Thomas Porter, Emmaline Gables, all of these factors had contributed far more to this unusual event than Anna had done herself. At bottom, all she'd done was fainted. He sighed. The problem wasn't, at root, how most idle people perceived it. To him, William Godstone, Anna's husband it was this: Anna had needed him and he wasn't there. Someone else had been, thanks be to God and heaven forefend that he shouldn't have been and that Anna should've fallen, after too much exertion over the weekend, to her peril. But to his mind, the person who should've been there was him; he was, after all, Anna's husband. But he hadn't been there, he'd been away. What was more, he was now only just learning of the event, five full days after its happening. He wasn't content.

Upon his return to the lane, Theo came bouncing up to him with the new puppy in close pursuit, 'Papa, Papa, come and see what Ivor can do!'

In truth, Ivor was more powered by enthusiasm than by Theo or by any discipline, but the sight of Theo being matched in boundless energy by the doting puppy almost put all thoughts of any disquiet from Will's mind.

'Here I am, here's my son, here's his puppy – Ivor did you say?'

'Yes, Papa, do you like it?'

'I like it very much indeed,' he said picking up the puppy and inspecting it seriously. 'And here's my wife,' he kissed her on each cheek, 'with our babe in her arms,' he nuzzled Sam who giggled, as Will laced his arms about them both, 'what could there be to worry about?'

'You've heard then?' asked Anna, tilting her head against his.

'I have, as you can imagine in Heartbourne, with suitable brevity and no great matter made of it at all.'

Anna, who'd been dreading this moment for five full days, for more reason than one, with the full force of her own guilty judgement upon her soul, half laughed and half choked at Will's gentle irony.

Will continued, oblivious to his wife's distress, as he scooped Theo up into their huddle, 'And I can imagine how little it has been spoken of, among female gatherings about the village all week, as they have so many other pressing political affairs to be concerned about, in what must be, to give them the credit they are owed, their frantically hectic lives.'

Coughing and laughing, Anna handed Sam to Will.

'Play with Theo and the puppy, will you ever? I need some water.' Their hands grasped each other's as she left.

Will watched his wife as she re-entered their home. She was a good and beautiful woman, if a little pale today. He loved her dearly and yet their time was spent so often apart. How could he take the care of her he wished to?

'Papa, what's wrong?'

Will turned to his eldest son, 'That's the beauty of it, Theo, there's nothing wrong here. We just need to take good care of your mother and make sure it stays that way.'

Ivor, tired of waiting more than a minute and a half for some attention, began to tug on Will's trouser hem. After suitable protestations about this offence and some dancing around into the front garden, ostensibly in an effort to get the puppy to stop but more obviously to an adult eye, to jig both Theo and Sam about together playfully as they laughed, Will deposited Theo back down on the ground and settled himself on the front bench to watch with pleasure.

He didn't have to wait too long for Anna to return.

'Ivor's progressing well, wouldn't you agree?'

Anna took Sam and seated herself beside Will, 'He's proving to be a remarkable new addition to the family, I would say.

'Coughing gone?'

Anna nodded and met Will's eye briefly, before turning to Sam on her lap.

'Here, Theo,' Will tossed him a small ball but pitched it just beyond the open garden gate, where it rolled past the waiting pony and cart. 'Oh I'm sorry, my son, let me go...' Will began to rise.

'No, Papa, I can get it!'

Theo proudly led Ivor, clapping his way down the path and through the gate.

'And the other supposition taken from the incident...?'

Anna met his eye, 'Oh that, yes, I believe there may've been something in it for a moment, but only for a moment, I'm afraid, Will.'

She looked into his eyes and attempted to speak but tears simply rose to her cheeks and fell in their own silent statement.

'The fall...' was all she managed to utter as he gathered her into his arms.

As Theo returned to the garden, he noticed that both of his parents were brushing away tears with their wrists. He stood still as he saw them looking at each other and with a wisdom beyond his years, perhaps inherited from Anna herself, he realised their weeping had nothing to do with the length of time it'd taken him to persuade Ivor to follow him back into the garden. He walked slowly down the path to the bench.

'Mama and I have cooked your very favourite supper, Papa.'

Will turned to Theo and smiled stroking his arm, 'Now isn't that, just the heartiest welcome home, any husband and father could wish for?'

Will spoke the words genuinely and with a generous spirit. This time, the unintentional irony, on more than one point, stung Anna's soul.

Chapter Ten

'In response to his own pensive and sorrowful mood, Will doted on Anna all weekend. In response to her own feelings of guilt and mourning, in a move most out of character, Anna allowed him to. In truth, the personal and physical ramifications of the fall and the miscarriage had sapped her vitality to an extent she hadn't fully recognised, until the opportunity to rest, to hand over the reins of responsibility to her husband, had presented itself. She'd wanted no one until he returned; now he was here.

It represented a shift in the usual terms of their relationship as he fretted about her comfort, plumped up her pillows and brought her warm soup he'd prepared himself. She'd submitted to the order for bed rest only after Will had called in Doctor Snelling, to have it issued by a higher authority but when after that, he frequently quoted other – Doctor's orders! – some of which appeared more credible than others, she didn't question them. She allowed Will to assume authority over her wellbeing and was quietly amazed at the tenacity with which he stuck to the task and the thorough way in which he carried it out, all weekend. She felt very humble, in receipt of such goodness. Chidden, indeed, would not be too strong an expression for it.

Anna found herself, in a passive way, amazed at how unusually people were behaving. For example, on Sunday morning (having had all her possible needs and more anticipated and a laden tray placed on her bedside table) she'd been left alone sleeping, while all other souls gathered for Morning Prayer.

When she started from her dreams some time later, she could've sworn that what'd disturbed her was Millie's voice, raised in what sounded like impatience. Impossible, thought Anna, as she shifted her head a little, for Millie lived only with her widowed father, who was something of a recluse and somewhat gruff. Timid little Millie Price would never dare to raise her voice to him, would she? Anna had rarely ever heard raised voices next door and not at all since Millie's husband had died, about a year ago now.

However, when Anna raised her head not twenty minutes later, who should she see in the garden assisting Will fix the (now rather famous) high trellis? None other than Mr Osborne himself, who Anna hadn't clapped sight of in a year.

So it continued. Will insisted that Anna remain in bed for another two weeks, as ordered by Doctor Snelling and only agreed to depart for work on the basis that Anna agreed to do nothing. Anna felt quite struck by the manliness of his demeanour, as he kindly but firmly laid out the terms on which he wished to leave arrangements in his absence.

Millie, Retty and Mrs Gables were to be given full run of the house and Anna was to allow them to look after both her and the boys as, Emmaline was not backward in pointing out, 'She jolly well ought to have done from last Monday onwards.'

Retty smiled wryly, squeezed Anna's hand and declared herself surprised and delighted not be the one being told off and told what to do next. Mrs Gables batted her arm. Only Millie seemed a little sad as the party began to leave Anna's chamber, having seen from her complexion that she still wasn't strong at all.

'Will, may Millie stay, just a short while? I feel I owe her something of an apology.'

'Just a few minutes then, Anna. I spoke privately with Millie yesterday,' Millie nodded in confirmation, 'and I believe she's not vain-hearted enough to view your reticence last week as a personal slight.'

Millie settled herself quietly beside Anna, 'It's not you that owes me an apology, Anna, it must be quite the other way round, I'm sure. How could I not have noticed you were so poorly?' she took Anna's hand in hers. 'And all those stupid remarks about another baby, when we all knew about the fall.'

'You were busy helping Retty cope with *the* Mrs Gables, Millie.'

'Huh, yes and sometimes it was the other way round, believe you me; she can be a sly one that Retty Gables. But, Anna, you look so pale, even now. How could I not have noticed? I'm your closest friend and I live next door...'

Anna felt more alone than she'd ever done in her life. Here she was, surrounded by people who loved her so dearly, yet because, because of him, Raphael, because of what'd happened between them, she had to stay alone. She couldn't explain to Millie her chosen solitude in quite extreme pain the week before, not in any terms that would do at all. How could she tell Millie the truth? How could she tell her that she'd hidden from her the bruises and the miscarriage and encouraged her to go to Retty's because she feared she was herself to blame? She feared that everything was all her own fault, while the innocent people who loved her, all now appeared to be blaming themselves.

'It wasn't your fault, Millie. I just reacted in a funny way, I can't explain it.'

'Did it make you think... of *her*?'

'My mother? Yes, it did,' Anna answered quite honestly. 'She lost her life and now I've lost his or hers, who's to know? Millie, I didn't even realise I was expecting, I was just so busy with Theo's party and everything, I must've been distracted, I don't know where my head was,' she stumbled, 'all the signs were there.'

'You did seem giddy and a bit, well, vacant once or twice, you know, like cows go.'

If circumstances had been different, Anna would have laughed out loud at such Millie Price frankness. Instead, she smiled at Millie and stroked her hand in return.

'You do still seem a little lost, even now,' she said gently. 'We're still here though, Anna, when you're ready.'

Anna was still blinking away tears as Will returned and ushered Millie away. How strange it seemed, that it was easier to hide the complexity of it all from Will, than from Millie. Moreover, in a village the size and character of Heartbourne, however was she going to hide from its carpenter and future harm? She closed her eyes but she dared not sleep, for dreams it seemed, were no longer her friends.

Chapter Eleven

'Having never written in his absence before, Will wrote each day and his letters arrived from Tuesday to Friday. Anna wrote back from Tuesday to Thursday and awaited (for only the second time with anticipation) his return on Friday.

During that week, Mrs Gables, Millie and Retty spent most of their daytime hours attending to Anna and her sons' needs. After working hours, Millie and Retty returned home to attend to the requirements of their menfolk. Mrs Gables (her supervision not being necessary once Henry was home) moved, with one of her three great trunks, into Anna's spare room for the duration.

Under close supervision for a while each day, Samuel was allowed to sit up next to Anna. He babbled and took great delight in playing peek-a-boo or marvelling at the pretty bubbles Anna blew from a pot of special mixture left by Uncle Christopher. Once or twice he dozed off in her arms and she allowed herself to doze also; the warmth of his small body and the vanilla smell of his head comforted and calmed her.

Theo was allowed to come and sit with her when he arrived home from school each day. The puppy, Ivor, was considered far too boisterous for Anna's condition but Theo's chatter was full of his exploits and scrapes, particularly on the day when Theo arrived home from school to universal panic among Millie, Retty, Mrs Gables and Judith, as Ivor hadn't been seen for an hour or more and no matter how they searched, he wasn't to be found.

Theo proudly related to his mother, how, with calm authority and composure he'd walked past the four harassed women to the inglenook fireplace. He carefully moved three wooden boxes, stacked like steps on the edge of the left hand settle and stood up in their place. He reached across to the inner ledge of the low, great beam and withdrew a small, sleeping, black bundle.

'He likes to sleep up there, Mama, when he's tired and I'm not there but I do hope he doesn't try it once he gets too big or I don't quite know what'll happen.' Theo explained.

'He'll fall down, not know what's happened and take to sleeping on the hearth rug like any normal creature, I expect, Theo. Life's a bit like that; you grow and change without realising you have done, you make a mistake because things aren't the same and don't fit any longer, you take a tumble and looking at your bruises figure out what you need to alter, to stop that happening again.'

'Life changes all the time, doesn't it, Mama? Sam's sitting up on his own now but he can't talk yet but if you know him he can tell you what he wants quite easily, can't he, Mama?' Theo went on without waiting, 'And yet, I can't remember when I couldn't talk at all. It wasn't a long time ago for you and Papa but it is for me. Time's funny like that, isn't it?'

Anna smiled at her little philosopher and agreed. Time and change were peculiar phenomena indeed. A week could change your whole world irreversibly. Whether or not, however, the change became irrevocable, she mused after Theo had left, depended on your reaction to it. She drew her small writing slope back onto her lap and continued her letter to Will.

That evening, after the boys were asleep, Mrs Gables came in to read to Anna. This was one of Anna's favourite parts of her unusual days in those two weeks, for it reminded her of the last, quiet, intimate times spent in the company of her father before her marriage, when she would read to him of an evening.

They began with Milton's, 'At a Solemn Music', which, brought up as a child of the clergy, was one of Anna's favourites. As the room fell silent, Anna's thoughts began to wander. It took her a while to notice, that Mrs Gables too, had fallen silent.

'It's very generous of you to be here, Ma Gables,' Anna spoke softly, not wishing to appear either sentimental or superficial.

'I do hope you're aware of how I appreciate your kindness and attention.'

'Humph.' Emmaline looked at her and pulled in her left cheek, resting it on her jutted out jaw. 'To a certain degree I am merely making amends for our communal neglect of you last week; I don't take full responsibility for it, for my attention was naturally with Henrietta and you, my girl,' she stopped and chewed on her cheek disapprovingly, 'were nothing short of quite reckless in regard of your own health and welfare. Two boys and a puppy? In that condition and circumstance?' She leant back in her chair to regard Anna critically.

Anna looked down at her handkerchief and followed the main thread in the pattern of the lace with her fingertip, instinctively knowing that her response was not yet required.

'I will, however, say this in your defence; if your own dear mother had still been alive, the oversight, omission, neglect, what have you,' she waved it away with her hand, 'would not have occurred. Your mother would've known you'd gone off to a peculiar meeting place and your mother would've recognised the meeting as being with that most Protean of creatures in manifest: namely Grief.'

Anna lifted her head from her handkerchief lace and looked at Ma Gables with new eyes.

'Yes, I've known that Proteus myself, I don't mind telling you, Anna Godstone, although, if I continue speaking, my words are to remain between the two of us solely, if you don't mind?'

Anna simply nodded.

'It was many years ago now, for me, but you see I don't blame Henrietta for her manifestation, her Proteus, her drinking. I mean, I ask you, I should've come sooner! Three babes, Anna, three babes! You've just lost the possibility of a child, not to be underestimated; hardship and grief are not to be treated as matters of competition where only the most grotesque deserves our sympathy. However, may I ask you, just for one moment, to lay aside your own thoughts for a short while and consider her journey? Three times she has borne babes down the canal to what should've been life. Three times she's held their perfect, tiny, lifeless bodies in her arms. Never has she seen her own babe open his eyes for the first time and attempt, so calmly, to focus on her face.

'With me, Grief came from a similar source but in a differently directed stream. I'd had a son born fit and well. He was growing robustly and the world seemed to sparkle in my eyes as I regarded him. All that, suddenly changed. I gave birth to a daughter, Annelise, we called her, as I cradled her silent body and wept.

'It changed me. I changed. I became bitter and critical of all I saw about me. I believe I must have been,' she halted and checked Anna's countenance, finding nothing disagreeable, she continued, 'somewhat quarrelsome. My boy Henry, the schoolmaster, Mr Crouch, the shopkeeper, Mr Turner, the innkeeper, Mr Congreve, our neighbours, too numerous to mention, my husband, Abraham, all received my thoughts and judgement un-tempered with any grace or measure. I must've been most forgetful of both The Lord's Prayer and Matthew, Seven, Two.'

'Forgive, that you might be forgiven; judge not, for measure for measure...'

'Indeed, the same. You would all have been children back then; you, Henrietta, Millie...I must have appeared to you, I don't know how.'

'For-midable, might be an appropriate term for it but...' Anna faltered.

'Spit it out girl; don't splice your words to me in this room.'

'Well, forgive me if I seem somewhat impertinent but it strikes me, Ma Gables, that for you to sit here describing how you can see, perhaps, the imperfections of your former ways of going about, that something must've happened, something to make you see...' Anna twiddled her handkerchief in her hands, searching for a gentle expression to describe her thoughts.

'Something must've happened, you reckon? For me to see the distance I was erring from a proper, fruitful path? The distance I was setting between myself and His grace?'

'Ma Gables, you're being too harsh on yourself, for as surely as Henrietta is now, you were, in your troubled condition, I do

74

pray, among friends?' Anna emphasised her last word with meaning.

Emmaline contemplated Anna for a while and then smiled, 'I believe you are your mother's daughter, Anna, in more than name alone, for it did indeed fall out as you say. It was, however, only after time, much time and much forbearance and forgiveness, that I began to recognise the case.

'With me, it was Abraham who proved my steadfast friend. You young women seem to have each other, in and out of each other's houses, living in each other's pockets, almost so much I'm surprised your husbands get a look in on your thoughts.'

'I protest, you are unfair!' said Anna, suddenly worrying that maybe the comment wasn't as far from the truth as it should be.

Emmaline leant back and smiled at Anna, 'I believe I like your sparky, forthright character, my girl, anyhow, maybe I'm right and maybe I'm not, but we digress. It was Abraham who never criticised or commented on my demeanour. When I raised my voice, he returned me kindness. When I spoke of an argument, he remained calm. When I engaged in battle, he would simply kneel by the hearth and pray, I knew not what for back then but I can guess at it now. Undeterred by what I saw as a lack of husbandly backbone from him (I fear I will have a frightful list to answer to, when I stand before the Almighty, Anna) I continued as I was, for about ten years.

'Then, one evening as we sat by the fireside opposite one another, he spoke to me very patiently in his tone but nevertheless, in a way he'd never done before.

'He asked if he might trouble me to recall an incident outside the village stores earlier in the day. I called it to mind and asked him, what of it. I blush now, when I think of my tone. He caught my eye directly and said that he thought I might've been softer in my words to Molly Jenner. He pointed out that she was expecting, for no less than the fifth time in seven years. He asked me to note, that as a newcomer to the village upon her marriage, and with such prompt and heavy subsequent matronly calls upon her time, that she had few close friends in Heartbourne and probably valued her friendship with me, and the attention that I, who was quite highly above her in worldly estate, had paid her over the years. He said that he might mention, that Molly probably valued the friendship more than I'd ever realised. He went on to say that he thought I may have not noticed, as I swept rather grandly past her, having finished my very public reprimand, the look of hurt and upset which passed across her countenance. He asked whether I'd noticed that he hadn't followed me immediately into the shop. I admitted, I had not. He explained that he had halted, to enquire as to the health of her husband and four sons. He asked if I'd noticed that he hadn't immediately followed my departure from the shop. I admitted, I had not, sufficiently mortified by this point not to admit that my attention had been too engrossed in noticing the disorder of the young Jenners' attire and footwear, as they scuffled about playing by the village pond opposite. He explained that he'd remained, to order half a dozen apple tartlets and pay for their delivery to the Jenners' cottage, in time for their family tea. With that, he shook the *Sussex Advertiser* he'd borrowed from Mr Turner and retreated impenetrably behind it.

'I sat, stilled. For two hours I didn't move, except to close my eyes as I smarted involuntarily from time to time at the recollections which were assembling themselves in my mind.

'At our usual hour, Abraham arose and I went to rally myself to prepare our hot milk before bed but he put his hand on mine and simply said, 'I will fetch it for us both, tonight, Emmaline.'

'Such haughty pomposity, such thoughtlessness, such a manifold score of occasions, so much unkindness, met with so simple and faithful a love. When we marry, Anna, most of us do so in a giddy whirl we call love, which is in fact, mainly passion. What happens next is largely a matter of luck. How someone else will act as a spouse cannot truly be known until they are one, until they are tested by the trials it brings to attach yourself to another imperfect soul for all days and then of course, if you discover that your choice was a bad one, it's too late.

'I myself, on the contrary, consider myself to be among the most fortunate of all souls who have ever entered into this Holy Estate, I jest not, my child.

'In the following weeks, I took it upon myself to assume the Christian, child-like humility of a pupil. I considered myself chidden by Abraham and by God himself, through my good husband. I was, however, like all mortal beings, fallible and a creature of habit. Although most of my actions and deeds became more thoughtful and considered, such as my visit to Molly the next day to make amends, I still found myself occasionally erring, until a small cough, or a gentle touch of Abraham's hand, or a glance in his direction revealed a look I did not want to fully muster itself, corrected me gently and put me back on a path with my Maker.

Emmaline paused, 'If you have one of those more unusual marriages, Anna, which I believe you do, which began founded not so much on giddy passion as liking, suitability and parental guidance, a marriage which rather than burning with superficial sulphur, takes some organic growing into, if you find yourself, after the salamandrine fires of other weddings have burnt down, with a husband as true and faithful to your union in difficulty as Abraham was to ours, you will find he steadily grows more handsome to you, than the prettiest face in any village could ever be.'

Anna's sight was absorbed in her handkerchief lace as she willed herself not to cry. Very slowly, she stretched her hand out towards Ma Gables, who covered it with her own and sighed.

Chapter Twelve

'Anna, dressed in suitable travelling clothes, wavered a little watching the perpetual movement of the tall slender poplars which marked the village boundary. In their majestic row, blown by the westward wind, their tops bowed forward to the east, where she and William were destined with their two sons. It was now late May and as she looked across, the fruit trees in the well-tended garden she was leaving behind were in blossom and about to flourish. Her roses were robust and about to bloom. Leave them, however, she must.

'If you had spoken to Anna quietly just a month before and told her that on her husband's bidding she would be leaving her father, her friends and her birthplace within weeks, you would've been met with a sceptical smile; Anna would've thought not. That, however, was before. Since her fall, Anna felt altered, less robust. William on the other hand now seemed to have gained a new stature in his words, his bearing and in their relationship as husband and wife. Anna felt sure she would rally in due course; the spark of her vitality was not lost, just subdued for the time being, and not without reason.

'Heartbourne too, was altered. Quite to its astonishment, it had acquired a new inhabitant, who to be blunt, was simply beyond its genteel reckoning. With the breaking of May, Violet De Vine had burst upon Heartbourne with considerably more force than your average spring thunderstorm.

'I must, however, explain things in their proper order.' Elise halted and looked upon Freddie. 'Come with me to the table young man, you look weary.'

'I'm not, Grandma, I'm just unhappy. Why do they have to leave Heartbourne? Won't Theo miss his friends?'

He took his grandmother's hand and leant on her in order to jump down from his high stool.

'Oh, Theo was young enough to make new friends, Freddie, and he had Ivor now, don't forget.'

'Oh, Freddie, let Grandma continue, will you?' said Catherine, with an air of impatience.

'They really did have to go, didn't they, Mother? For the sake of everybody?'

'Yes, Anna felt that they did.'

Freddie, at just seven, was just young enough to submit to being settled upon his grandmother's lap as she continued her tale. Predictably, for those who'd been alive and vital on God's earth for longer than he, before very long, he was dozing in peace.

'Three weeks after fainting, Anna had been allowed to arise and potter around her house and garden once more but not to do any work. Will had come home that week and agreed that Anna's nursing team could be disbanded, on the condition that Millie remained close to Anna during waking hours. I say that Will was home, which he was, however Anna couldn't help but feel he was somehow preoccupied, almost elsewhere, as he whistled while fixing the broken leg on the nursing chair that had sat lopsided for the last year or more, or as he hummed to himself, while painting the new replacement window sill that he'd promised their landlord he would attend to when they'd moved into the cottage.

'Tell me, William Godstone,' said Anna, flipping back the quilt for him as they settled down on that Sunday evening, 'what's on your mind?'

'Aha, you've noticed?' he asked jovially. 'Well, I'll confess there's something afoot but I don't wish to speak of it before I can be more certain of effecting its happening. I will, though, at this time ask you this, my beloved. How would you like it if we were to spend all our days together as we have this weekend, Anna? If I were always in the same house as you? If we were always to share the pleasure of our boys as we lay them in their cots at night? If I were to have the joy of waking to you and waking them up each morning? If I were never to let you fall,' he took her under his arm and kissed her head, 'without being there to protect and guard you?' He rested his head upon hers.

'I think I'd like that very much indeed, my love,' she said nestling into his embrace, 'but there's no great call for a stonemasonry gang in a small village such as Heartbourne, we can paint a pretty picture but we can't eat imagination, Will.'

'Oh, there may be another way but I wouldn't want to press for change, if it wasn't what you wanted, Anna. I'm delighted though,' he looked at her most tenderly, 'if the picture I paint is one you'd wish for.'

Anna was puzzled but tired, so she kissed him and allowed herself to fall asleep in the security and strength of his handsome arms.

The following week passed peacefully and Anna began, very slowly, to regain her strength. Doctor Snelling was still very insistent that a diet high in liver, red meat and cabbage be followed and that no physical exertion, including gardening, was to be undertaken. The word haemorrhage was mentioned briefly but not dwelt upon, as Anna was now plainly in steady recovery.

That weekend, Will came home whistling. As he climbed down from his driving seat he bore a smile as broad as Sussex itself.

Over supper, he conversed with Anna and Theo jovially before insisting that Anna should go and rest in the parlour while 'her boys' washed up for her. Only one small breakage occurred, which Anna heard fall and smash on a flagstone but she wouldn't have dreamed of commenting if they had broken six cups and plates between them, so great was the kindness which prompted the fulfilment of the task.

When 'her boys' came through to the parlour, Anna was attempting to sooth Samuel to sleep but he appeared to be anything but sleepy as he patted Anna's cheeks and giggled, trying to pull himself up to her shoulder, to gain a better vantage point on the world.

'Let me take him for a turn around the garden, Anna, it's not chilly tonight. You read to Theo.'

Will relieved Anna of Sam and she was able to relax. The, at times exhausting persistence of caring for an infant, had become somewhat more shared of late. It was just one of the ways in which Anna felt a newer, mellower and more mature partnership was growing between them. If she'd known at that time, that partially due to her fall, Sam was to be her last child for ten years, she may've been more covetous of her time with him in infancy. We are commanded, however, not to seek to know the future but instead to trust and in this instance, it was as well that that was the case.

When the children were asleep, William wrapped a shawl around Anna's shoulders but then instead of sitting down, he put a finger to his lips as if to indicate a secret and disappeared off into the kitchen once more.

Anna heard him clattering about making an extraordinary amount of noise for someone who seemed to believe that discretion was, for some odd reason, required.

When Will re-entered he was carrying a tray, laid with a small cloth, which was just as well, given the several spillages that had occurred on route from the two generous jars of eggnog which sat on top of it, frothing with promise.

'Eggnog!' cried Anna, 'Why, Will, it isn't Christmas!'

'Full of wholesome ingredients that'll build your strength, Anna, not to mention a small draught of brandy to steady your nerves, for I've a surprise for you, my dearest.'

'Do you now, I thought you were merry about something. Tell me, which should I have first, the eggnog or the surprise?'

'Oh, the eggnog for sure, Anna.'

Anna sat and sipped, saying nothing. For all of Will's new found thoughtfulness and sense of responsibility, she was aware that the impetuous side of his nature was yet to be calmed or overcome. She smiled, met his eyes and waited almost teasingly, as she supped the delicious mixture, most usually reserved for Christmas Day.

'Well, Anna,' Will could contain himself no longer, 'do you feel a little fortified?'

'Err...A little, maybe, but just a few more sips might be advisable, if I am to be shocked.'

'Oh, Anna, your spirits are coming back to you quite wonderfully, I see.' He beamed and shook his head as a giggle escaped her.

'Now then, I must first impart the news which makes my proposed surprise possible. The Pippingford Masonry Gang has been awarded a contract in a proud and fast growing town not ten miles from here. The leading family thereabouts and the townsfolk between them are to share the cost of greatly extending and grandly adorning their current house of worship, a plain built church, which is deemed to be becoming all too humble for such a mighty and upcoming centre of commerce. The work, an advancement on which has already been paid in ready monies, is expected to last at least three years! Three years, Anna, in one place, day and night, week by week for thirty-six months, no fewer!'

Will's exuberant excitement was enchanting to behold and Anna found herself, as she quite often had in recent weeks, admiring his handsome features and sturdy physique. How she could've formerly taken them for granted, not noticed them almost, she couldn't fathom.

'Why, Will, that's tremendous news, steady work and little travel for three years solid, you must all be very pleased and satisfied, praise God!'

'We are, my dearest, we are indeed but do you see for us, for our growing family, it presents an opportunity? Anna, let us be sober for a while. Do you remember, just after your fall, when I was so grieved not to have been here to support you, protect you or even tend to you after the event? How aware I am that had I been here, the order for bed rest would have been immediate and maybe the extent of the after effects of the trauma would've been less? Do you remember how I asked you, a short while ago, if you would like us to wake each and every morning by each other's side? And lay our sons to sleep together?'

'I do, I do indeed. Do you mean to travel the distance each way and back, every day then, Will? I'm afraid I don't grasp your meaning.'

Will travelled across to Anna's chair and, almost kneeling, grasped her hands in his own, 'I've had the assistance of a friend in the town where we are to be based. He's found for us a suitable cottage, Anna, on the outskirts of town, so that the garden, Anna, it was a stipulation of the request, is really a very decent size for a town dwelling. The landlord is known to our friend and he's a respectable man who may be trusted. The proposed rent is very reasonable indeed, on account of our connections with this gentleman and the landlord himself, who's known your father since he was a boy.' Will stopped and looked into Anna's eyes. 'What do you say, Anna, to being together as a family, with me in my rightful place by your side, there to protect you always, that, God willing, no perilous danger may come your way again?'

Anna looked into Will's hope-filled eyes, carefully maintaining a calm exterior demeanour. The turmoil which moved around within her was unexpectedly veering in his direction; how could she say no to such chivalrous intent? How could she deny such graciousness in the face of her cloistered, guilt-fuelled feelings? How could she have turned from this man before her now and looked at another?

Anna opened her mouth to speak but she faltered. She closed her eyes; how could she turn down such an escape from her present trouble? She'd not ventured back into village life since the miscarriage but if she stayed, encounters with Raphael were sure to be unavoidable. Leaving, departing, living elsewhere hadn't even occurred to her as a way, an exit, from her predicament.

'I...I...' she stuttered, unable to articulate anything of her thoughts to Will.

He placed a finger gently to her lips, 'Hush now, I've startled you indeed, I can see. I did think that I might've given you an inkling of my thoughts the other day, but maybe I didn't. I see disquiet on your face, leanings in both one direction and another and what could be more natural? You've lived here all your days and I'm asking if you'll leave to be with me. You can still stay, Anna, if you wish. I want no commanded wife who lacks the spirit I love in her. If you'd prefer to stay, I might come home mid-week to stop a night and we could still be together more often than we have been so far in our union.'

He halted for a moment and stood up, lifting Anna and then seating himself on her chair, with her in his lap. He leant his head upon hers, 'I want no answer from you tonight, no, not a word. I want you to take a week. I want you to consider, I want you to think, for there was never such a great one as you, Anna, for mulling things over, I know you that well.'

Anna smiled. She found out and grasped his hand. It was true, she was forever a one for mulling things over and coming to a conclusion in her own time, she wasn't quick in decision like Will.

'Well, if you'll not be offended by my taking you up on your kind offer, then I think you may be the better for it by the end of the week.'

'Take your week, Anna,' he looked into her amber-brown eyes, 'I say, I will have no commanded wife, I want you, back again to me, whole.'

If he'd known of his rival, if he'd aimed to win his wife's heart for his own, he couldn't have chosen in any one of his steps over those precious spring weeks a more fortuitous way of achieving just that ambition. The fact that such steps were taken in total ignorance of the whole, made them all the more enchanting to his young wife's heart. She would take her week, she would consider her step, take stock, take time to come to terms with the magnitude of it all. It would grieve her to leave. Yes, it would but her father was always so busy and in demand, if she visited monthly, he wouldn't much notice the difference, she mused. Millie, Millie was another matter. It had only been a year since she was widowed, still childless. Then again, over the last few weeks, a friendship appeared to be growing thick and fast between herself and Retty. They shared an almost unholy sense of humour and Millie seemed to be blossoming into the role of elder, wiser friend in a way that was improving her confidence considerably. Perhaps it would be better for them almost, if she, Anna, did move away. Ma Gables surely couldn't stay forever; Abraham must be wanting her home, so although, as Anna thought on it, Emmaline had come the closest any person had ever come to being a mother to her in all her life, staying in Heartbourne would not prolong the tender experience.

'I haven't asked you,' she sat up suddenly from her reverie, 'where, Will? Which town is this you propose we move to?'

'Aha, well in that there's a pleasant surprise for you, I'm almost sure, for the aspiring town is none other than Frampton, the abiding place of your new found friend, Mrs Gables herself. Might, Anna, her friendship and company go some way towards mitigating the loss of Millie and your father? Might Emmaline and I provide a new family to you? But, Anna, whatever's the matter, no, don't try to get up!'

'I must, but I must,' Anna's head was spinning, Frampton, Frampton, home to none other than Nathan Lunsford? And the letters, Uncle Christopher's letters, how could she have forgotten, where were they? Where had she put them, if anywhere at all?

Anna struggled to move forward, the last place she'd seen the letters had been in the spare room, 'The letters, the letters!'

Will held her steady, 'What letters, Anna? Why ever have you come over so peculiar, so sudden? What letters?'

'Uncle Christopher's letters, he left me some letters, I swore to keep them safe, Will, and I've forgotten them completely. Why, they must've been in the spare room all the time, but Emmaline....'

'Anna, Anna, calm yourself, I have the letters, all three. Anna, sit down, here, now.'

Anna sat back down but she struggled to retain consciousness, 'The letters, Will...'

'I have all three, numbered in green ink, Anna. All is well, Anna,' he rocked her like a child and kissed her forehead, 'all is well.'

Chapter Thirteen

'Will was set to depart for work on the following Monday, on time and with a decided liveliness in his gait. Anna felt the liveliness to be hopeful but tempered, in a more considered habit which was perhaps beginning to establish itself a little within Will's demeanour.

As she wished him good-bye, standing outside to do so for the first time since her fall, Anna considered herself to be blessed once more. The morning May sunshine shone down upon them as Will held her in his arms. The aroma of his masculinity seized her senses and she became almost a little bashful.

'Until Friday,' he whispered softly in her ear, 'decision day.'

He raised her into the air like a child and span her three quarters of a circle, until she shrieked with laughter and he feared to do her harm, in her still delicate state. Instead of continuing, he placed her gently to the ground and steadied her by her hips.

'Until Friday,' he kissed her on each cheek and swung up onto his seat, departing with a fond wink, a smile and a cheerful whistle.

That week, accompanied by Millie on a score of quite transparent pretexts, Anna began once more to travel around in the village about her business. She was not yet strong enough to resume the series of requests for kind duties her father had begun to issue to her once more but quite quickly on this occasion, Emmaline spotted the discomfort and pronounced that, 'Without the need to concern the good pastor, all could be accomplished if good friends were to oblige.'

Such obligation, dictated by *the* Mrs Gables, was not to be ignored by a soul. Retty, Millie, Judith, Bessie, Molly Jenner, Frances Marchant and more besides were summoned to Her presence each and every morning of the week, as a sharing of visits to the sick, the needy and acts of kindness were distributed and taken on, as individual circumstance allowed. The Reverend Thomas Porter was not disturbed with the extent of his only daughter's still fragile state of being and yet, the more feminine aspects of pastoral care within the village flowed on uninterrupted in their babbling spring passage. Thus, the fabric of the parish was maintained, while Anna was left feeling strangely disencumbered, unnecessary; if pushed to it, the parish could indeed, she thought, spare her.

By Thursday, everyone was becoming accustomed to the new way of things. Molly had made three new friends in the village through acts of generosity with her time, directed by Emmaline. People were beginning to see old Molly in a new fashion, as she was indeed herself. Peggy Thornton had even gone so far as to ask in her three youngest children for a current bun, after Molly had sat with her father so long, that Peggy was able to fetch items from Mr Turner's shop and prepare the entire family's evening meal, without constantly fearing for her father's safety if she did not ascend the stair and come back again, at his every roar and call.

Judith had delighted the day of no less than five elderly parishioners with her arrival and the advent of a tender moment in their declining years; that of a new born babe in their arms, while Judith took pleasure herself, in fetching them some tea.

Millie was taxed with both running errands and affixing herself to Anna, so that no further harm through omission could be allowed to occur. Even Retty, although Millie was not constantly aware of what task she was on, or where she'd been bidden, appeared in general, to be rising to the occasion admirably. All in the village of Heartbourne, seemed well. Until Friday, that was. On Friday, everything changed.

As she lay in bed on Friday morning, Anna consciously realised that, in the absence of her mother, she'd been fulfilling the role of a village priest's wife since the age of around fourteen. The idea that she could be free, that Heartbourne would continue in its way and that its inhabitants would continue to support each

Cay Towner

other, was a conscious recognition of her ability to leave. All the same, it would be hard, she thought. Millie had become such a constant companion but then again, the words of Ma Gables rang in her mind, '...living in each other's pockets, almost so much I'm surprised your husbands get a look in on your thoughts.'

Everywhere she looked, every companion she spoke to that week, had been known to her since her birth. How could she leave? How could she even think of leaving her father alone? And yet, her father was never really alone. He was either with his own sacred thoughts or in the company of churchwardens or parishioners, overseers of the poor, choristers or bell-ringers or most seriously, engaged in the most quarrelsome meetings of the vestry, where no two gentlemen among the parish officers seemed ever to agree with one another.

She was unsure, uncertain but then, in her most tentative moments, the image of Will by her side rescued her. His steadfast strength was creating a whole new marriage for her and her boys. Surely, such a marriage for a future was a fortune only a fool would turn aside from. And yet, it was still so hard, to take that step, to commit her soul to leaving her precious Heartbourne.

Then, with no small measure of trepidation in her heart, she considered the prospect of sharing a dwelling station with none other than Nathan Lunsford himself. She found her mind sitting a ghostly vision of Nathan Lunsford in the pan of a set of brass scales, while as she turned her sight, balancing his weight in the opposite pan, sat a beaming, beautiful, Raphael. How, and so quickly, had the mind of a Christian woman come to this? She put her hand across her eyes and squeezed them tightly, to make the vision go away.

Anna turned back the bed sheets and sat up. She knew that by the time she re-entered them, her decision would've been made and conveyed to Will, her husband. She prayed for guidance and a thought occurred to her; in each place there was one man to be avoided. In Heartbourne, there were but three hundred and fifty parishioners or so, whereas in Frampton, a grand and growing town, there would be many,

88

many more hundred inhabitants than that. Will had said that their cottage was on the outskirts of town and did Nathan Lunsford have any idea of who she was or her connection to Christopher Coates? No, he did not. In a town one could enjoy a certain level of anonymity. Uncle Christopher had spoken of the disadvantages of not being known or recognised in other places but maybe, under the circumstances, this would be of advantage to her. In Heartbourne, everybody knew each other and each other's business, only too well.

Later that day, Anna and Millie were sitting on a bench by the village pond. It was a new and unaccustomed sensation to Anna, to have time to rest and idle in the middle of a working morning. Her eyes were lightly closed as she took Dr Snelling's advice and allowed the gentle warmth of the spring sunshine to permeate the skin on her face and uncovered arms. She half-listened to Millie's chatter as she cherished the warmth and weight of Samuel as he slept on the rise and fall of her chest.

Millie's gossip about stubborn old Mrs Smithers being caught walking the High Street in her nightdress, somewhat confused, at five o'clock in the morning, raised Anna's consciousness of the need to mention the case to her father (or maybe Ma Gables) to see if some progress might be made towards her care. The sun bore down upon her near contentment; even Millie's gossip was a kind of care in its own way, which sought out a natural way of working things out between Heartbourne folk. If she chose to follow her husband, to be wedded to him, as was now most truly her humblest desire, Heartbourne, she felt, in God's hands, would be well.

Anna was still silently praying to this effect when a most unholy commotion broke out in front of the village stores.

Unbeknown to Anna and Millie, while they'd been passing a pleasant half hour beside the tranquil pond, a disturbance had been brewing in their very near presence. Mrs Gables, accompanied by Retty Gables (as she often now was, sometimes through obligation but sometimes through choice) had been assembling a basket of provisions to be taken up to

John and Rachael Durrant upon the celebration of their fiftieth wedding anniversary. Both parties of the marriage had been unwell of late and hadn't been abroad for some days. Ma Gables had gathered for them both food prepared by her and purchases, in a broad basket which Mr Turner had pronounced, 'A luncheon fit for the Duke of Newcastle himself!'

Upon leaving the shop, Emmaline had suddenly missed in her packages the Warwickshire cheese that Rachael was so very fond of. 'Mr Turner must've been so keen in his haste to tot up my expenditure that he has quite forgotten to place it in my basket! It must still be sitting all wrapped up on the counter. I'll return for it, Henrietta, he'll realise his mistake in a moment, I'm sure.'

With that, she placed the luncheon basket filled with all manner of delights, including a handsome bottleful of orange shrub, onto the bench which sat under the low stone wall of the store's forecourt. As Mrs Gables bustled back down the path to retrieve Rachael's cheese, Retty's attention was caught by the sight of Anna and Millie, Anna in particular. She wandered a few steps through the gateway onto the street as she gazed at Anna relaxing, maybe asleep through Millie's chatter, with the slumbering Samuel on her breast. A brand of hot jealousy seared through her chest, which tightened as her eyes bleared over with tears. Realising the indignity it would cause her to be seen publically in such a state of disorder, she fumbled for her pocket handkerchief and covered her face with it, giving herself, so she thought, a moment to recompose herself. Before she had recovered sufficiently to face the village, she heard Ma Gables let out a shriek.

Retty hastened back over to her, 'Whatever's the matter, Ma?'

'Why, the basket, Henrietta, where has it gone?' Mrs Gables looked about herself in confusion and, owing to her rather stout constitution, appeared a little like a small dog attempting to find its own tail again.

Retty, having just that moment rallied the strength to button back in her own emotions, remained calm but became confused, 'I don't understand,' she said looking hopelessly at the empty space on the bench where the basket had been sitting, 'where can it have gone?'

Both women then looked about them from side to side, at the grass, at the air, at the wall, at the bench. In their disbelief, they looked at each other in horror. There were people inside the shop, others by the pond and Mr Congreve supervising a delivery over at the Gun Inn but no-one was to be seen hurrying away from the spot on which they stood, let alone carrying a rather sturdily weighted down broad basket.

'Thief! Thief!' Mrs Gables was not a woman to remain silent under such an affront. 'Thief! Thief! Look to your bags, I say!' And she began walking around erratically about the forecourt in indignant disarray, waving both her stick and the Warwickshire cheese. 'Thief! Thief! Who will go seek them out? They cannot be far! Assistance, we require assistance here, now, I say!'

By this time, all those in the near vicinity had gathered around the spot from where Emmaline was hallooing. Mr Turner and his customers had come out from within the shop, Millie and Anna and several others besides had come over from the pond and Mr Congreve, George Jenner and the delivery men had all been drawn across from their business.

'A thief, you say?' Mr Congreve seemed particularly curious, 'Why, what has gone missing, my good woman?'

Ignoring for the moment what she considered to be an impertinently over-familiar form of address, Mrs Gables went on hallooing, 'Thief! Thief! We had a basket of baked and bought goods, not to mention a good measure of orange shrub! We had got it up and together on account of the Durrants' anniversary and on account of them both being poorly for the occasion and now, it's gone! Thievery, if you will believe it! In Heartbourne! Who will go looking? Who will rally to our assistance in our hour of need?'

At the shocking sight of Mrs Gables' distress and subsequent appeal, four of the men folk gathered quickly organised themselves into a posse and dispatched themselves about the village, having first garnered a description of the missing goods from Retty. Meanwhile, Mrs Gables was urged by Mr Turner to come inside and take a seat and some tea, for he was sure that the condition of her state could not be good for her health and he would not see her weaken her constitution in this way, for, as he stated clearly, a sick wife was a poor return for a husband in this life, as he himself knew well.

Mrs Gables was recovering with her tea and the surprisingly knowledgeable and considerate company of her host, when there came a quiet tapping upon the door. Mr Turner arose and spoke softly to the caller for a few moments before admitting him. It was Mr Congreve. Mr Turner indicated that Mr Congreve should sit in his own chair across from Mrs Gables, who he then addressed carefully.

'Ma'am, this gentleman has one or two questions he would like to ask you and then one or two incidences he would like you to know about last evening, if you are sufficiently recovered?'

Her curiosity raised, Emmaline answered, 'I am in robust health, I do assure you, speak man, if you will, for I am no tender spring primrose underfoot.'

'Mrs Gables, am I correct in my understanding that the basket, taken in broad daylight from the bench, was full to the brim with victuals and strong drink?'

'Victuals and strong drink, Mr Congreve, for the luncheon was to be a celebration; there were all manner of delights, except for this Warwickshire cheese, I still have the cheese at least Mr Turner,' she humphed. 'There was a bottle filled with orange shrub and tucked away underneath, a modest tot or two of Nantz, perhaps, or so was my thinking, an addition to the Durrants' usual nightcap for this evening.'

'And, if you will forgive my impertinence...'

'Whenever anyone utters those words, I find the universal answer turns out to be, 'no', but you may ask me anyway; impertinence seems to be becoming an almost modern disease, an affliction you younger generations find hard it to keep free of when conversing.' She tapped her stick twice on the floor, 'Fire away, what holds you, Sir?'

'Young Mrs Gables, she wasn't out of sight at all, over the course of events?'

Mrs Gables, who had half guessed after the enquiry in advance, raised herself up upon her stick as she inhaled deeply before fixing a piercing stare upon Mr Congreve.

'Whatever the opinion of this village regarding my daughter-in-law, I tell you, Mr Congreve, if so much as a thought of stealing from either myself or John and Rachael had even crossed her soul, she would be on her knees in prayer for forgiveness as we speak, not, as she is instead, gone home to prepare early the Scotch collops that were to be for her own supper and Henry's and mine as a replacement for the missing pork pie, that the Durrants might still have their celebration without needing to have any knowledge of this grievous wrong, this very grievous wrong, committed in our midst, here, here, in very Heartbourne, Mr Congreve.'

'I pray you, please, please, be seated once more Mrs Gables,' Mr Congreve had risen himself and was indicating graciously for her to sit back down, 'for I only needed to ascertain the point clearly, for the benefit of others in the village, that, when they ask, I might say that I did enquire and that it could not have been the case but if you will, on this occasion, forgive the impertinence for it was not for my own benefit but merely a question asked, to silence the clacking tongues of them with little or no grace in their souls here about, I do assure you. Please, be seated, Ma'am, for I have details about an incident last night I feel you and all about should know of, for your own protection.'

Mr Turner's intimation, of the possible imparting of new knowledge about 'goings on', had not escaped such a seasoned village matron as Ma Gables. She allowed herself to be persuaded that the affront to Henrietta was not a personal slight, as Mr Congreve had explained, but a necessary query, to silence idle gossip. She descended back onto her chair.

'Last evening, a similar but lesser event took place that I, not knowing how to account for it, took to doing nothing much about but scratching my head, Ma'am. I understand that there was a great pie and some haslet and tartlets and cheeses and all sorts prepared for the old couple's special day?'

'You are correct. Continue, if you will.'

'Well, it just seems no coincidence to me, that's all.'

'You must explain, Jeremiah, you have given her only a hint of it, tell Mrs Gables your brief tale, my good man.'

'I was about to, Mr Turner! Give me my time, I say!'

'Proceed, if you will, with your narrative, Mr Congreve, for I must surely follow Henrietta quite soon in an attempt to reassemble some semblance of the kindness we intended for the Durrants' luncheon; it would not do for them to be waiting into the afternoon, that indeed, would not be a kindness at all.'

'As I was about to say, it was early yesterday evening when it happened. I'd fetched for myself the last piece of a light pudding and a half a pint of Honey Bee Ale and had assembled myself at the small table in my rear yard, underneath the cherry blossom, it being such a fine evening as it was. Mrs Congreve then let out a shriek, which it simply isn't in her character to do often, so I thought I'd better go and investigate. I covered over my supper hastily with my clean handkerchief, to keep off any opportunistic flies and went off to see what the matter was. It turned out, Mrs Congreve had knocked over an ornament that'd been her mother's but it was not broken, so all was well. When I returned to my table, however, my pudding and my ale were gone! The tin plate and handkerchief were lying there alone, next to an empty ale pot! 'Well, I'll be jiggered!' was all I could keep saying to myself, for although there were several servants about the place, no-one Mary and I haven't known since they were bairns was on the premises. None of them would go thieving a piece of light pudding or drowning a moment with an all too hasty gulp of ale.

'As we lay in bed last night, Mary pointed out that the side passage next the slaughterhouse was the most probable point of entry and exit. I wondered if we should fix a gate across it as the galley door is so often open during service hours and our loss could've been so much greater. Mary, however, as is ever her way, gave the Christian response that it was to be hoped, if not presumed, from such a modest piece of pilfering, that the perpetrator must've had more need of a slice of light pudding than my great belly did. I thanked her kindly for the accuracy of her comment, thanked her very much indeed, three times over, 'great belly' indeed and so it was we went to sleep a chuckling at our loss and not a crying for it.'

Emmaline was not in the mood for such humour and Mr Turner was obliged to suppress his amusement at her glare.

'Today's event, however, casts maybe a different light on it, do you reckon?'

'Maybe it does, and maybe it doesn't,' said Emmaline thoughtfully, 'at any rate I think it is a matter for the vestry, will you report it to them, Mr Turner?'

'I shall relay all the particulars, you can rely on me Ma'am, we have a meeting this evening and it will be done, the parish officers shall know all.'

'Well, I thank you for your kindness, Mr Turner, and for your intelligence, Mr Congreve. We have in our midst a person plainly in great need; either of the charity of the overseers of the poor or of a jolly good whipping. Which, we shall see, you mark my words, for there are no hiding places in a village as small and characterful as Heartbourne. You will call on me directly, if the four men dispatched come back with any news?'

Assurances were made and Mrs Gables took her leave and made her way back to Buttsfield Lane, where she found Retty, Millie and Anna all in the kitchen busy remedying the losses. As she watched Retty working unprompted amid her friends, no longer sat in a shawl of self-pity as she had been at Theo's party, Emmaline felt a tear descend her cheek. One man's loss, took on a whole new meaning. Perhaps Abraham would have to do without her for a while longer but the hope, that the basket from which she now lifted the whimpering Samuel, would one day host a small Henry Gables, that was not lost, was not lost indeed.

Chapter Fourteen

'Anna and Millie took the back path home; Anna was still weak and prone to weariness and she wished to avoid the shower of enquiries that would be bound to descend upon them like arrows, if they walked home along the High Street.

As they reached the top of Mill Lane, at the junction between village and fields, Millie offered to carry Samuel who kept struggling to be free from his mother's arms. As the babe was transferred from one woman to the other, something in the narrow, wooded path that stretched down the eastern side of the field caught Anna's attention. Millie was engrossed in tipping Samuel back and forward again to make him chuckle and didn't notice at first that Anna had stepped away.

'Anna, what?'

Millie stopped as Anna placed a finger to her lips and pointed in the direction of a scarlet shawl which was just visible from their position, draped over the side of a patch of hawthorn in the woods, about sixty yards away. All of a sudden, they heard a peculiar noise which shortly repeated itself, followed by a raucous laugh and a sigh. The noise was a hiccup.

A singing voice of sorts started up, 'Oh Petal dear, why do you ramble?' which halted periodically, as further hiccups ensued.

Under the cover of, 'Oh Petal dear', Millie whispered urgently to Anna, 'I'll never keep his Lordship here quiet, you wait while I go and charge Judith with him,' she touched Anna's arm, 'and don't go in there till I get back, Anna Godstone, we don't know who she is or what she could be like. I'll be like a flash, don't lose sight of her now!'

With that, Millie dashed off, as silently as she could, with Samuel. Anna tentatively stepped forward, one pace at a time, working her way around in a quarter circle that she might find a vantage point where she could see but not be seen. It was impossible to move silently, as the new spring undergrowth covered unseen dead twigs, which snapped beneath her tread as she made her way, as stealthily as she was able, across to the scene. While the singing and hiccupping and laughing continued, she worried not. She grew quite close to a spot she hoped might offer her a sight of this creature, when her skirt became caught on a hawthorn bush. As she stooped to free her garment, she caught sight of Ma Gables' basket sitting on a tree stump. She went to release herself but suddenly found herself stopped, unable to move, as none other than Raphael De Vine stepped out of the woods on the verge of the opposite side of the narrow path.

The effect his near presence had upon Anna was unmistakable. For all that her new found awareness of her husband and of her own capacity for passion had awakened in her a more fervent interest in her marriage than had existed hitherto, this had happened just at a juncture when William was too afraid of causing her harm, to make love to her.

Now, as Raphael stood not ten feet from her crouched form, an image of intimacy streaked itself across her mind. She closed her eyes but the image only came into sharper focus and she was forced instead to remain with her eyes open, fixed inescapably upon the real form of Raphael before her. She could smell the unmistakable aroma of linseed oil and she wondered what task had required its patient application in his workshop that morning.

'Well,' he addressed himself to the drunken woman who was still just out of Anna's sightline, 'you've decided to make an appearance at last, I see.'

'Ah!' she laughed, 'It's Raph-a-el, my angel, come to rescue me, my Raph-a-el Di-Vine!'

More cackling followed as Raphael folded his arms and looked upon her with disdain. Anna was desperate to understand and to see this woman who addressed Raphael so mockingly. She took her eyes away from him and attempted to free her skirt from the hawthorn but her stooping had caused it to be caught along the length of a twisted row of spikes.

'Have you come to get me, Raphael? Have you come to get what's yours?'

Anna leant around, stretching to catch a glimpse of the woman, only to be starkly horrified by what she saw. It was not her dishevelled appearance, her ruined hairstyle or the shabby state of her attire. It was not the sight of the discarded remains of the beautiful luncheon prepared by Ma Gables or the (now empty) bottle of orange shrub on the ground. It was the sight of this woman, her torso propped up against a tree trunk with her skirt hitched up to her knees and her legs akimbo, stroking the material which covered her private parts lewdly, while she beckoned Raphael towards her with her other hand.

'Have you come to claim your husbandly rights?' she cackled again.

Anna couldn't help herself; she yelped in horror and tore herself free of the hawthorn, not caring in her anguish about the ripping to her skirt. As she disentangled herself in haste, she found herself propelled in her state, not away from Raphael but instead towards him. The last rip freed her and she stood on the path, physically trembling before him, her hands held up as if to protect herself from the unwanted vision she couldn't disentangle from her mind.

'Anna? Anna?' He turned back to his wife who had now covered herself sensibly and was striding towards them.

'Your wife?' asked Anna, in an unguarded moment she later feared she'd come to regret.

'And what, may I ask, do we find here?' Raphael's wife glared at Anna and back to Raphael who was staring in anguish at Anna's distress.

'Nothing, nothing, Violet, you ought not to go judging others by your own, lamentable,' he placed emphasis on the word before repeating it, 'lamentable level of morality!'

'Oh, ought I not?' Her tone suddenly became more sober. 'But then let's see, what have we here?'

'We have a thief, a common thief!' Anna rounded on Violet in a fashion which quite surprised even her.

'If thievery of a husband is theft, then I do believe you tell the truth, my girl!'

'You speak nonsense: no one has stolen your husband; he stands here before you!'

'Oh, he stands before me all right but his eyes are all yours, I see what goes on here and I say the thievery is all yours, my dear! Tell me now; what would the villagers about here say, if you walked out of this wood with your skirt shredded, as 'tis, and *my* husband trailing in your path? Ha! Not so quick to call the odds now, you slattern, are you?'

Violet spoke these words in compete ignorance of the earlier predicament Anna and Raphael had found themselves in but the memory of it was scribed boldly across their mutual thoughts right now, in letters which they feared would become the indelible ink of village myth, if they failed to head off this latest unfortunate appearance. Luckily for both of them, as they both stood in idiotic fashion (as passion is wont to make numbskulls of us all) this was the moment at which Millie Price chose to re-enter the scene.

'Well, I suggest you don't think, even for one small moment, that discovery is an event you would be wise to wish for,' Millie was sauntering towards Violet with her arms folded and a look across her countenance Anna had never witnessed before, 'given the circumstances.'

Millie halted, face to face with Violet, with not above a foot between them.

Violet's temporary sobriety appeared to have left her as she swayed before Millie.

'And what, circumstances, might-they-be?' she asked, as if tired with the situation already.

Millie nervously darted her eyes over to Anna, who took up the helm.

'Why, the theft of a husband's eyes witnessed only by yourself and with only your word to back up the accusation. Your word, that is, versus the good word of the only daughter of the good pastor hereabouts, the Reverend Thomas Porter, the daughter who lost her mother at birth, right here in this village, where she's lived all her days. Your word, the word of a stranger and a common thief,' Anna waved her arm across the carnage left strewn about from Violet's stolen luncheon, 'not an imagined one.'

Violet belched loudly and staggered back to the tree trunk where she sat down. She looked about her at the littered ground.

Anna walked over to her and crouching down, spoke to her quietly, 'We'll cut you a deal, Violet, for I promise you that nothing has passed between Raphael and myself, nothing, that is, that should ruin your marriage or damn our eternal souls.'

'But something has happened, ain't it? Or you, Dame Lady Purity, wouldn't be crouching down, offering a drunken, thieving varlet like me, a 'deal', now, would you dear?'

Anna tipped her chin down just a fraction before raising it again and meeting Violet's eye.

'This is the deal, and this is what you will do. You'll take your scarlet shawl and go home with Raphael to sober up quietly. Not one of us will say anything about this meeting, again, ever. Millie and I will clear up this area and return the items remaining to their rightful owners. We will simply say this is what we found, and where we found it.'

'The good word of the good pastor's daughter, eh?' Violet mocked.

Millie and Raphael had drawn close enough to listen.

'You agree to the deal, or I shall call for the parish officers as witnesses, Violet. You have no witnesses to your claim, while we, are three.'

'Oh, have it your way,' she answered, petulantly throwing orange peel in Anna's face, 'I've long since stopped caring for the activities of his fruitless loins, I can tell you.'

'Violet, stand up and come home with me as you've been bid. This is a rare spectacle for an entrance you've made and enough is enough, I declare. Push me further and the marriage and the roof over your head with it will be at an end. I've been minded to put you aside quietly and in modest comfort for some time now and if your thoughts are indeed cast in that same direction, then perhaps the time has come for us to talk further. I would prefer it, however, if the conversation were a calm, frank and sober one and thus, it is not for today.'

With that, he lifted her from the ground and strode off with her in his arms, instructing her to make no further display of herself.

Anna sank to her knees with her face in her hands in grief and disbelief. She felt the comfort of Millie's arm and her warmth around her neck.

'Oh, Millie, there's something very sad for us that I must tell you.'

'It's all right, Anna. I kind of half knew. But I know you also, I mean, you're not about to leave your marriage for him, to leave good, kind Will, are you? You wouldn't do something so rash, for a man with no better judgement than to marry a creature like that, now, would you?'

'No, Millie, no, you're right; I wouldn't,' she rubbed a little mud from Millie's chin with her thumb, 'but I am, however, about to leave Heartbourne, for I fear, I fear, there's garlic in the field Millie, garlic and I don't know how else to rid it.'

As the tall slender poplars swayed in the breeze, Anna looked down at the brief letter she'd received from her Uncle Christopher, just a few days before.

My dearest Anna,

I do apologise but I must be brief, for R- awaits me downstairs. Confrontation over with best possible outcome for R-: she may rest at peace. I will explain all, when I see you on Saturday next but be reassured, for I believe no further harm will come of this affair.

May God bless you, my child, and all of us who continue to seek His comfort as we praise Him for its continued and assured return.

Yours in everlasting gratitude and affection,

Christopher Coates Esq

Anna returned the letter to her pocket, just as the sound of tripping hooves reached her ears. She stood in anticipation before her vision confirmed that the sound was indeed bearing Uncle Christopher to her in his smart, newly painted, blue and red Sussex wagon.

101

At the sound of his arrival, Will and Theo came bursting out to greet him, 'Uncle Christopher!' cried Theo, 'Come and see what Ivor can do now!'

'Why, hello and hello!' Uncle Christopher greeted the chaps with warm handshakes and attendant slaps to the shoulders. 'Hello and hello!' Theo looked a little taken aback at being buffeted about so, but as his father winked at him and smiled, he decided not to worry.

'I'm afraid Ivor's performances will have to wait until Frampton, Theo,' his father explained as Christopher drew his niece aside for a moment, 'for we've still a great deal of furniture to load onto your Uncle's wagon before we can pick up our speed and head away to unload it all again the other side.'

'Moving house does seem to be a very great deal of work, Papa. I do hope we don't choose to do it often.'

'Don't worry, Theo, we've no plans for it to become a regular event.

'Ah, Christopher, Jed and I were just attempting to move the kitchen dresser. Did you need a cup of tea right now or might we just accomplish this and then greet you in a fashion you deserve?'

'Aha, no standing on ceremony is necessary today, young Will, there's too much work in hand for all that. Show me the way!' Uncle Christopher burst into song, bowling William and Jed along, 'Let's sally forth together! Show me the way! Let's rise and go together!'

Anna smiled as she followed in the wake of the song. Uncle Christopher had always had the joyful knack, she thought, of making any event seem like a jovial, carefree party. What a blessing he was, indeed; all would be well, he'd reassured her again in their brief chat and at that moment, she felt that it would.

Theo thought that moving day would never, ever end. At first he was glad and proud to be a willing helper, coming and going with plants and pictures and wooden boxes of boys' things from his own room and placing them wherever he was asked

102

in his papa's cart or Uncle Christopher's wagon. After a while, however, he began to tire and carrying his own quilt downstairs to be packed, he jumped the last stair and knocked off a fully packed tea crate, a cup and saucer someone had carelessly left on top. It fell to the floor and smashed. He apologised a thousand times and helped Millie Price to clear it up, but all of a sudden, he didn't feel so grown up any more.

By lunch time, the two vehicles were laden so high into the sky that Theo wondered if the angels might have to lean down and stop things from falling off the top as they went along their way. God himself, he was sure, would stop the bumps from toppling them over completely into a ditch; maybe that was why the grown-ups had stacked it up so high, to make it easier for God and the angels to watch over as they travelled.

Theo heard his father announce that they needed to start thinking about moving off with the first loads, if they were to fit in the second trip to finish off before night fall. People from the village were gathered all around and the women had all started to hug each other, while the men kept slapping his papa on the back and shoulders. Theo decided to take Ivor for a last run up and down the lane when he saw the lace handkerchiefs coming out.

'Come on, Ivor, for you'll have to sit still for a long time on the journey,' Theo clapped Ivor along to race with him. 'We can't travel fast you know or the angels might drop something, right on our heads!' He slapped himself on the forehead and laughed at the notion, speeding off up the lane to say goodbye to his favourite view. Looking back down from the top of the lane across the village, Whyly lay to his west, the village and the church of his christening to the south, his school, his woods, his fields, his friends; he said his own goodbyes, glad that he had Ivor to come with him.

As he came back down to the departure party, he saw his mother standing with her head resting on her father's shoulder. Grandpa Porter had his arm around her and was speaking to her quietly. Her eyes were a little red but Theo thought he must've avoided most of the handkerchief business.

There was an attempt to get Ivor to go into a box with holes poked into it but as they moved off, Theo was sitting next to his father with the puppy half buttoned into his jacket, as some small measure of attempted control and safety. Ivor leaned out, nose sniffing in the air like the figurehead on a ship, leading the way forward. They were off.

Chapter Fifteen

'Anna, Sam and Uncle Christopher travelled along slowly in the wake of Will's cart. Anna attempted to quell her inner turmoil by distracting herself with thoughts of the difficulties of others.

'Now we're together for a while, Uncle, and Samuel is asleep...'

'Not that he'd tell our tale but I take your point, Anna, I do take your point. Hmmm, let me see.

'Ruth and I met at Brambleberry Hall and we, 'sallied forth together', just over a week ago now. We reached Nathan Lunsford's cottage at dusk but somehow found ourselves loitering a little at his gate. Ruth said she suspected she sensed a little of how Maria must have felt, when she attempted to follow Nathan, without having fully thought things through. Ruth felt afraid and said she was uncertain how to broach the subject with sufficient tact, in order to gain entry and achieve the conversation we wished for. I stated that I thought it simple, 'We march up his pathway, knock on his door and request to speak with him.'

'But, what if he denies us entry, Christopher? What if he won't admit us? Will we lose our chance, d'you think?'

I could see the anxiety on her face as her left eye twitched a little. I decided that action was needed and I opened the gate and ushered her through it, in a gentlemanly fashion of course, my dear. Half way up the short path, she stopped and started to sigh again. I stood and regarded her. 'We don't have to do this, you know,' I said softly. 'We could just go home and leave it to the good Lord, if you think it better?'

Ruth sighed, steadied herself and then inhaled, pulling herself up to her full height, 'No, I wish to go ahead, for Maria's sake, God bless her.'

At that moment, our attention was drawn to the front door as it creaked slowly open, just wide enough to give some sight of a stocky man with broad arms, untidy clothes, dishevelled hair and a shirt that lifted a little over a round pot belly.

'Can I help you at all?' he asked, his upper lip curling somewhat on one side.

'We were wondering, my good man...' I stopped as I noticed Ruth was making her way past me, travelling forward, one step at a time. She duly came before him and looked him straight in the eye, without speaking for a while. Nathan looked back, scanning her face pensively, as if some inkling of recognition troubled him which he couldn't quite place.

'Do I know ye, Ma'am?' he asked, with his brow furrowed.

'You did once, Nathan, but it was a long time ago.'

Nathan gasped at the sound of Ruth's voice, for it is a much un-noted fact that our voices age and alter a great deal less over time than any other aspect of our person.

'Her eyes and her cape, come again in the mist – but her mother's voice? What are you?' he raised his voice and pointed at her, having no object to wave in defence, 'What are you, I say, are you woman or spirit? And are you man or demi-devil?' he asked, pointing at me.

'Oh, I assure you, my man, I do nothing by halves.' I stared at him closely, attempting to gauge him and fright him in one but in his eyes...' Uncle Christopher trailed off as his horse plodded on.

'What, Uncle, what did you see in his eyes?'

'Despair, loss, guilt, shame, unless he were a very good actor indeed, a confusion of all these is what I saw but his eyes didn't rest with me long, for he was drawn, drawn back to Ruth's face.

He continued, 'Maria, mother of Maria, I mean Ruth, are you she?'

'I am and in my body still, unlike my daughter.'

He rested his outstretched hand on the door frame and closed his eyes as if in silent prayer. When he re-opened them, his chest was visibly rising and falling, 'You'd best come in,' he said.

Nathan ushered us into a small but respectable parlour, where he lit two candles and bid us be seated in the two Windsor chairs which sat opposite each other across the unlit fire. He fetched himself a stool, which he sat on between us, slumped as if all spirit had left his body. It was a sorry sight to see.

'Ruth, please tell me what you know and how you come to be here, over twenty years have passed!'

'I know nearly all, Nathan, nearly all and maybe, if I had any sense, I would be here with an officer of the law.'

'But, you're not?'

'No, I am not. I'm here to hear your side of things, Nathan, if you'll undertake to speak honestly.'

'Why? Why? Why don't you just hand me to the authorities, after all, I am responsible? The deaths of two good women lie at my feet.' His tone became flat and subdued.

'Tell us your tale, Nathan, that Ruth may hear it. In truth, that's all we ask.'

'Do I take it, you know...Annette? Maria?'

'That you were a bigamist to my daughter? Yes, I know, Nathan. You say that you're responsible for her death, but what I wish to know, is, are you responsible for her killing?'

'That too, yes, for it was my doing; if it hadn't have been for my treachery, she wouldn't have been afield that night, would she? No, she wouldn't.'

He answered his own question and fell silent for a while. Ruth appeared to be taking the inference that he felt responsible for Maria's death, but not guilty of her murder. She waited patiently for him to continue.

'It was all originally an error. A solitary sin. One slip, I erred, I was a young man and easily led by my cup and a pretty ankle. The ankle was Annette's. I was wrong to bed her, being already promised in matrimony to Maria, I know that, now. Know it well. But I was young, my only defence, a poor one, I know.

'I went back home and wed Maria, forgiving myself easily at the time. It was only around seven months later, upon my return to Frampton in my travels abroad, that I received a letter from Annette at my lodgings informing me that she was with child and that she declared the child upon me.

'By this time, however, Maria was also with child. What was I to do? I cast around in my head, searching for an honourable answer but there was none to be had. The closest thing seemed to me, at the time, to go ahead with what would appear to be the honourable action in these parts; to marry Annette. It was either that or face a bastardy bond from the parish officers and have to pay for the child, without the dignity of giving his or her coining legitimacy, in the sight of Christians here around.

'Three times the banns were read, three times I quaked to hear public objection, by the third time almost convinced that the Lord God himself would stoop down and cast off the Bible from the very lectern where the priest stood, to let all know there were just cause and impediment indeed. Your home, your village being three counties distant from Frampton, some ninety miles or more, no earthly objection came. Little did I realise the divine objection, the blight this act would place upon my days was to follow but slowly, only in the course of time. For them what knows of impediment and does not declare it, well, they get to hold their peace. For them what knows of impediment and goes ahead with it themselves; there is no peace to be had again. I know that, now.'

Nathan remained slumped as he stared into the cold, empty grate.

'I came to regret my act sorely, long before Maria's death, for the life of a bigamist is not one a soul would opt for with any degree of rational forethought. I was forever racked with feelings of guilt and misapprehension. I thought the fourth and fifth time the question were asked would end my disquiet, but that were merely the end of the very first chapter of it. Wherever I was, I felt I should be elsewhere, till I only ever felt somewhat at rest when I was where everybody thought I was; on the road, trading, with no wife beside me at all! I learnt the loneliness of a lie. I'd denied myself the comfort a married hearth should bring.

'When I heard, when I received your letter, Ruth, containing the news of Maria's death and the circumstances of it...'

'He trailed off as he fumbled for his 'kerchief, Anna. A grown man struggling for his strength in the face of two near strangers; it was a pitiful sight to behold his grief. I don't think, unless he's the face of a devil in an actor's form, that he could've been involved in Maria's bloody murder, truly, I don't.

'He continued presently, speaking of his self-loathing and self-blame following Maria's death. He spoke of how distraught he felt, that the only way to give up the sinful life for which his blameless wife had been punished, was to give up all contact with the daughter also. It was, he explained, during this period of time that the barrel and the bottle became a way of life with him, a way of life which became ingrained and then later led to further punishment for original sin.

'I drank to forget. I even thought...' he trailed off and regarded Ruth closely. 'Excuse my asking,' his eyes travelled over her brown cloak and back to her face, 'but how did you come to know where I dwell? Do I take it that you've been to Frampton afore? That you've seen enough of me to know my business? Of Annette and our child? That you've been watching me, all these years?'

Ruth dissembled as calmly as if she were a villain who did it every day, 'I have a relative, a cousin, who lives here about, who has done so for around seven years. When I made a visit to Frampton in the normal course of my trade, as I have done for many years and heard from her of the recent, infamous goings on, your name was mentioned, Nathan Lunsford. Your name, in connection with the possible murder and death of a wife. Well, you can imagine the misgivings which travelled through my thoughts, which have haunted them with the ghoulled faces of spectres ever since.'

'You believe I murdered 'em? That I took these hands to them both?' he made motion as if strangling the air as he leant in towards Ruth. She drew back and I was about to intervene when his hands dropped limply back to his sides, 'Well, I did and I didn't, Mother. I almost wish I could be accused and taken up for both of them, for the death of these two innocent souls is surely to be laid at my door; I can repent of it but not undo what is done.

'After Maria had been laid to rest, I was troubled with visions of her, day and night, whether I woke or slept, there she would be before me. I was so haunted with the prospect of her that I would see her before me in town, in church and in my dreams. When she came to me as near, close on as you are now, late at night I felt that God himself was blaming me for her violent death. I thought to kill myself but I still had Annette and our child to provide for.

'Eventually, I sank to my knees to Him in prayer and asked for His forgiveness, stating truly, as He would've known, that had I foreseen what would happen, had I ever guessed that my beautiful Maria would take to the road to pursue me and be set upon by villains, I would never have committed my sinful act. I lay before Him the case, asking Him to spare my second wife and child from my own sin, as He'd already punished another for it. I'm not ashamed to say that I knelt at the altar and wept for forgiveness, that no further harm would come of my errant, knavish behaviour.

'For a long time, although I didn't ever quite forgive myself, I believed He'd forgiven me; Maria's ghostly self left off from haunting me and life went on undisturbed and untroubled by further incident. Until recently, that was.

'My drinking, over the years, has got the better of me and blighted my life. I was both unwell and in drink when I argued with Annette, one night shortly after our daughter had been married and moved out to the edge of town.

'This particular night, after a furious row, I said something that let slip that I was already married at the time I'd married her, Annette, that is. She elicited the rest of the story from me in my incapacitated state. Horrified at the intelligence that her marriage had never been legitimate, she reasoned that, wretched as her life was with me, she had no duty to stay. In a wrung out state she must've left, after I was asleep, and fallen down the Devil's Ravine in her distressed condition.

'Again, I was distraught, for now my original sin had returned to haunt me in the incapacity and disablement of my second wife, which I felt to be my entire fault. Now, I rue my faith, for it tells me I must do myself no harm, but I know not how to live. The death of both these women is surely, I repeat, surely, to be laid upon my soul's report and I can repent of it but I *cannot* undo; I cannot undo what is done.'

'Anna, he continued like this and appeared to be in a pitiful state. Ruth suggested that there maybe was a way that he could make amends: to allow his daughters to know of their connection and meet. Nathan, however, was afraid, scared that he would be taken up by the law if his bigamous history were known. Ruth suggested that it could merely be put about abroad that the girls were cousins, that the truth only needed to be known within the family. Nathan, however, was still afraid that his daughters might think that the story of their lives was worse than it actually was: had not, after all, he challenged Ruth, she feared this herself?

'Nathan said that he felt that to lead his daughters to such fears and misgivings would be worse than letting them alone; that trying to ameliorate his own remorse, by harming their minds' peace, would only be a further sin. He was, it has to be said, Anna, very convincing. Ruth and I eventually nodded our compassionate agreement across the cold hearth, to leave things as they were.

'There is one salient point to report, that I must not omit, however. As we were leaving, Nathan passed what I felt to be a curious comment. He noted that we were very brave, if we did suspect him of murder, to come and brazen the matter out in this way. Ruth then told Lunsford of the letters but she declared them unread, Anna. She stated that the two persons with whom they were placed didn't know of the tale, simply that they are to be opened if, and only if, any unfortunate 'accidents' or 'mysterious fates' befall either herself or me.

'Lunsford, in a subdued voice, stated that, if it were not for the girls, he almost wished he could be tried and hanged for murder, for he declared he felt so guilty it would be a double relief to him both to be punished for his sins and to leave this world.

'Anna, I hardly need tell you, that as we made our way back through the chill night air to Brambleberry Hall, we rued the fashion in which a single error in youth can blight and destroy a man's whole life.'

'A person's whole life and that of their family,' said Anna, pensively.

'Yes, yes, you are to the point, Anna, as usual. In this case, a whole family stretching out to Ruth and the girls, beyond the poor dead women themselves and Nathan in his wretched state, who fears himself quite beyond redemption.'

'Well, the good Lord promises us that no one who truly repents is that and if only he could ever just drag his brains out of the bottle...'

'I agree, but it was not the moment to take up his cause; Ruth is content that Nathan Lunsford is telling the truth. She says she will pray that God grants him forgiveness and peace in eternity, for she fears he'll not feel it while alive. If, by some small chance he is dissembling, then she has done her best to tread a Christian path and his fate must again be with the Lord; she feels she has played her part and is sufficiently certain that she is right to believe him innocent, in order to resume her life in peace. Meanwhile, Nathan Lunsford may only cast about for comfort, which we fear he may not find.'

The driver's seat of the Sussex wagon fell silent for some time as they rolled slowly forward towards Frampton with the Godstones' furniture piled high, creaking and swaying behind them. As Theo had predicted, nothing fell off, nor were they pitched over, to their peril, in a ditch.

Anna, however, remained quiet and thoughtful.

Chapter Sixteen

'Anna awoke the next morning, for the very first time, to the sounds of town life. Will laughed as she stuffed her head under the pillow like a child, 'Well, how noisy they are, do they not know the hour?'

'They know it as well as you, now come on, we must rise, my sweeting.' Will kissed her and got up.

'The rising I don't mind, it's the caterwauling, banging about, crying out so, and oh, so many vehicles and horses, that I'm not accustomed to.'

'My dear, as you saw when we drove through town on our way here yesterday afternoon; this is one of the quieter parts of town! Why, you'll soon grow used to it.'

'I'm not sure I shall,' she frowned, emerging with disordered hair.

They were interrupted by Samuel's morning song as he began to practise his latest, newly acquired sounds, while freeing his feet from his bedding that he might grasp them with his small, soft hands as he sang. Will picked him up out of his cot with a swing and he giggled as his father took him over to Anna, who was still forbidden to rise in haste. As Anna sat up to receive Samuel and nurse him, Will sat beside her.

'Is it really so very bad, Anna? I mean, if you turn out to be unhappy, we can return, nothing is lost here.'

Anna looked into Will's concerned eyes, 'No, no, not so very bad, Will, just different, that's all. I've awakened all my days to the sounds of sparrows and robins, of blue tits and swallows or cooing cuckoos in the spring. I'm more used to hearing cockerels before breakfast, than the sounds of delivery carts and their drivers whistling at the horses and the maids.'

'You could make a gentle start in the garden, if you like?'

'I could indeed, I noticed it looked freshly cleared when we arrived yesterday. Now who d'you think could have done that, Baby Samuel?'

'Oh,' said Will grinning, 'we have a very considerate landlord, perhaps it was he.'

'Will Godstone,' she kissed him as he rose, 'don't ever grow dishonest, for I swear you are the worst dissembler on God's earth.'

'I'll take that as a thank you, shall I?' he asked light heartedly, smiling and tapping the door frame as he left to awaken Theo from his dreams.

Over the week, Anna did attempt to start adjusting to the different ways of life in town. The noise, she soon gathered, was just the beginning of the differences in manners, which were abundant and manifold. In Heartbourne, she'd always been Anna Porter, the Reverend Thomas Porter's only daughter, whose mother (God bless her soul) had died in childbirth. She was a known, loved and respected figure whose time spent in acts of kindness was not lost on the many of those around her who'd themselves (or their relatives) been recipients of her simple benevolence, of quiet unassuming gifts of time, food, flowers or the like. Reading to the sick cost not a penny, she mused, but was always a powerful remedy for low spirits and a tremendous lifting of the weight of the clock hands in their cycle, for at no other time in one's life but in sickness, do they weigh and strain so in their round, as she herself knew from recent weeks.

However, here, in Frampton, who was she? A newcomer? A stranger? A passer-by? All three. As she ventured into the centre of town and the High Street, to fetch her modest purchases each day, she found herself buffeted about, knocked asunder by the shoulder, if she didn't mind out for the next passing porter with a tray of pies upon his shoulder, bound for a destination, where, by Anna's reckoning, Time's hands must rush along dictating pace beyond all reason to its watchers in that place, if the haste of these men was anything to go by. The hurry, the noise, the bustle, all jangled Anna's senses. The alienation she felt from the dead pan eyes or no eyes at all. Even the shop assistants' voices were curt and efficient, not courteous and soliciting as she was accustomed to.

As she walked back on the Thursday, to the cottage merely called home, Anna felt herself longing for Sunday that they might go to church, perhaps meet some people who would speak to them kindly and maybe, somehow or other, start to become friends. Not one of her neighbours had called upon her all week, an omission which would never have happened in Heartbourne, for the delight of everyone's pleasure. Even Abraham Gables was away for a few days, visiting Emmaline, Henry and Retty, having caught a lift in that direction upon the return of the Godstone party vehicles for their second load on moving day. Anna felt strange and alone. However, you are never alone with the Lord, she remembered, and she prayed on the road home, for friendship and for company to fill her days.

Once Samuel was asleep, she placed him in his crib and opened the nearby window. This looked out onto a narrow path and then a bare patch of soil which, sheltered by the lee of the house and yet being south west facing, Anna had chosen as the place to start a modest herb garden. On her way out, in addition to her fork and trowel, she picked up a short, three legged stool that had belonged to Theo in his infancy, so that she might make progress gently, without the risk of further injury to her health.

Once outside, she approached the sheltered spot around the corner of the cottage and was immediately struck by the presence of a sheet of grey tarpaulin spread carefully over what looked like two short towers. She approached the towers with curiosity and pulled off the tarpaulin to reveal two smart stacks of bricks, fashioned in the old slim style, just right for the formation of neat, separate sections for her herbs. She sighed out loud with pleasure. On top of the baked red bricks lay a single white rose, which Anna lifted to reveal a cream label which read: *With my love, from Will x.*

Anna fetched her potted cuttings, which, she noted with pleasure, had travelled from Heartbourne remarkably well. She placed them down by the rich, dark earth and returned back down their wallpaper strip of land to the water butt, to fill her can just half full of water, as closely instructed by Will. As she made her way slowly back to her prospective herb garden, she became aware of voices just beside her on the path parallel to the one she trod. The speakers, separated from sight and awareness of her presence by a tall privet hedge, did not guard their words or tone. The voices sounded tetchy and irritable. In spite of her better self, somewhat starved of the natural entertainment of day-time interaction with others, she silently placed down her watering can to listen the better.

'But, I don't need to be tethered like a wayward goat, unable to wander free-willed about my own garden, Jessie.'

'Now, you know the instructions left by the Master, Ma'am, you're to rest and consider your health, not go gadding about as you please at whim! Mercy save us, you have no appreciation of how pale you still look to those of us who must watch you each day with fear and fret! If you were to stumble out here and take a turn for the worse, there'd be the devil to pay with him and his mother and more besides!'

'Don't pull on me so, Jessie, I am not a child to be chidden thus! What harm can a little air for ten moments do? I just want to breathe and be free!'

'No, now stop that, Ma'am, no spinning about I say, stop, stop now or we'll all be for it! Ma'am, do you want to stop spinning so and stop waving of your arms, like a freewheeling faerie, or shall I call for the Master?'

The light laughter of the younger woman ceased. An air of self-pity now accompanied her words, 'Oh! Very well, back I must turn like a well herded beast to its stall, so it seems.'

'Why, you ungrateful girl, a stall! The Master provides you, who art in truth no better than me in rank or virtue, with a grand house such as this and you've the cheek to refer to it as a stall!'

'Why, 'Denmark's a prison', Jessie, didn't you know?' the voice sounded listless.

'This isn't Denmark, girl, why, have you lost the westward side of sensibility now? This isn't good, not good at all.'

The voices were now receding back to the house but were still strong enough for Anna to catch, 'Nothing's either good or bad...' as the voice trailed out of earshot.

Anna finished the quotation for her, 'But thinking makes it so.'

Rankled by both what she'd heard and the coarse aroma of the privet flowers, her nose wrinkled involuntarily and she decided to move on. As she approached her stool, she stood down her can and stopped to look at the house next door. In a village, greater houses and lesser ones were separated, at the very least, by a pathway and a broad garden. Here, people's dwellings were mixed, higgledy-piggledy, so that not unlike other streets she'd passed through, here was their cottage, a modest, well-kept family home, cheek by jowl with a much grander residence, a white double fronted house, with wide bow windows at the front and no care for the tax over eight, judging by the wealth of smart fenestration she could view at the rear from her small, narrow estate so nearby. And yet, Anna considered, this cottage was a wide manor of delight to her; full now with a sleeping infant, a white rose before her eyes and later would come more pleasure with Theo's return, a family meal and the now firmly burning furnace of desire which existed between herself and Will.

Anna took up her trowel and looked at the healthy array of herbs before her that had travelled so well; sage, rosemary, thyme, marjoram, mint, carefully separated – it was no good. She looked back over to the white prison. Then, she put down her trowel, picked up her watering can, refreshed her waiting herbs and went inside to get changed.

Chapter Seventeen

'Anna, dressed in her Sunday clothes, with a broad basket of modest gifts upon her arm, pulled in her middle, pulled herself up straight and knocked upon the grand, polished blue door of her neighbour's residence. There was no reply. Uncomprehending, as serving folk were plainly at home, Anna knocked again. This time a harried, plump and red cheeked servant came to the door, that Anna recognised by her voice to be none other than Jessie herself.

'We will have no hawkers here! You may take your basket of wares and your nerve,' Jessie stepped forward almost knocking Anna from the top step, 'and you may depart!'

Anna was aghast.

'Knocking on the door at the Master's entrance, I ask you!' Jessie started to depart, complaining.

'But, I am no hawker,' Anna suppressed a slight smile of confusion, 'I'm your neighbour come to visit –'

'We have no desire for neighbours who visit.' Jessie's voice remained clipped and austere, 'I thank you and good-bye.'

Anna stood and gasped, before gathering herself and announcing loudly, 'Well, I do declare, in all my years upon God's good earth, I have never been met with such manners in any company! Tell me, are you the lady of the house, for you are not dressed as such?'

Jessie appeared a little taken aback at Anna's sudden assumption of authority in the exchange. She looked at her again, yes, well dressed but in last year's fashion, so presumably in cast offs from her mistress, and yet, for all her basket on her arm covered over with muslin, she did not possess the air of an inferior personage, far from it. Jessie was perplexed.

Anna took advantage and continued, 'Where my husband and I are from, if a person of genteel breeding calls upon another, it is the norm for the lady of the house to decide whether or not she is to be admitted. Does not the same apply within this household? For I had taken it, from its appearance, to be a house fit for visitation from a pastor's daughter but if it is not, I shall depart gladly. I cannot, however, account for how widely the news of my treatment may spread about the town, for I'm sure you are aware how idle folk are apt to prattle and I'm sure I wouldn't be able to take responsibility for this household's fame, if my ill treatment were to gain renown.'

Anna stood stiffly bearing the countenance of an eminently respectable woman in very high dudgeon. She wondered if she'd over-egged it a little, not being accustomed to conducting herself in a fashion Mrs Gables would consider to be a laudable response to such impertinence. Instead of folding in humility, however, she thought of the young woman's words, stood on the threshold of her prison and stared on resolutely at her gaoler.

Before Jessie could fathom whatever to do, a laconic voice sounded from behind her at the foot of the stairs, 'Jessie, show the lady in, would you please?' The owner of the voice swept past Jessie whispering audibly, 'Where, may I ask, are your manners? What would the Master say, if there were to be gossip?'

Outmanoeuvred... Anna thought, raising her eyebrows but avoiding a smile, as she picked up Samuel's carrying crib and stepped forward. Jessie was obliged to give way.

The inside of the house was elegant and tasteful both in its understated architecture and décor. As Anna came to know, during her first conversation over tea with Verity Cortaise, her husband was a successful corn merchant, a self-made man whose mother had come from a little money but had married a man with none. Driven on by the desire for a lifestyle and status, which he'd regularly watched his grandparents enjoy, but not his parents, Michael had worked hard at his lessons, paid for by his grandpapa. His industry, coupled with a certain native wit for bargaining to his own benefit, had caused him to rise well enough. Verity, however, Anna noted, didn't look much like a flushed bride of a mere six months. Maybe, like herself, Verity had married too young. Her age, though, was hard to determine, for although she both looked and sounded not above twenty, a pale, wan complexion and a listless air about her made her age seem indeterminate.

Anna was careful during the conversation to listen more than she spoke. She spoke enough, she did hope, to gain the young woman's interest in an acquaintance with a neighbour, but not so much that a person cloistered from the world, as Verity did appear to be, would seek the comfort of solitude once her visitor had gone.

Anna's balance was well judged; she not only learnt a great deal about the young woman and her husband's family but also managed also to solicit a return visit for the next day. This, however, was much to the consternation of Jessie and indeed Michael's mother, who quite patently viewed the connection with a parochial priest's daughter, the wife of a stonemason to boot, to be beneath her daughter-in-law.

The view of Michael himself appeared to have been swayed by Verity's father. He'd made a rare visit to the Cortaise household that day during which he stated that he believed his daughter, although, he admitted, still sickly, and not in sufficiently robust health to be generally out and about in company, to have been too much, for too long, in solitude. He argued that it was only natural for a young wife to seek out and enjoy the company of another such as herself. Moreover, he argued with more gentleness and compassion than Verity could remember seeing in him for many a year, that a priest's daughter, who lived only next door, was nothing less than a gift of an opportunity to provide companionship for Michael's young wife, whilst avoiding any physical exertion or indeed, any foreseeable moral risk.

Upon hearing Verity's narration of these events, Anna blushed at recent recollections, when placed next to the credentials her background seemed to be providing her with among new people.

For Verity, however unexpected her father's intervention and her husband's acceptance of it seemed to be, it was to her advantage, so she simply accepted it.

'Maybe, despite what they say in ballads and plays, once in a while when Fortune spins her wheel it does rest up in a mortal's favour.'

'Verity! How can you think so? Why, the good Lord is in charge of all and although you appear to have been in the doldrums a little, it seems to be His plan for you to come out of them now.'

'Poppycock!'

'I beg your pardon?'

'You heard me, poppycock! 'In the doldrums a little', why, I've never been out of them my whole life, by my reckoning. I can't remember a day of my own when my boat sailed freely, when I was able to steer from the helm my own direction and have that power of will over my destiny that I see given to others but not myself.'

There it was again, that streak of self-pity Anna found so hard to stomach or advise upon. Still, she must try, she thought, to steer young Verity onto a more Christian and fruitful way of thinking.

'But the real freedom comes, Verity, when you give up the helm and hand possession of it to your Creator, loosing yourself from that pride which believes you know what's best for your life. Surely, you've been taught that since you were a girl?'

'I've been taught by those around me to do as I'm instructed or catch it. I've not been led by any 'benevolent being', who, you never know, might've had my interests at heart once in a while, there's no telling.'

'But there is telling, Verity...Verity?'

Verity had straightened up and stiffened, while her eyes darted about below a deep frown, 'I mustn't blab about all this, I forget myself, it was a condition of my being allowed to come here that domestic matters remain private, and oh, now I've gone and, and, oh no!'

Verity sank back down in her chair, knocking over her tea cup with one arm in her distress. Annoyed at herself over her concern for the lace edged tray cloth, now covered in dregs and tea leaves, Anna crossed over to Verity and put an arm about her shoulders.

'Hush now, hush my dear! There's no harm done here, if your husband is a very private man we needn't mention again our conversation here today; the conversation itself was private also!'

'Oh, but there's no such thing with me you see! I've recently been taken with the affliction of speaking while I sleep and I cannot guard, I find, the slightest anxiety from escaping from my lips while I slumber. Oh, it's so unfair!'

Verity fell again to sobbing and, despite Anna's best attempts, could not be led to believe that little, if anything, had been imparted through her speech, for at least a quarter of an hour. After this time, she was gently persuaded by turns, that not much had been said. Eventually, persuaded more and more by her own reasoning, rather than by any punctuations Anna managed to occasionally insert, between sobs and cries and by minor alterations to the memory of the offending comments, that nothing, in fact, had been said at all that could be deemed to have broken her word of promise to her husband. Indeed, she sniffed one last time, nothing at all.

Pacified at last, she was at length persuaded to take a turn about the garden, to allow her composure and complexion to settle a little before she returned home. They'd barely entered the garden, however, when Verity suddenly took fright at, well, Anna knew not what.

Verity jumped backwards in her shoes, right into Anna's carefully prepared but as yet un-transplanted herbs.

'Oh no, my shoes! My beautiful shoes all covered with dirt! Whatever will Jessie say? Oh, why did I have to have been wearing such light blue satin? They are quite ruined! Oh, why did I think I must wear such pretty shoes, to come here of all places? I even have pieces of pots in my stockings! Oh, get them off me, Anna, do!'

Anna obliged as best she could, attempting to calm Verity that she might move away from the precious cargo she had trampled by this time in places almost to oblivion.

Hearing, Anna presumed, the continued commotion Verity was creating, Jessie appeared from the side gate of the Cortaise residence looking like a Gorgon on a mission. She bore down toward them and with much tutting and grunting, not to mention disapproving scowls, she rather roughly, led the simpering Verity away.

Anna was afraid to admit to herself, fearing her response to be rather unchristian, a sense of relief at Jessie's intervention. As she surveyed her decimated stock of herbs, she counted a total of eight main stems broken, with a purple sage and marjoram crushed, she feared, beyond repair.

'Oh blast!' she cried beneath her breath, not wishing to offend anyone but frustrated beyond her usual patience. How foolish and naive she'd been, to attempt to recreate her friendship with Millie Price. And oh, how so very much she missed her!

As she set to, completing the transplanting she now wished she'd undertaken the day before, she tried not to allow her uncustomary ill temper to get the better of her. I must focus on what is good, on what the Lord has given, not what he's taken away. She stabbed at the soil with her trowel. Theo is settling well at school, the children seem nice (even if their parents lack the manners to call upon a new neighbour) and Sunday will surely bring new friends. I must focus on what is wholesome and Will and I...

Anna floated off into a passion filled reverie, for what her days lacked in interest and intimacy, her nights, she considered, far more than made up for. She felt as though she'd slept like an infant through her marriage till this time; conjugal communion and motherhood had left her still virginal in passionate consummation. Will had, of course, noticed her awakening, likening her to a tulip, whose warmth had thawed her winter snow. It was as if a more timely spring had arrived for them and the intensity of the pleasure of it all still brought a touch of crimson to her cheek and neck. The fact that the catalyst for her throwing off of innocence had been...well, it didn't prevent her from recognising that it was Will she'd fallen in love with, not for a second time but in a deeper, surer sense than she'd ever felt before.

Anna returned to her now somewhat diminished stock of herbs for replanting. As she continued her work, however, she found herself singing a most ancient ballad from the store of all man's time.

Chapter Eighteen

'The days and weeks bustled on in their round about her and Anna, with Will's gentle support, slowly began to acclimatise to life in town. Theo was the first of them all, truly to set up camp in Frampton, inviting friends for adventures in the garden, returning visits and going out to play so that Will was obliged to learn all his new haunts, in order to fetch him and Ivor back each night for supper. That was part of the joy of their new family life, though, that Will was there to do so, that during the week days and evenings, Anna was no longer raising the boys alone.

The warmth of June days permeated their cottage walls as the mellow afternoon sun streamed in through their open windows. Abraham Gables looked on, while the four Godstones played in relaxed comfort, while he drank his Sunday afternoon tea with them, as was becoming his habit in Emmaline's absence. He watched and observed, he noticed, a family who felt blessed. He was also touched by the pleasance of the boys' growing familiarity with him, for if Anna's attention was called away to the kitchen and Will and Theo's play became too boisterous, Samuel was wont to crawl over to Abraham's upright legs and sit between his feet with an arm wrapped round one calf for support, as he laughed at his brother and father's antics from a safe and secure position at the periphery of the rug.

The flood of pleasure Anna began to enjoy in the constancy of everyday family life and marital harmony soon outweighed any temporary loss she felt to the busy-ness of her days. Indeed, she started to notice, on the three or four days a week when Verity did visit, that there is nothing like an excess of unsought company to make a soul value the comfort of none. Still, she'd sought the alliance and, she remembered, with good reason. Anna found, through her frustration at Verity's seeming inability to pass a picture without leaving it knocked crooked, or drink some tea without its being split, or pass a vase of sweet peas without the vessel, the table and the rug on which they were placed all being in mortal peril of damage, that the most appropriate place in which to pass the time with the young Mrs Cortaise, was in the garden. Here, her damage did not impact on the weight of the week's laundry and what Verity stumbled over, trod down or knocked asunder, Mother Nature, at this flourishing time of year, repaired with speed.

After a period of time, however, the necessary exertions of establishing a well-stocked garden in high summer began to pale the attractiveness of the activity for Anna's young, sickly companion. Verity took, Anna presumed for this reason, to turning up dressed in fine clothes unsuitable for outdoor work. Persuaded by Anna's insistence that she needed to be in her garden, Verity would arrive suitably dressed, after a fashion, only to find excuses to return indoors. Anna presumed that Verity still hoped the manners of a priest's daughter would oblige her hostess to follow. Anna purposefully failed to fall in with this imagined device, allowing Verity instead, after some initial anxiety, to return indoors to comfort and entertain Samuel, if he'd happened to awake and cry while Anna was still working. In spite of her habitual flightiness, Anna noted that when it came to the baby, Verity seemed able to focus her attention sufficiently to ensure that he remained intact, with no damaged articles to his person, by the time Anna deemed it wisest not to leave him alone with her less than robust new neighbour any longer.

On the first of September, one week before Samuel's birthday, everything altered. Verity had used her habitual excuse, namely Sam's awakening, to totter back inside the Godstone cottage. On her way back to the house, to Anna's dismay and annoyance, Verity had taken fully three paces over her herb garden, next to the parlour window, to shorten her pathway by what? One step? Anna was incredulous. She stood with her wrists on her hips, surveying the latest damage and ruing the fact that at this time of year, Verity's regular, 'little mistakes', as she called them, would start to take considerably longer to heal.

Anna set down Theo's old stool and began to attend to some rather crushed sage, muttering as she did so. Verity was probably fortunate that Anna was a priest's daughter, or the muttering might have turned to cursing, as she realised that nearly half of a newly established thyme had been trampled upon. Her irritated thoughts were unexpectedly turned aside as she felt a gentle tapping on her outstretched back. She turned around. It was Samuel. Having taken his first steps only the evening before, he'd seen his mother approach through the window and made his way outside to be with her. He laughed joyfully at the novelty of his success and possibly also at the look of bemused surprise upon Anna's face. She sat up and he buried himself in her lap, giggling. Anna was amused at his delight and she bent down to kiss his head. He held up his arms and Anna noticed a piece of something sticky in his left hand. She looked closer. A piece of mint cake. Not a thing either she or Will would've given an infant. She looked at Sam's face and recalled, not that she'd ever thought about it before, the regularity with which Verity would be wiping it, when Anna returned inside the house. She remembered taking it as an indicator of good care, surprisingly thoughtful care of her son and how Verity would take up a bottle of Sam's milk as she put down the cloth. Now, as she surveyed the sugary mixture smeared across Sam's cheeks and lips and chin, she was less impressed. And it begged the question, if Samuel, complete with sugar filled distraction was here, then where was Verity?

Anna crept like a thief about her own house. She'd deposited Sam safely in his high chair, still complete with his mint cake, before setting out. She stalked slowly from room to room, wondering at the meaning of it all, for as she searched, she could espy nothing of any sufficient value to tempt a far wealthier neighbour than herself to turn to thievery.

Verity was not downstairs. Curious. Curious and disturbing for she couldn't recall Verity ever having been invited upstairs, why would she be?

As Anna swung open her bedroom door, Verity started, shrieked and dropped a page of the letter she was reading to the floor. It was covered in neat rows of distinctive handwriting, in dark green ink. With rather dull predictability,

Anna noted coldly, Verity began to sob. On this occasion, however, Anna felt absolutely no compunction to comfort her. Instead, she entered into a somewhat surreal state of being; nothing was as she thought it'd been. Verity's whimpering, like the crying of an untended cur, became a background noise. A flow of steely chilled resentment seeped through Anna's veins, removing any trace of warmth. To Anna, it was like becoming another person she didn't recognise but to go to Verity, to feel any compassion for her at this moment, was an impossibility. She looked towards her mother's writing box which stood opened on her chest of drawers. She remembered the intimacy of the moment when her father had given it to her, on her eleventh birthday, in a coming of age ceremony in his study. Now, the privacy of its rosewood sides and carefully polished keyhole stood violated.

Verity sank to the floor and continued to snivel. As she descended, Anna experienced a second cold front assault her senses, as she noticed the envelope which Verity dropped. It bore a smart number two on its top right hand corner: Uncle Christopher's second letter, as per his strict instructions, never opened by Anna, lay unsealed and read, strewn across the floorboards. The sensitivity of the material contained in the letter, the capacity of it to irrevocably harm innocent people and the uncle she loved so dearly, impressed itself upon Anna severely enough for her to break free from the cold winter of her anger and step forward to gather up the sheets.

Remaining without speaking, she satisfied herself that the contents of the two letters were restored to their rightful envelopes before locking them back in her mother's smart box and, for the first time in her memory, removing the key.

Anna strode to the door and without turning back addressed Verity with chilly civility, 'When you have composed yourself, you may come down and explain. I would strongly recommend that in your rather self-indulgent sobbing, you do not raise the volume in my absence sufficiently to rally the awareness of Jessie. To bring the attention of anyone to the contents of these letters, let me make it clear, would incur my permanent displeasure.'

Anna had chosen her words carefully; she wanted to know, she needed to know for the sake of Ruth and Uncle Christopher, what in God's good plan this could all mean. She'd been unable to restrain herself from communicating her disdain but she had deliberately left open the door to forgiveness. In this life, she reminded herself, as she trod back downstairs, we all need forgiveness. Unbidden, a glance of Raphael's marbled blue eyes, his curly black hair and the sound of his voice sped across her mind. In her current mood, she banished them. She took, however, the message from her Maker: 'Let him who is without sin...'. Look past the sin to the sinner, Anna Godstone, she told herself, hoping dearly that Verity would take a few moments to compose herself, that she might adjust herself also. At present, she simply felt incensed.

Chapter Nineteen

'Verity did indeed take some time before descending the Godstone staircase and entering, with her head bowed down, into Anna's kitchen.

'Sit at the table please,' said Anna curtly, avoiding eye contact while pouring the tea she had prepared. 'You can do no harm in here, short of breaking the cup and saucer themselves, I suppose.'

The irony of these words stood out and imprinted themselves upon Verity's mind as she sat down in a silent and nerve-shocked state: the capacity not to harm this good and kindly neighbour, who'd befriended her so unexpectedly, now seemed to be beyond her. It seemed whatever course she chose, whatever she did or said, after the shock of what she'd just read; damage, harm, destruction seemed to be forces she was born of, they were inherited, inescapable factors in her life. The enormity of it all bore down upon her, suffocating her efforts to breathe to speak, to utter a word of her history and her own tawdry role in what'd happened; in the tragedy of her own mother's death. As she stared at the grain of the pine wooden table before her, she attempted to control her breathing and gather her thoughts. She needed Anna to understand, the only way to lessen the harm of it all, was to tell someone everything, to tell all: to make *him* pay. I must grow stronger, she told herself, I must grow stronger or he will surely, surely, one by one, kill us all!

Anna, her attention distracted for a moment by Samuel's attempts to gain Verity's attention (and who could wonder after how many pieces of mint cake?) remained for the last few moments of her life oblivious to the revelations Verity was about to disclose to her and the extent to which they grievously outweighed the contents of her uncle's optimistic missives.

Verity took the moment to stir the sugar into her tea and raise the little blue and white cup, trembling slightly, but not so much as to spill its contents before they reached her lips. She placed store in her ability, as she secured the cup back down in its saucer and raised her gaze to meet Anna's stern enquiry.

'My maiden name,' she rather blurted out, 'my maiden name, I don't think you know and I'm not supposed, under any circumstances to tell you, although until this day I didn't know why, but I must tell you now, for us all. For I know you believe me to be stupid and silly and trivial and maybe in some ways I am but not in all, not silly enough not to realise that now, all must be told.'

Anna remained rigid, 'Are you aware, Verity, that you have not yet actually said anything coherent?'

'I am, I am working up to being coherent, I shall be coherent for I must be, I must tell you...'

Verity was interrupted by Samuel's cries of frustration at being ignored. Anna took him from his high chair and placed him on her lap.

'What is your maiden name, Verity?' Anna's impatience was plain as she attempted to wrestle her own empty tea cup from Samuel, who'd grasped it from its saucer.

'Lunsford, my name is Lunsford, daughter of Annette and Nathan.'

Anna started and her cup careered off the edge of the table and span across the room. Anna watched, mesmerised as it bounced, oh so slowly, once, then twice, three times across the red brick floor before colliding with the iron grate and exploding into a thousand sharded pieces. The room remained silent in the aftermath.

After a while, Anna spoke in disbelief, 'Nathan Lunsford? Nathan Lunsford is your father? The man who persuaded your husband to allow you to come here? The man who...'

'Yes, but back then I didn't know why, Anna, oh please you mustn't blame me, I was in ignorance of so much and have been beholden to him in a way no soul would wish to be since, since...' Verity drew deeply, breathing through her strong desire to stop and weep.

'You're Nathan Lunsford's daughter? Why, did he command you to come here and spy upon me? To seek out and read my uncle's letters?'

'To seek out (but not read) the letters in green ink, yes, that was the task I was charged with, under threats, Anna, threats even you would shrink from yourself, I'm sure.'

Anna suddenly became aware of the tremolo in Verity's voice and she halted herself and regarded Verity, as the girl placed her fingers upon her temples and rubbed them round in agitated circles with her head bowed down.

'Go on, Verity,' she still commanded but her tone was softened. 'Take some tea if you need to but you must explain.'

'I must explain, I must explain but I must start from the beginning and I'll only be able to accomplish the task if you, Anna, if you understand that I'm in need of forgiveness, for I've done wrong, I've been weak and not strong and I must become strong but without your forgiveness, I cannot do it Anna, I can't do it alone: I haven't got your loving God but only Michael and Father, who each have played a part in my treachery! Oh, Anna, only say you'll forgive me and I shall draw the strength to tell you all!'

Was there ever such a call for pity? This child of twenty or so, who sat before her was starkly terrified and when Anna considered how altered her position in the whole seemed; Nathan's own daughter bidden to treachery, to find the green inked letters, Anna found her mind galloping forward, but no, first she must forgive and then listen.

'Oh, Verity, you do have my God, every yard as much as I do, if only you knew it. Listen, Verity; no don't weep, for as you say, you must tell all you know but know also, that we're asked to forgive one another by God, just as he promises to forgive us. Verity, whatever you've done (and from what you've said it would seem you feel responsible for something quite serious) if in telling me, you tell God that you're sorry, you'll be forgiven as you speak the words. You'll find you have a sense of peace that no longer requires my forgiveness, although you'll have that also, indeed you have it already, now.'

Verity lifted her head and smiled weakly. Anna poured her some more tea but refrained from moving from her seat across the table, for she needed Verity to remain sensible.

'Where is the beginning, Verity?'

'It appears that the beginning was before my creation, although that was all news to me, frightening news, however, when you consider my position. My story begins here in Frampton, where I grew up with a drunken, argumentative father and a mother so consumed in always rowing with him and being angry that things weren't different, that I didn't much figure in their attention on life.

'When my father, then, introduced me to a handsome and wealthy young man, why I leapt at the chance of escape from the dull monotony of my parents' endless battles and my mother's sobbing keeping me awake at night. I also enjoyed the attention he paid me before we were married, who wouldn't? He brought me posies and said kind things about my hair and he even gave me a puppy, a white Scottish terrier I called Dolly.' Verity stopped, as a soundless tear carved a track through the white powder on her cheek.

Dignity, in the face of adversity. Anna noted the progress.

'But, you have no dog now?' she asked gently.

'No, Michael said it was a silly name and that he disliked having her in the house and on the furniture, so he took her away a week after we were married. He also took away his attention to me and replaced the compliments he'd formerly paid me with insults. I took to weeping uncontrollably, I couldn't help it, I'd even awake in the morning and when I remembered the state of my existence, would burst into tears. They called for the doctor and he pronounced me, 'feeble', whatever that means. To me, it means they have the right to imprison me and keep me indoors and from the world at large.

'I went to my mother and begged for her to intervene, but she refused. She said that I'd followed my father's wishes, in marrying young, that I'd left her to cope with him alone and that, in short, I'd made my bed and must lie upon it. I came home and retreated to the library, my husband's books being my only world and my escape from the scolding Jessie and the viperous tongue of my mother-in-law.

'Thus things stood, until one night, when the house was awakened very late with a beating on the servants' door. Between sobbing, a voice was crying out to be let in. It was my mother. I sat up in my bed, afraid to move. The banging and the crying went on and in spite of my disappointment in her; I found I could listen to it no longer. Unable to understand why nobody else seemed to awaken to her distress, I tiptoed to my bedroom door. My mother was still beating on the secluded side door and moaning. I opened my door to find a chair placed before it, with my husband upon it, reading a book. He didn't look up at me, instead, he simply turned his page and ordered me to return to my bed.

'But, my mother!' I said.

'I shan't sanction such a disturbance at my house.' His tone was icy and his eyes remained upon his page. 'If we ignore her, she'll depart and people, maybe even my mother, will sleep through this disgraceful public display. If she's admitted, she'll make a regular habit of creating scenes or worse still, expect to move in permanently, on top of you, which was not a part of my arrangement with your father.' He raised his sight to glare at me, 'I command you to return to your bed.'

'Could I've slipped past him quickly and made my way downstairs? I could've, Anna, I confess but to my shame, I didn't. I was weak and in my weakness, treacherous to my own mother's need. Cowed by my husband, I turned on my heels, turned my back and took the coward's way.' Verity paused, tearless and still, 'That night she fell down the Devil's Ravine.'

Anna's thoughts were a pitchfork battleground of competing realities; what did all this mean? Were Uncle Christopher and Ruth safe from Nathan? She doubted it, this nerved racked child before her plainly hadn't been; 'my arrangement with your father', exactly how far had Lunsford controlled this poor girl's destiny? She needed Verity to go on.

'Take some tea, Verity; remember we all need forgiveness, even from ourselves.'

'But, how can I forgive myself? My mother never spoke to me coherently again, although she did communicate quite clearly that she didn't blame me. She did that with her eyes and her touch, even though her speech was taken away and when it started to return, that's when...'

'Take some tea, Verity,' said Anna, leaning over and covering Verity's small, fragile hand with her own.

Verity sipped some tea and continued, trembling a little, as if cold, 'I arose to the news of my mother's fall and the demand of my father that I returned to my childhood home to nurse her for him. Michael seemed changed in his attitude towards her and strangely compliant with my father's wishes. I returned, and for a few days, my mother and I were quietly at peace with one another. While my father was out of the house, I told her how truly sorry I was and wept upon her shoulder like a child. In his absence she cradled me and although unable to feed or dress herself, or not to dribble as she ate, she kissed my head, Anna. That is forgiveness, is it not?'

There were tears in Verity's eyes, as Anna nodded and squeezed her hand, gently.

'What happened next, I'm guilty of still, for my lies have held back the truth and justice, for I fear, Anna,' her voice dropped to a whisper, 'for the safety of us all! Those letters, Anna, if I tell you and he already knows of those letters, am I guilty of placing you in danger also? Or, do I protect your Uncle Christopher and 'R', a kind of relative of my own? And, do I really have a sister?'

Having no higher authority to seek guidance from, Anna followed her soul and simply told the truth. This time, Anna smiled and forgave Verity for weeping.

'That is the only good news in all of this, oh, Anna, how can we resolve it all?'

'First, I believe you do have to confide in me. Second, I believe you must promise to tell no one else about it. Then, I feel, we'll probably need some time to think it over, to make a careful plan, Verity. I mean, your father doesn't yet know you've found the letters, does he?'

Verity shook her head, encouraged by her understanding of Anna's meaning.

'What happened, though? I believe you told the authorities your mother died in her sleep, peacefully?'

'I lied, Anna, I lied. My father was gradually becoming aware of the reconciliation between my mother and myself but she

135

hadn't sufficiently recovered to warn me how severe the danger of his knowledge was. From my naive position at the time, I was the one who was to blame for her condition. So, my parents had rowed, yes, but they did that with monotonous predictability. How can I've been so stupid, to not realise that this row must have been different? 'Secret' and 'sister', her only clear words, I didn't realise what he'd told her. How could I, when I knew nothing of it? How obvious it all seems, now, today. She must've realised her marriage to him was an unlawful sham and come running to me, her only real, living relative.'

'This much, I'm afraid from other sources, I did already know, only not that you, my dear Verity, were Lunsford's daughter yourself!'

'Only, I turned away. I didn't know the part he'd played in it all; his guilt that she knew of, that if she were to recover the power of speech, it would undoubtedly be to her peril, unless she were to escape from him. I didn't know enough to save her, either the first night or the second she was in danger!'

'What did happen each night, Verity?'

'On what turned out to be my mother's last night, Pa came home from drinking, slid in like a snake and overheard me attempting to help mother to speak again.

'Fa, fa, fa, or way, way, way,' she would say repeatedly, as if learning to speak anew like a child; Fa, fa, fa, way, way, way. This went on for some time, before she suddenly decided to repeat the two words she'd managed previously, only this time adding one more.

'Secret, secret, sister, sister, secret, secret sister, sister, sto, sto, stones.'

She began waving her arm as if throwing corn to the ground. I started up and sought out my old school slate and a piece of chalk from the dresser, but by the time I'd turned around, my father was standing between my mother and myself with his legs almost astride her and his arms upon the elm arms of her chair.

'Now, don't ye think,' he leant in close to her, 'don't ye think, it were best for all of us, Verity here included, very much so, if you were just to rest in peace, my dear?'

'He guided her outstretched palm from its place of action to her lap, and held it there. I couldn't see her face, it was blocked from my vision by his torso, but her moan, oh, her moan!'

Verity gasped and placed her hands across her face to hide herself. She gasped twice but then, to Anna's surprise, instead of folding into tears, she pressed on rapidly, 'I tried to protect her Anna, I did. I declared that peace was indeed what she needed, and refrained from declaring peace from him, at least. I announced that I would sleep with her for the night and that he might rest or slumber where he willed. He made no answer to me but nodded and then stared at my mother a while. Then he slumped into the chair opposite, that I'd just vacated, and glared into the fire.

'As quietly as I was able, accustomed to my father's sudden mood swings in this state, I raised my slender mother from her seat and slowly assisted her passage across the room and up the stairs, to the sanctuary (or so I thought) of her bedroom above. As I undressed her, she began to weep and once I had secured her bed jacket, I crept in beside her and, for the first time in my life, put my arm around her shoulder as she laid her head upon mine. I kissed her and we slumbered.

'Some time in the night, I awoke with numbness in my arm, from the warm weight of my mother's body upon it. Half asleep, I withdrew my weary limb and turned over, to sleep once more.

'When I awoke in the morning, there was an unpleasant aroma and a dampness to the sheet. I turned to my mother and sat up, aghast. There she lay with a pillow over her head. I wanted to cry out, but I feared to. Terrified, my tear-bleared eyes searched around the half light of the room but my father's form wasn't there. I was alone. I lifted the pillow from her face. I felt relieved that her eyes were closed but utterly distraught at the notion they would open no more.'

Now, tears criss-crossed down through Verity's pale face powder. Now, Anna clasped both her hands in her own and spoke softly to her, 'You don't have to go on, maybe that's enough, for now.'

'But I must, I must, for he killed her, Anna, with his hands and then tied a noose around my own neck and so I didn't know what to do or who to complain to!'

'How, Verity?' Anna squeezed her hands and then poured her some more tea, adding sugar and stirring it well.

'To send that message, not to hide the deed but to leave that pillow in place. I know my father's messages well of old: the leather belt on the arm of his chair; my small oak stool placed by the garden door; instead of my plate, the key to the lock of the cellar on the table before me. He was and is a man of messages, and those feet in the letters, Anna, make no mistake, Maria's un-booted feet, that was a message; those feet would never follow him again, he'd made sure of that.'

Anna rose up but then sat back down swiftly, as a swathe of fear swept through her veins dragging her senses to bent knees.

Verity continued, 'Of that, however, at the time I knew nothing but the message, the pillow, my mother's dead, urine-soaked body beside me, I understood all that. Quietly, I lay back down and stroked her hair and sang to her.

'After a while, he came in, 'You'd best come down,' he said, and left.'

Verity paused for a while. Anna, ashamed for having judged her and now in perfect understanding of her turmoil and fear, stretched out and stroked her cheek kindly.

'I needed to shift for myself and in a somewhat detached state of mind, I couldn't hurry. I found I spilt the water from the pitcher and was obliged to clear it up. I found myself unequal to the fine finger movements needed to dress and button myself up. I found myself unable to fix pins in my hair but that they fell out or dug in.

'Finally, I said a lingering goodbye to my mother, kissing her blue-white cheeks so keenly, wishing I could bring dear life back to her soul.

'I descended to the man called my father. I opened the door and walked over to the chair where my mother had last sat. I seated myself opposite him. I bowed my head, afraid and disbelieving.'

'Don't you sit there feeling prim and righteous, my girl. You think I killed your mother but it wasn't me that did for her. You see, I know. I might've put my hand upon the pillow to keep you safe, because I know. She came a knocking at your, oh so sturdy door, but the trouble is, she knocked in vain, now, didn't she?'

I sat up straight and looked at him, 'How do you know? Did Michael tell you?'

'I had no need of Michael, child. I was there myself. I saw her knocking on your servants' door, to avoid you the embarrassment of a commotion on your door step. I saw her crying out, to ruthless care, so it turned out. I saw and heard her turned away, with your name mentioned.'

'No, it wasn't! I sent no message, she wasn't turned away!'

'Oh, but she was; a rough wench, not much more than your age, came and spoke in the briskest, coarsest terms. I thought she must have come from Billingsgate, myself.'

'Jessie. But, I sent no message, I was denied also!'

'That's what you say, but will your servants and your household remember it thus?' He paused, eyeing me beadily.

'And then, there's last night. You see, to some it might seem that you, in the face of your mother's returning speech, made excuses to lie with her for the night. Having sent her away from your own house in distress, you were suddenly, oh so keen, to come and nurse her here. Then later, with only the two of you in the room, there she is, cold dead in the morning!'

'You'd see me swinging from a gallows for what you've done?' I asked him, trembling to my soul, Anna.

'Rather that, than look down at my own feet swinging loose! But it doesn't have to be that way, Verity. It was your mother, who was foolish, who put herself in harm's way. It was she, who, knowing a little too much, went out to pronounce it to the world. It was she, who strayed and fell in the pitch of night, who knows, maybe a little distracted by a devil throwing stones, to direct her to her fate.'

'It was you! All along, you were there!'

139

'She was warned but she took no notice, took it upon herself to go and tie the knot for my noose instead, my child. My wife, should've known me better. My wife, should've taken my advice. Question is, will you, Verity,' he leant forward, 'my child?'

'I looked into the pitch of night myself, Anna. If eyes are windows to the soul, as they say, my father's soul is surely with Beelzebub!

'The rest, Anna, you know. He coerced me into falsehood and perjury to provide him with an alibi. I forgave my mother utterly for turning me away, for he now seemed to control my husband also: in my fear, my dreams became, indeed still are, haunted by the spectre of my father, of the courtroom, of the gallows being erected with my name above them! Either that, or I become my mother, running but stumbling in the night, and then, then I hear stones, small pebbles skating across the ground until they hit my ankles, smarting my bones! I have become clumsy and nervous in my lack of sleep, but Michael cares not, he simply calls for the doctor, who doubts my good sense and gives them all reason to hide me away. Michael seems often to do my father's bidding, although he does no one else's, not even his mother's.'

This salient point was not lost on Anna but she returned to the main, 'So, your father, based on false blackmail, obliged you to seek out my letters?'

Verity nodded, 'But I was not supposed to read them, he believed them to be sealed. This is the third time I've had the opportunity to go upstairs and read them. Anna, forgive me, for can you imagine, thinking yourself alone in the world apart from him, to discover you have a sister?'

'Yes, I can, and I am quite jealous of you for it; but for nothing else!'

The two women both smiled at the grim humour and Verity appeared to relax a little.

'Anna, I have trusted you with my life in order to protect your Uncle Christopher and 'R', what is her name, the grandmother of my sister?'

'Her name is Ruth, fittingly; the epitome of pity inspires its return once again.'

'Ruth, my sister's grandmamma. And my sister?'

'Do you know, I don't think it came up, for my uncle related the tale to me over the fireplace one night, does the letter not mention it?'

'Ah, no, it will have to wait, then. Still, the knowing Anna, the knowing bolsters my resolve; in protecting Ruth, I protect my sister from losing the only mother she has in this life.'

Suddenly, Verity's capacity to travel through her tortured history, which Anna had marvelled at, given her usual frailty of spirit, became understandable. For the first time in her life, maybe to make amends for not having slipped past Michael to her mother's aid; Verity was being heroic.

'Listen, Verity, we need time now, time to consider what to do.' Anna covered both of Verity's pale hands with her own, browner, more robust pair.

Anna had planned to go on, to praise Verity and give her a little of the maternal warmth that she was so bereft of, but their conference was interrupted by a rough, loud rapping on the door. It was Jessie, sent to enquire as to the reason for Verity's extended absence and to rectify it.

Instead of panicking, Verity arose slowly and stood tall. The two women squeezed each other like sisters themselves, encased in secrecy and union, in conspiracy against none other than Nathan Lunsford himself.

Verity left the cottage without any prompt rescue to furniture or ornament being needed. She answered Jessie's stern remarks with a frivolity which would not have revealed the sinister sobriety of their last hour's conversation, even to the seasoned ear of Sir Dudley Rider himself, had he been around to witness the case. Not for the first time that day, Anna was impressed.

Once alone, she strode up the stairs to her writing box and wrote out a hurried, brief letter, on the writing slope at her dressing table. It was later than she'd realised though and as she sealed the envelope, she heard William enter and halloo

141

below. She crossed back to her mother's box, slipped the letter inside and locked it up, tucking the key away in her pocket.

Chapter Twenty

'As soon as Will and Theo had left the next day, Anna slipped out to post an urgent letter to her Uncle Christopher. As she came out of the Post Office she was startled when she met face on with Will, apparently still on his way to work.

'Why, who've you been writing to, Anna?'

'Oh, no one, no one.'

'So, you've been into the Post Office for some other reason?'

Anna saw his point, 'I was just posting a letter, for Verity, in a way.'

Will stared at her. They were both very conscious of the conspicuous nature of their conversation, standing as they were in front of a building which in many towns might well be described as a very hot spot for gossips. Anna remained mute, frowning, cursing her own stupidity as she looked on a rather unkempt man who hadn't shaved and whose belly protruded a little from under his shirt.

'I'll see you later then, Anna.' Will sounded somehow disappointed and Anna was remorseful. Should she have just told the truth? Most likely not; mentioning Uncle Christopher's name in so public a place would quite possibly have been a very foolish indiscretion. She felt alone again, just as she had after the miscarriage when she couldn't explain any of what she felt to Will. She hated secrecy and yet for now, until she'd warned Uncle Christopher and Ruth of the palpable danger they were all in from Lunsford, she felt she'd no choice but to wait.

As she walked home, Anna felt as though a surreal aura surrounded her life: Uncle Christopher, Ruth, Verity and she were all at dire risk of harm. Lunsford was indeed a double murderer after all and a great dissembler to boot, tricking Uncle Christopher and Ruth into believing him so utterly remorseful, while all the time manoeuvring his position. More chilling than that, not only had he murdered two wives and mothers with his bare hands, he had also threatened, through the instrument of the law, to add vicariously a third to the list;

his very own daughter, Verity. As Anna passed by chatting shoppers and bustling tradesmen, the uncaring mêlée rolled on unawares. Neither did she care for them, as in her distracted and solitary state, even with Samuel on her hip, she hastened home.

Once indoors, she waited nervously for Verity to come. She attempted to distract herself from the gravity of the situation with the usual round of household chores. She stopped, however, after she'd broken a second blue and white tea cup, the third to be destroyed in two days. What would Will make of it? She didn't know. She knew enough to be certain he wouldn't call in a doctor and use such distraction and clumsiness to label her and lock her away. She now understood a great deal more about Verity than she'd ever expected to. As she swept up the latest porcelain casualty in the affair, she realised with humility that she was just beginning to gain a small inkling as to how anxiety-stricken and terrifyingly precarious life must have become, for such a fragile, young vessel.

Afraid to venture outside, for fear her demeanour would reveal the altered state of things should Lunsford be watching, Anna took Samuel into the parlour and allowed him to amble around the furniture and travel about on his own two feet as he felt able. She provided him with a willing and congratulatory audience and his confidence grew with her flattery, praise and applause.

When Samuel came to her and lay upon her for his nap, having learnt how from her time of recuperation, she rested also and inevitably slept. Perhaps, due to exhaustion from nervous anxiety, once asleep, Anna slept on. Samuel was still an infant and with no adult indication of when to rise, he slept on too.

Will was mightily surprised to arrive home to a quiet house, not quite set in order as it customarily was. Theo, he was aware, was with friends until supper time but he was a little concerned when he found Anna asleep with Sam in the parlour, at that hour.

He ascended the stairs and went over to Anna's writing box. The key was still absent. He sat for a short while on the end of the bed and then returned downstairs to awaken the slumbering pair.

During the night Anna awoke to Will's voice soothing her as he drew a cool, wet flannel across her brow. She was soaked in perspiration as was the sheet beneath her. Focus as she tried, she was unable to utter any sense in her words to her husband.

Anna slept fitfully rising to consciousness only to slip under once more. Sometimes she was aware of voices, Will's and another, who talked like a doctor, although not Doctor Snelling but a stranger, who knew nothing about her. She wrestled with the fear he wouldn't care for her but only his fee. She wanted Doctor Snelling but his voice didn't come.

Sometimes she heard Ivor scratching at the door to go out and sometimes she heard Theo's thrilled voice or Sam crying out in abandoned babyhood laughter.

Mainly though, for the next three days, although she had no inkling of the time, she slept, sometimes well, sometimes badly, tossing in distress and moaning in anguish, about what, Will knew not. She made, however, after her initial failed efforts, no attempt to speak again.

On the fourth morning, Anna woke with a clearer head; the fever had broken. She was still weak but found sufficient strength, propped up against her pillows drinking tea, to enquire as to whether Verity had called.

Will sat beside her and looked into her eyes, 'Anna, praise God, you've been restored to us! You're not, though, my dear, by any means the only person here in Frampton to have been struck by this fever. It has attacked mainly the elderly and infirm; you yourself, my dear, are plainly still not back to your full strength but you are, in what the doctor hereabouts referred to as your 'underlying condition', of 'robust constitution'.'

Anna smiled at Will's mimicry of pomposity, glad that though more supportive and responsible, he'd not lost his playfulness of heart. Her smile evaporated, though, at the sight of Will's thoughtfulness and contemplation before he spoke on.

'Anna, you're probably unaware that you turned a corner early yesterday evening. You're awake now because you've slept and rested, not sweated and tossed.' He paused; Anna looked down and waited, while running her forefinger along the satin stripe of the white quilt.

'Verity came down with the fever at the same time as you, on Tuesday. Her fever has not yet broken, Anna.'

Anna heaved a sigh of relief: Verity was not lost.

'She remains, with her underlying fragility of health, in danger. I'm sorry.'

Anna tipped her head back against the bedstead, 'Oh, don't be sorry, Will, Verity will be just fine, I'm sure of it. I'm sure.'

'But, she's still in danger, Anna.'

'I know she is, we all are Will, but I believe Verity's made of sturdier material than that very spire you're building on St Mark's, even if she is obliged to keep the fact discreet from others.'

'Anna, what is it you know? What's all this secrecy that keeps you from me so? We've been through this before, Anna, and look how much better it would've been if you'd have spoken earlier; you mayn't even have been lying here now, having narrowly skirted Death's swathe once more.'

Anna looked at Will squarely. He was right, of course he was.

'I shall tell you, Will, just two questions first. Has Uncle Christopher written?'

'No, Anna, he hasn't. Why, was he the recipient of your covert letter?' Anna nodded. 'I should never have allowed you to stay down by the fireside with him on Theo's birthday. All these letters between you, tell me, Anna, what skulduggery is here?'

'I shall tell you now, my love, you're right, I should've told you on Monday, I should've learnt and not been a fool again, forgive me, I hate this separation from you, truly.'

Will shuffled forward to her and held her elbows in his strong, warm palms, 'Anna, I'd forgive you anything, if only you'd come back to me and stay with me always.'

'But don't you have to be at work, Will?'

'No, they've given all of us with sick ones but no relatives to hand compassionate leave, unpaid though, I'm afraid.'

'That's fine, Will; God's providence here is in giving us time, for there's much to tell and I'm afraid, Will,' her voice trembled and she calmed herself but then repeated, 'I am afraid.'

Chapter Twenty One

'Anna scanned her mind, trying to ensure she'd relayed all of the many details of the case to Will. Will sat silently, deep in contemplation.

Theo was at school and Sam, to avoid risk of infection (as he had been all week) was spending his day with Abraham Gables, who was of an age in life where he could chose to work each day or not, as suited him best.

'I'm not best pleased with your Uncle Christopher, I must say.'

'Oh, but don't say that, Will; had we not known, think of how alone and in danger Verity would be now!'

'You've a point, I suppose, for surely, if the villain won't risk the green inked letters continuing in existence...'

'Then he has no plans to allow Uncle Christopher and Ruth to remain at large either.'

'Let alone risking Verity's continued blackmail holding firm, given her instability.'

'I fear with Verity, he is only biding his time, for another 'accidental' or 'tragic' death so soon would doubtless re-arouse weighty suspicions.'

'Our problem right now is that she's on her own, next door and in immediate danger. After all, there could be no suspicion if Lunsford wasn't in or near the house and her heart failed from the fever!'

'With Michael Cortaise's allegiance, such an appearance could easily be managed. Will, I suspect there's blackmail there also.'

'I agree.'

'All it would take would be a pillow...'

'Blackmail is a powerful tool...'

'Oh, Will, either one of them could do for poor Verity; to whom do we turn, without risk of harming her?'

Will lifted his hands, palms upward, and looked at her.

'Of course,' said Anna, 'how stupid of me.'

She placed her hands together, placed them within Will's, and quietly, together, they prayed.

Will and Anna were villagers, not townsfolk and still unaccustomed to town ways. Quite often, once the household was up, the lock on the latch was lifted and it occurred to no one to press it home until nightfall had come once more. Such was the case this Friday morning and Doctor Carroll, who'd grown quite fond of Will over the course of the week, and who was accustomed to accessing the private areas of people's lives, thought nothing, when his tapping with his cane received no answer, of entering and ascending the stairs to the Godstone bedroom.

As he halted to listen at the door, he presumed his eavesdropping would last but a moment, just sufficient to ensure no embarrassment ensued. As he listened on, however, he consciously chose not to interrupt Anna's account: Annette Lunsford had been his patient since a girl, and, owing to complications, he'd delivered her of Verity himself.

His grievous suspicions surrounding her death confirmed, once the room fell silent, he tapped and slowly entered, without waiting for an invitation.

'Excuse my manners, if you will, my young friends but you see, desperate situations call for desperate remedies.'

'Why, how long?' asked Will, jumping up.

'Long enough!' Doctor Carroll announced, and walked with his cane around the bed, until he arrived at the bedside chair. He sat down and regarded the couple before him. 'You're right, we have to intervene, to save Verity's life from that murdering vice.'

'You have access to her and influence in the house...' Anna offered tentatively.

'I do, indeed, I can command if I choose and today, I believe I shall. I shall outline my plan but briefly to you good people, for after your tale, Anna, I fear that it is imperative we act with alacrity.'

Without the chance to fully assimilate the wonder of this proffered assistance, Anna and Will listened intently and gratefully, as Dr Carroll explained his devices and plans. Anna

149

thanked the Lord he was a Christian man, for such intelligent capability in immoral hands... she put it from her mind, determined not to become tainted by her current experiences.

Dr Carroll explained that the recent outbreak of fever had caused the safety of the common health in Frampton to rest in a precarious state. Owing to the steady spread of the potentially fatal infection, he'd set up a temporary infirmary to which he'd been assigning the most dubious cases of recovery. The infirmary was housed in a comfortable and modestly furnished dwelling owned by the parish church, which had happened to be vacant at the time of the potential epidemic. The priest of St Mark's had gladly handed over command of the property to Dr Carroll upon this occasion, for the benefit of all.

'I propose I go next door and insist that within the hour, Verity be moved to the infirmary, where I may take control of her safety and wellbeing henceforth. Lunsford, by my reckoning, will still see this as an opportunity to rid himself of the threat Verity's continued life poses to his own. Michael Cortaise, as you've rightly guessed by my estimation, appears somehow, in some way, to be beholden unto Lunsford. Now, he might or he might not be prevailed upon to ease his current domestic dissatisfaction, if it could be done with Verity under his roof, but I know Michael, he's a coward, he'll not risk an act of such magnitude in a public domain, no matter what duress Lunsford might bring to bear upon him.

'No, if we move her, I believe we set a trap for a man emboldened by previous successes and escape from judicial notice. I suggest we place a close watch upon Verity, both within and without the infirmary, and then we wait for Lunsford, we wait for him to make his murderous move.'

'Forgive me asking,' Anna enquired, 'for you're further acquainted with me, than I with you, owing to circumstances, but who'll be to watch? Who do we know or trust with such a task?'

'My dear girl, my name is Henry and my brother's John, and although we are not the Fieldings, in this town, I am the doctor and my brother John, is Justice of the Peace. From what I know of you already, which is a great deal from your manner of telling this account and your compassion regarding this unfortunate girl; I tell you, from this time on, you have friends, Anna, friends in places of high note.'

'How can we thank you?' asked Anna simply.

'It is I that must thank you, my child, in this case, for I've known these two good women and have watched them suffer at the hands of Nathan Lunsford for far too long. Now is the time for action. I must step next door with speed and put plans into motion.'

Dr Carroll arose and nodded to the pair as he made his way towards the door, where he hesitated, 'I'll send word this evening of how things lie. If a messenger knocks, it will be a servant of mine, so do not fear. I'll tell him not to wait but to slip a note under. I doubt very much Lunsford will trouble you tonight; he's not yet as far ahead in this as we three. As you said yourself to Verity, Anna, he does not yet know the letters written in green ink have been found, let alone found and read. May God bless you and keep us all!'

Anna tapped Will on the shoulder and he jerked out of his thoughts and remembered his manners.

After he had shown Dr Carroll out, he returned to Anna's side, 'Never again will I grumble to the Almighty about his tardiness in answering prayer; you've got to admit, Anna, that was pretty instantaneous.'

'Each time I fear, I then find he's gone ahead before and provided; God's providence, in a doctor we barely know, Will! Will, what are you doing?'

'I'm just peeking, Anna, I want to see Verity brought out from that white prison and carried away to safety.'

'Come away, Will! What if Lunsford were to see you and suspect? We mustn't alert him to the state of things or our advantage in the matter will be lost. Will, come away please or I fear you'll place us all in a tower of cards! What if he takes fright and absconds himself? Do you want to live in fear forever more?'

Will came away from the front window slowly and reluctantly, 'Why, Anna, your mind's grown fanciful with all this intrigue; Lunsford knows not of a plan to undo him made but five minutes ago in this room. My mind misgives about you, though.'

'Why, Will, whatever do you mean?'

Will stepped over to her and sat next to her once more.

'Anna, is this all? Is there anything else holding you asunder from me? Only sometimes, you seem as a different person, one I don't know from the Anna of last snowfall and before. I know there've been changes between us but I thought they were changes that were bringing us closer together in our marriage, Anna. Only now do I discover, that since we've been closer in union in our love-making, all the time you've been apart from me, involved in cloaked liaisons and affairs I know nothing of...' he trailed off.

Anna placed her face into her hands. Her soul quaked and she knew not what to do. She had but the beat of a bat's wing to decide, for if she took any longer, Will would know that she'd not told all, not all.

'How am I to take this? Do your hands cover guilt, Anna?'

'No, not guilt, Will,' she raised her head and met his gaze, 'but remorse. All my life I've thought myself wise, and maybe a little older than you in my soul but of late, the decisions I've made seem to have kept me away from you. I do see that and I'm truly sorry for it.'

Anna looked into his eyes, hoping he'd not press his point home. Will looked back.

'I see,' he said simply.

Anna glanced away for a second, no more, but when her eyes returned to his she saw that in that moment, a chasm had opened up between them. She wished she hadn't, wished she'd not looked away but it was too late: Will had read her.

Now, as things stood, Anna and Will were cast beyond each other's reach.

Chapter Twenty Two

'They'd felt so close, finishing each other's thoughts almost, as they'd discussed Verity's fraught situation. Now they were apart. Will retreated downstairs where Anna couldn't follow. Anna retreated into tortured contemplation; she had to tell Will or estrangement would follow, perhaps not separation from him physically, for he wouldn't leave her and Theo and Samuel, she knew. But, the look in his eyes, she'd seen it outside of the post office the other day; disappointment, mistrust, judgement. She couldn't bear it, she had to tell him or the devil would make play and what conclusions he might conjure in his thoughts, she dared not think on.

Nothing so very much had happened, had it? She tried to persuade herself but the effort was useless. Thought after thought darted through her mind, each thought carrying with it a stinging tip as it landed home, penetrating her consciousness with the poison of guilt: the camellia; his marbled blue eyes; his athletic form; his voice, as he carried Samuel across the bedroom to her; her confusion in the woods and unseemly outburst of consternation upon the revelation that the crass, thieving varlet before them, was none other than his wife.

How could she bring this to her marriage, how could she tell Will? Yet, if she didn't...

Downstairs, a little later on, Will watched alone from a dark corner of the front casement window as Verity was stretchered carefully, supervised by Dr Carroll himself, into a grand, covered carriage bearing the Pelham Arms, no less, complete with the Pelham Buckles on swags.

How typically ostentatious of Michael Cortaise, a carriage borrowed from the Duke of Newcastle, First Lord of the Treasury himself. Will's mind revolted at the superficial nature of the 'tender care' on display for all to see. It lacked sincerity, a weakness he'd never once thought to find within his own marriage. Enough, he sat down heavily. Verity was being driven away to comparative safety; all the poor child had to do now was survive both the fever, and an attempt at her murder, and she'd be fine. His mind reeled and reeled. Did he really know his wife at all?

For the remainder of the day, Will and Anna remained apart. Will steeled his resolve against her, unless she were to become honest once more. Even when he felt sure his resolve would weaken, when in her sweet presence (for he must take her food) he found her asleep, exhausted from the fever and the weight on her soul, he supposed, of her continued duplicity. About what, he knew not for certain, but some semblance of words had spilled out during her fever; his heart misgave and he was sorrowful in the extreme.

That evening, after the boys were in bed, each of them waited for news; Will in the parlour, Anna upstairs. Anna couldn't help thinking how much easier it would've seemed, to listen in their old cottage back in Heartbourne, where their souls knew every heartbeat of the house; each creak of each frame in the wind, the noise of each wall as it settled for the night. Here, there was noise from outside one moment, movement in the beams and slates another, and then, periodically, Ivor's scratching to compete with.

No knock came. No note appeared under. At length, Will determined to waste no more rush lights, having barely earned a shilling all week. He ascended to Anna, and blew out the wick's light, in silence.

In the morning, Anna awoke. For a brief moment she held no memory of the estrangement between herself and Will. Then, suddenly, during mid-stretch, she halted. She felt alone, nauseous from grief and shame. She opened her eyes but without turning, she knew that there was no Will beside her.

Before she was able to collect her thoughts further, the long awaited knock came at the door. Anna started up and her mind flew to Verity's safety as she listened. She heard Will step to the door but not open it. The note must have been slipped under, just as Dr Carroll had promised, only a little later than he'd hoped. What did it mean? Was Verity safe? Was she well? Wary of sudden risings but in the absence of Will's footstep on the stair, she swung her legs around and rallied herself into a seated position on the side of the bed. She paused and her eyes fell on a tray of uneaten food still left from the day before. Some soup. A little finely cut bread. A fruit scone. William must've prepared it for her. She felt unworthy of such love. She longed for her mother, she wanted Ma Gables and felt jealous of Retty's good fortune to have her by her side. She wished for her Uncle Christopher. Oh, why hadn't he come or sent word, at the very least?

A tear fell on her cheek which she was still brushing away when Will entered the room. In his altered state of mind, he mistook her grief for something it was not. He interpreted her attempt to subdue her sorrow as yet another act of hiding away emotions not fit for him to see or know of.

Although he hadn't meant to, he spoke to her curtly, 'Verity is safe.' He left the room abruptly, placing the note bearing Dr Carroll's hand on the bed next to her.

'Will!' Anna called him back but he walked on down the stairs. Had he heard her? She didn't know. More tears fell before Anna was able to gather herself calmly enough to read the letter.

Curled up, like a subdued child under the quilt, she read Dr Carroll's rather ornate writing.

Dear William and Anna,

First, let me cast your fears into abeyance: your young friend V- is safe from harm, for the moment, at least. If you will forebear your further curiosity, however, I feel I must tell this tale in its rightful order.

I attended your friend, my patient, yesterday morning and immediately advised her removal to our temporary infirmary, in accordance with our plan. I met, however, with some resistance from her husband, who was desirous of seeking the opinion of the C-family physician, who travels down from London upon request, as and when the family require his attendance, so I believe. I instantly feigned alarm at the delay of some hours this course of action might incur, stressing with some vehemence, within earshot of the servants, the on-going risk to the entire household of V-'s continued presence. Self-interest being ever a spur in the flank of human motivation, news was suddenly uncovered among the staff, that the said physician was not currently in Town but merely down at Horscroft, not fifteen miles away. Unable to dissemble further without suspicion being aroused, I was obliged to come away, while a servant was dispatched with a missive.

You are not, my friends, without sufficient sense to realise the strain of demands upon my time, given the current circumstances in our town. I went about my patients and my numerous tasks, I must confess, with a keen apprehension and pre-occupation regarding V-'s mortal safety. After two hours, my fear broke out into agitation, causing me to utter a hasty and unconsidered reprimand unto my assistant, Hubert. Humbled, I asked the Lord's forgiveness, collected myself, offered an apology and then excused myself in order to return to providing the protection of my presence in V-'s 'condition', shall we say.

Upon my return to the steps, I was met by a messenger being sent out to find me. The physician had sent his apologies but found he was unable to attend poor V-, being already caught up in attendance upon the Duke of Newcastle's wife. The aforementioned gentleman, however, upon hearing of V-'s condition and the terrible fear for her (emphasised by my stark warnings) offered the assistance of his very own carriage, in some small lieu of the attendance of Dr Berryman. Relieved, I set forth to make arrangements for V-'s swift removal from the C- residence. You may, perhaps, have witnessed this much from your humble abode your good selves.

I was careful to have V- installed in a room on her own, although it housed one other bed, allowing me to place a screen within it, behind which a thief catcher was stationed, a man known to my good brother. Two other such men were positioned around the infirmary posing as porters. The room I chose was bathed in silver-grey moonlight and therefore, by no means fully dark, even at that hour. Outside, in the locality, were no less than six watchmen, all alerted to the case and primed to keep approaches and entrances under a constant vigil. Just narrowly opposite was stationed the local constable, sent there deliberately earlier during the day, before V-'s arrival, ostensibly to keep guard over the post office, after that theft of a sack of mail earlier this week. He stood before the door of the post office with his hands behind his back, giving him full view of the infirmary before him.

The scene was set. We waited. For once, I was glad of the mundane tasks demanded of me, to maintain the best to be hoped for chances of those souls unfortunate enough to be housed within those walls. I grew tired but found myself unable to sleep and was comforted only by the knowledge that V-'s own fever had broken, that she slept without perspiring and that, if we could but preserve her through this one night, she would in the course of time be well once more.

Once or twice, as I moved quietly around the ailing house, I heard odd noises from V-'s chamber. Upon investigation, though, they turned out to be nothing more that the appointed thief taker's snores issuing from behind his screen. Irritated at his lack of care for such a sober duty, I jerked him awake by his shoulder each time, grateful that there was more plentiful and regular watch outside.

Possibly less tolerant in nature than of normal, owing to a much greater stretch of consciousness than God intends for our poor souls, on the third occasion of his odious snoring, this time quite loud enough to wake poor V-, I marched into the room, grasped him by the shoulder and escorted him out into the corridor. Once there, it became obvious that the man was inebriated. As it happened, as the man stood before me, swaying and squinting with his left eye, another of the thief takers, although one I had never seen before, was passing by. I motioned for him to step over to us but before I could speak, the first man indicated that he needed to step outside for a moment, to ease himself, a direct result of his imbibing, no doubt. In a whisper, I accused him of being in a drunken state, whereon the two men began to bicker about whose fault it was. The first blamed the second for his condition, while the second stated that he didn't pour the beer down the man's throat himself. You can imagine my frustration. I interrupted them sending the intoxicated man to relieve himself and reassigning each other's duties to them. Once back inside the bedroom, Verity stirred, and I decided to sit with her a while, after I had settled her new protector behind the modesty screen.

After some time had elapsed, I dozed, but as a professional doctor is capable of, after many long years of service, I dozed without fully sleeping. I was, in consequence, easily aroused by some movement but I chose not to stir. I opened my eyes slowly. I soon realised that the sound came from behind me and that the new thief taker and not V-, was moving. With moon behind me, as he came around, I could see the man, secure in the knowledge that he would be unable to see that my eyes were open, just a little. I wondered if maybe he also needed relief, but then he moved stealthily over to the spare bed. I thought maybe he too was lazy and intended on going to sleep, but he didn't lie down – instead he took the unused pillow in his hands. He stalked over to V-. As he lowered the pillow onto V-'s face I jumped up, intending to cry out for help but the fiend, dropping the pillow, swiftly grabbed me by the throat with such vehemence that I was taken without breath. He started to strangle me, pressing harder and harder upon my windpipe crushing my ability to draw in air. I struggled and with my arm knocked over the screen but before it fully fell, disorientation overtook me and a darkness began to descend upon my vision. I tell you, my friends, at that moment I feared for my continued presence here on earth and found myself wondering if I was yet fit to meet my Maker.

The screen, I believe, must have fallen and clattered as the thick-set hands around my neck pressed me to the floor. Hearing movement below I only felt as vibrations, I believe the devil thought the better of it. To my relief, by God's ordinance, and just in the nick of time for me, he withdrew.

I have been told by others present that the murderous man, now known to be Lunsford, ran from the room and then the house, hallooing that a villain was in V-'s room strangling the doctor. Thus, pretending to raise the alarm and rally help, by the time some water had been fetched and I had regained my senses and the power of speech, Nathan Lunsford had long since departed from all sight, from all sound, from all light.

In the commotion V- had been awoken, awoken in time to recognise the figure and form of her father as she held the unsought for pillow. With quite remarkable dignity and composure, she conveyed this fact before requesting some tea. She then asked me to relay all the particulars to her of the incident. She asked, most firmly, that I did not omit any detail out of nicety. She desired to know the whole truth.

When she had listened, she calmly called for pen and paper and she began to write. I feared for her stamina but she insisted she wouldn't rest until all had been recorded; of that night, of her mother's death and that you, Anna Godstone, are in possession of letters, which it is now requisite for you to deliver up unto the law.

The third thief taker was questioned as to his part in the affair, he too being a stranger to all around. He declared he had no prior knowledge of either of the other men within the infirmary that night, stating that it was the first man who'd appeared to be 'recruiting' for the night in a local hostelry, offering wages well worth buying him a beverage or two. My brother was not best pleased with this particular and owing to the near fatal harm caused to his only surviving brother, notably myself, he has ordered a likeness be carved and for 'Wanted' posters to be pasted up in profusion all about the town, to ensure above all doubt, that Nathan Lunsford stays away, for ghastly fear and mortal dread of being taken up for his life, hung by the neck and gibbeted for all manner of man to gawp on as dire warning.

My dears, I shall in any case be visiting you in the course of my duties this afternoon to check upon Anna's progress; if there are any other particulars you wish to know of, you are simply to declare them and all shall be told.

Until that time, I remain humbly your servant,

Dr H Carroll

So it was over; Lunsford had escaped but his villainy was known and he was unlikely ever to return, unless he'd no more life left in him than to last to the next assizes, or so she hoped. Verity was safe, but what about Uncle Christopher and Ruth? Anna grasped the letter once more as her eyes flitted through for the sentence she sought. There it was, just as if she'd known all along. But of course, she'd been ill. The entire town might know of the robbery of a sack of mail, such a thing was not common, but certainly not unheard of, and would undoubtedly have been posted in the *Sussex Weekly Advertiser* and spoken of at length by all. All except those sick in their beds, with husbands who desired not to converse with them. Again, the weakness of isolation swept through Anna's limbs and she felt weary.

With great effort, conscious that had things been different, she would have called for Will to help her, she fetched some clean stationery and her writing slope. Poignantly, reminded of the last time she had written letters while in bed, she sat down to scribe one letter and a note. The first was to Uncle Christopher, enquiring as to whether he'd received her earlier

159

letter and relaying to him the momentous and startling events of the past week. She pointed out that it was probably wise for him and Ruth to be a little on the lookout but not too afraid, for now that Lunsford's history was known, he had nothing to gain by their deaths and everything to lose in the risk of being taken up in any attempt to harm them out of malice.

Much the same, she thought, might be said of herself and Verity, not now, for any attempt to visit Frampton would surely be an act of insane idiocy but in the future, when Time had dimmed memories, embellished fantasies and wrought Age's changes on Lunsford's face... Anna decided not to dwell on the notion and returned to writing.

Apologising, if her words were unnecessary and a slight to his sensitivity, Anna pointed out that the heavy mortar which must be delivered to Ruth, that her daughter had indeed been murdered by Lunsford, was bound to resound through her senses with a mighty force. This might, however, be cushioned in her spirits if followed by an immediate focus on the fact that she had, beyond all seasoned doubt, saved the life of her granddaughter's half-sister. By bringing the particulars of the case to Christopher Coates, she had facilitated the good Lord's intervention in the piece in good time; Verity was still alive.

Anna ended her letter to Uncle Christopher with a humble request for confirmation that he had received it, that she might recuperate from her illness without fear for him and Ruth, beyond that measure which was unavoidable with a character such as Lunsford at large.

Anna then took a new sheet and wrote a brief note to Judge John Carroll, confirming the background of the letters she was sending to him through his brother, certainly having no further desire to keep them in her possession. She then took her correspondences and slipped them into her writing box, turning the key and placing it back in her pocket, which sat on the dresser.

Anna moved back to her marital bed and sat down. She felt the chill of the morning September air across her arms as she ran her fingers along her goose bumps while in thought.

Suddenly, Anna heard a commotion of delight issuing from downstairs; Samuel was laughing loudly and Theo was apparently making announcements before Will's laughter joined them. Her boys. Together. Of course; Samuel's first birthday breakfast.

Chapter Twenty Three

'A few days later, when she was sufficiently recovered, Anna did attempt to explain to Will about Raphael De Vine. From the very mention of his name, however, Will frosted over and the conversation did not go well. Her thoughts ran over and over it in the following weeks and it was all of her dreams when she awakened in the night, that and visions of Nathan Lunsford once more attempting to take Verity's life, or her own, or Uncle Christopher and Ruth's together.

That nothing amounting to a 'sin of the flesh' had occurred, she knew Will understood. Unfortunately, that something amounting to a 'sin of the soul' (as he had bitterly quipped) had, was now an irrevocable part of her marriage. It had happened, Will knew as much, and he didn't appear to have any immediate intention of forgiving her.

The fact that Anna's womanly awakening had coincided with these events, was not lost on Will. He'd accused her of acts which she simply wasn't guilty of; betrayals of the mind that would've been odious to her during moments of passion, but her word on this, or any other matter, was now doubted by her suspicious husband.

A visit home, to seek the solace of friendship from Millie or the benefit of matronly advice from Ma Gables, was comfort beyond her grasp; she dared not even suggest it, for fear of her motives being called in to answer for themselves and unfavourable judgement being placed upon them, with no further evidence being required.

Will steadily distanced himself from her, never sufficiently to raise any public concern, especially before Abraham Gables. In private, though, he began to live almost without her. He would leave the meal table without a word, taking the paper into the parlour and closing the door behind him. He would announce that he was going out with Theo and Sam, who he took to calling 'my boys'. If they were ever alone together, he paid more attention to Ivor than he did to Anna, even treating Ivor with an occasional gift but not Anna, even on her birthday.

The children were too young to notice such a slight and not one person in Frampton knew her well enough to be sensible to the changes within her marriage.

Verity, as Anna had predicted, turned out to have sturdier piers to her constitution than had previously been believed. She stayed on at the infirmary way beyond a time strictly necessary to her recovery, making herself useful in small measured doses to Dr Carroll. She proved herself quite capable in matters of bookkeeping and, once she had regained sufficient strength, small errands which took her out into the world. Both Dr Carroll and Anna (who became a regular visitor) started to notice a marked change in Verity's demeanour and bearing. Her trips to the High Street afforded her a new independence, long overdue for a young woman of twenty. Others found she possessed a lively manner of speaking, an ability to see humour in the commonplace (about which others merely complained) a delight in young children and a natural ability to amuse all about her. These charming qualities, all the more delightful for Verity's own lack of awareness of them, started to turn strangers, who often began with a morbid fascination in her case (which made folk only too happy to speak to her as if they knew her, whether or not they had done before) into acquaintances.

Owing in large part to Dr Carroll's wise precautions, an outright epidemic of fever was averted in Frampton and by way of recoveries and funerals in turns, the population of the infirmary began to dwindle.

Meanwhile, the elderly rector of St Mark's, now rapidly declining in the scope of his abilities each day, was desirous of gaining repossession of the dwelling, that a new curate might be installed there who would be able to help him maintain the services and blessings required by the townsfolk in their round. A kindly and perceptive man, he'd noted Verity's continued presence and one day came to speak privately with Dr Carroll regarding the circumstances of her case. They spoke sombrely for about twenty minutes, before adjourning to consider most carefully, how, in the eyes of God and the compassion of Christ's command, they should proceed in acting for the child, for that, as the rector remarked, was apparently still her condition, both in body and in soul.

The following day the rector returned and quietly requested that Dr Carroll accompany him on a visit to Anna Godstone. They sent ahead a note, but Anna was not surprised by their calling; she had been a close witness to Verity's trembling responses and subdued manner, and ability to knock over any crockery, or indeed whole pieces of unsecured furniture, whenever any reference to a return to her marriage was made by Doctor Carroll. The stark difference between this lack of composure and the steadily growing confidence and self-assuredness she displayed in the company of common townsfolk or other church folk, when she accompanied Anna to help polish the silver or the choir stalls, was discussed with concern in Anna's parlour that morning.

It had been a surprise to the rector, but was not to Anna, that in the course of his care for Verity, Dr Carroll's concern that her recovery might be complicated or jeopardised, should she unwittingly overexert herself if in the early stages of pregnancy, had been met with an emphatic reassurance that no such circumstance was possible. Upon further delicate enquiry, Dr Carroll had come to the realisation that Verity had only the dimmest notions of how such an eventuality might even take place. She had quietly and unemotionally stated, that she did not mind the kind doctor knowing, that she and Michael had always had separate sleeping arrangements and he'd never once disturbed her after she'd retired for the night.

The rector, in his capacity as a man of God with a duty to care for all of God's children, reminded them of their Christian duty to care also for Michael Cortaise in their handling of the matter. Dr Carroll and Anna graciously agreed, pointing out to the rector their suspicions that Michael too, in his own way, appeared to have been prey to Lunsford, in some nebulous shape or form the substance of which, Anna declared, she really could not guess at. Dr Carroll, as a very experienced man of the world, had his own theories but judiciously chose to keep them to himself before the rector.

Anna, a little falteringly, for fear of appearing unchristian but desirous to lay bare before the rector the factors impounding upon Verity's ability to cope with the notion of returning to her marriage, carefully relayed to him and the good doctor the circumstances Verity had been subjected to, before she'd first met her; Jessie's bullying, the pronouncement of her supposed feeble mindedness and her subsequent confinement. Anna went on to relay Cortaise's behaviour in more detail than Verity had included, in her account of the night her mother had fallen down the Devil's Ravine. She particularly emphasised the words that had resounded around her own mind: 'no part of my arrangement with your father'.

Anna decided to place her finger upon the thorn the three of them were surrounding, 'It would, in my opinion, be no Godless act to annul a marriage that has never been a union on earth, never mind before the Lord. It might even be a form of release and absolution for Michael also, even if we were never to hear him say so.'

This viewpoint, in its bold honesty, on the hitherto unspoken but most obvious release route for Verity, plainly impressed both Doctor Carroll and the rector.

'A form of absolution, for Michael also, yes, I do see...' the rector mused out loud.

'If pressed into the union not of his free will, like a man enslaved upon a galley in the swell...'

Anna kept buttoned in the desire to give way to a wry smile, admiring Dr Carroll's style from within.

'He might be freed from pressed service he cannot perform, that by your accounts, make him grow bitter. For the oppressive demeanour you describe in your tale of him, does not fit with the studious and God fearing boy I once knew.'

'An annulment, though,' said Doctor Carroll, moving deftly towards an endgame in his quest on Verity's behalf, 'would leave her in a precarious state of affairs financially, with no parents to provide for her and the former Lunsford dwelling returned to its landlord already.'

'Hmm, the vestry wouldn't be pleased if we threw her welfare onto the parish in such a way.'

'There now,' Anna allowed herself to smile a little, 'I may be able to help.' Anna proceeded to explain to the two kindly patriarchs sitting before her (such opposite examples of the two who'd previously held sway over Verity's life) Verity's open joy and delight, when Anna had confirmed the news that she possessed a sister, much the same age as herself.

'You, I'm sure, can imagine how God-given, gracious and welcome such a blessing must've been for Verity, who discovered this knowledge not long after the death of her mother had left her on the earth, or so she'd supposed, with no other blood relative than Lunsford.

'Since that September night, when Lunsford attempted to murder Verity, I've received letters on the matter, not only from my Uncle Christopher but also from Ruth. The letters were my first direct contact with Ruth and I quickly understood how she and my uncle have come to be friends; they both display an openness of heart, a direct manner and a kindness not afraid to tread an irksome path. In short, Ruth has possessed the foresight and wisdom not to shirk from the troubling and weighty duty of relaying the truth of her parentage to her granddaughter, Amelia. The narration of the dark history was managed tactfully but conveyed wholly and without omission. Ruth explained to me, in her letters, that she believed it to be her duty to take such a path, fearing that maybe otherwise after her death, if she'd been anything less than honest with the child, that Lunsford might take his advantage, re-enter her life and take revenge upon her for the acts of her grandmother against him.

'Amelia was deeply affected by the revelations made to her by her grandmother. For a while Ruth feared that yet again, she might not have taken the right course of action. She feared that Lunsford must've laughed at her, 'haunting', simply using to his advantage her naivety of the world.

'With a strong desire to comfort Ruth's soul, I wrote back, suggesting that we might alter the current ending of the history by bringing to Verity and Amelia the only essential goodness to come of it all; that they have been given each other. I received a response from Ruth not two days ago, telling of how overjoyed Amelia became at the idea and asking me to approach the matter with Verity.'

'Hmm, yes, I see where you're going, young lady.' Dr Carroll prompted the rector.

'Oh yes, oh yes, I see; might it be possible for you to write back to this grandmother, delicately explaining the condition of Verity's marriage and asking if she may seek the sanctuary of a wholesome home with her only living relative?'

'I'm sure,' Dr Carroll said, ' from her execution of numerous mathematical or scribing tasks for me, that Verity would be capable of earning a modest income to contribute to her own support; cosseting has made her restless, not idle and keen for activity and she's a pretty enough girl to have around the place.'

'Very well, I shall write this very morning, gentlemen,' Anna halted a little before asking, 'and Michael Cortaise?'

'Leave him to us, Anna, after all, you may have noticed, Rector, that he has not once visited her at the infirmary, let alone objected to her absence from his house.'

'Hmm, is that so? Well, maybe we are being directed in the matter as you suggest then but I would counsel that we hold at bay any proposals until we have secured an alternative future for the girl. Do we all agree?'

Assent was roundly confirmed and the meeting drew to a close.

A few days later, Anna was not surprised to receive two letters; one from Uncle Christopher and one from Ruth. She was somewhat aggrieved, however, that they both appeared to have been read by William, her husband, before they'd reached her.

The letter from Ruth confirmed what Anna had hoped for so dearly; far from seeing the suggestion that Verity come to them as an imposition, Amelia saw the arrival of a sister in her life as a joy she'd never hoped or sought for, which far outweighed the loss of an imagined dead father's good reputation. Ruth confided in Anna that, to her, this was a double relief; forming first a kind of atonement for any culpability she might bear in

167

not having prevented Annette's death and secondly, a form of security in a family bond she feared she could not provide for her granddaughter forever.

Anna turned to the second, unsealed letter, somewhat chagrined at the difference in how she was treated and respected by these different people in her life. Her uncle's letter was full of praise for the role she had and was continuing to play in the affairs of his dear friend Ruth. It outlined a possible timetable and arrangements for Verity's removal and subsequent installation with her new family, which allowed for a visit of his own to his dear niece, so long overdue, for which he humbly apologised.

Anna set to and quickly scribed a note to Dr Carroll indicating that all was well and the proposed private meeting between Michael Cortaise and his brother John should now be arranged.

She then sat back and sipped her tea alone, wondering how a visit from Uncle Christopher would feel, given the current strain within her marriage.

Chapter Twenty Four

'That year, late October brought bitter winds which bit the cheeks and clenched the toes and brittled the bones of ordinary folk, as they shivered about their business, in Frampton and all Sussex.

Michael Cortaise had been prevailed upon by Judge John Carroll, who'd referred to certain tests which his brother could conduct, with or without Michael's consent, which might confirm the veracity of Verity's assertions. Such tests, however, would be unpleasant for Verity and might also, the judge hinted, jeopardise the privacy of a quiet annulment. Michael Cortaise was not a fool; thus freed from Lunsford's authority, he signed the necessary paperwork, unobtrusively shut up his house and moved with his mother to Brighton.

Dr Carroll and Anna had attempted to sit Verity down quietly to explain the news to her but keeping her stilled or even seated proved to be impossible, once she'd garnered the kernel of what she was being told; in short, she was ecstatic. Anna expressed her concern that Verity might be a little sad to leave her newly formed acquaintances about town but the thought of Amelia ('Amelia, what a beautiful, delicate name, don't you think?') sent Verity into such imaginings of a life beyond her barren marriage, that all such minor points dwindled into insignificance. Frankly, thought Anna, after the previous year, who could blame her?

A date had been set for mid-November, when Uncle Christopher would travel the significant distance from Ruth's home village in Wessex, in order to collect Verity. Anna awaited his visit with considerably less enthusiasm than usual and little delight; she was sure that he would be bound to notice the awkwardness and distance that had developed between her and William.

As it turned out, however, no such intimate observation was made for Uncle Christopher's attention was very firmly elsewhere. Much to Anna's surprise, although it seemed so obvious once you knew; Uncle Christopher had ceased to be a bachelor. He arrived in Frampton not alone, but with his new wife Ruth and step daughter Amelia in his company. Now, thought Anna, all was explained; his recent neglect of her and remarkable failure to materialise, even after the night Lunsford had escaped. How could she not have foreseen this? No matter, she thought, for he seemed to be even jollier and more booming than she'd ever seen him and she was truly glad for his happiness. It almost took away a little of her own sorrow, just to see it. The larger than expected gathered company also avoided any peculiar scenes, for rather than an intimate meal at the Godstone home before Verity was taken away, Uncle Christopher proudly announced that they were all expected at the Maiden's Head for supper, by way of a familial and nuptial celebration fitting the occasion.

And very fitting and very jovial (and very noisy) it was indeed.

The next day, Anna took particular comfort in the simplicity of Samuel's affection and company, for otherwise, as she walked amid the diminished greenery of her winter garden, in the first snowfall of the season, she felt very alone.

Chapter Twenty Five

'A year later, if you'd have asked a fellow worshipper from Saint Mark's of Frampton for a description of Anna Godstone, you'd have been given a portrait not a soul from Heartbourne would ever have recognised. For all that Anna had grown up motherless, she'd always possessed a very sure perception of who she was and her place in the world. Now, this was gone.

Her father's position had given her a role full of kindness she felt bidden to fulfil by God, and He'd seemed not to object to her quiet way of carrying it out, alongside her ordinary life as a friend, or a wife, or a mother, as Time dictated in her round. The people of Heartbourne had trusted their priest's daughter's judgement and sought her advice, but as even the memory of her involvement with Verity's case diminished, she began to lose all trust in her own wisdom; was not, after all, her poor judgement to blame for the disjointed state of her marriage? Even this, she didn't know, as she found herself wheeling from fantastical scenes in her mind, where she became angry with Will and demanded his forgiveness, to moments of self-judgement and condemnation, where she laid the sole blame for their estranged misery on her own, weary shoulders. Once, as she'd stood in a lane waving him off to work, she'd believed herself wiser than Will and more seasoned in her judgement. Now, she believed she knew nothing, least of all who she was, or who between her and Will was right or wrong.

Such self-doubt wrought changes to her demeanour; she was less confident in meeting people and shied away from invitations. She avoided company, fearful that the intimacy of female friendship would demand knowledge of her past she found it hard enough to face within her marriage. The idea of letting the painful truth loose to roar about upon her character, before the unforgiving world at large, was unthinkable.

Truly, isolation is starvation to the soul and so complete was Anna's solitude that she became morose. At times she was somewhat tetchy with her sons. Such moments drew dark moods of disapproval from Will, as unbeknown to Anna, he leant further and further towards the conclusion that she was disappointed in her marriage, and wished not for him as a husband, but another.

Meanwhile, Anna yearned for nothing but the peace of forgiveness and the warmth of understanding and a return to the joyful times of the past between them, times that now seemed like a fantasy, a vision of happiness placed in her life to drive home the bitter winter-tide of their life as a household now.

The following spring, upon the nervously hopeful news from Emmaline, that Henrietta was with child once more, Abraham Gables gave up his battle to persuade his wife that he was not born to lead a bachelor's life. After a week in which he'd managed to cinder his supper (so carefully left by the maid) three evenings in a row, too distracted by his reading to remember its warming, he'd expostulated that enough was quite enough, so loudly, that his neighbours three doors down were well aware that things had come to a head.

The next morning, he delegated his entire workload to his most senior partner in the firm and went home to pack up for Heartbourne.

By late afternoon, having packed rather more than was usual for his regular short trips back home, Abraham decided to make his way to the Godstones' on this occasion, rather than the coach station.

Anna was dismayed, desolate. For eighteen months, she'd been hoping for Ma Gables' return. Now, for all that Abraham declared his removal to be only to be temporary, until the infant was born (for he knew he'd no hope whatsoever of Emmaline's return before such time) she feared that once the grandchild had been held in each of their arms, the idea of detaching themselves from family life in Heartbourne would seem alien to them both.

Once Abraham had secured Will's services, to carry himself and his luggage back south, he enquired as to the possibility of Anna's accompanying him, to visit her father, who was, he believed, quite unwell. Will, however, despite Abraham's polite attempt at persistence, was adamant that Anna couldn't be spared, that they'd no one to leave the boys with and that work was far too pressing, with the imminent completion of the lofty spire in hand, for any leave of absence to be considered.

As he travelled down the short brick path back to the street, Abraham Gables was saddened and pensive in the light of Will's response. The Reverend Thomas Porter was an ageing man, who'd not seen his daughter above three or four times, in what was now, nearly two years, since Will and Anna's departure from Heartbourne. And indeed, on those occasions, the priest himself had made the journey to Frampton. Anna had, noticeably, not returned to Heartbourne even once.

Abraham started down the street but stopped, suddenly aware that in his distracted state and with the mildness of spring weather not alerting his hands sooner, he'd left his gloves behind. He turned back and approached the front door with his hand up ready to knock, but then he quickly withdrew it. He listened, and then turned away, leaving his gloves for the morning.

Chapter Twenty Six

'Two days after Abraham's departure, just as the Godstone family were clearing up after their Saturday dinner, there came an unexpected knock upon their cottage door. Anna started, looked up and smiled involuntarily.

'Why, who could that be?' asked Will, rather ill-temperedly, 'Banging with a stick like a...'

'Beadle? No, it couldn't be.' Anna spoke out loud to the emptying room as all three of the male Godstones trooped out to answer the door, the boys following noisily their father's strides, their feet slapping in on the flagstones as they went.

'Abraham! Back so soon? And Emmaline, what a pleasure, I'm sure, do come through.'

Anna rapidly dried her hands on a cloth expecting to go and greet this most unexpected visiting party. She stopped, however, as she heard Abraham addressing himself to Theo. He was sending the boys out to play in the garden. Theo agreed readily to the request of his old friend, who had become quite a grandfatherly figure in his life. Anna put her cloth down on the draining board as she listened to Abraham maintain his assumed authority, requesting that Will accompany him into the parlour. Then, there came a quieter tap on the kitchen door.

Ma Gables entered and leant upon her stick, fixing Anna in her sight and chewing on her left cheek a little. Before Anna was able to command her pent up emotions be still, they burst through like a siphon and she sobbed so loudly, she feared the boys would hear her. She held up her hands to her face, trying not to issue forth any further pain. As she cried through her hands, failing to control her sorrow, there arose to her broken figure, the bosom of a mother's love.

In the parlour, still assuming control, Abraham asked William to be seated. Positioning a chair opposite, he sat down and considered Will's countenance for a moment.

'Abraham, you command me in my own home, which I tolerate out of time honoured respect for an elder, but may I ask, why? And why, may I ask, is your wife with my wife, alone, without my consent or approval?'

'Oh, I think you know why, young man, either know or can guess, or ought to be able and since when, may *I* ask, did a good Christian wife need her husband's permission, to speak with an older, respected matron?'

Will's eyes darted to the left, before returning to Abraham. Both men regarded each other. Neither one spoke.

In the kitchen, Ma Gables had settled Anna before the fire in a Windsor chair, under a blanket, with a cushion behind her head. She then fetched for herself an ordinary stick backed chair, that she might sit closer to Anna than a grander seat might allow. Anna attempted to protest and reverse the arrangement, but she was, as no one ever had been, any match for Ma Gables in an argument, no matter how kindly.

'Anna, my child,' she spoke softly, taking one of Anna's hands in hers, 'if you were able to choose, if you had the free choice of anything in the world, and I mean anything, what would you want to happen next, to be your future? Paint me a picture, Anna, of your tomorrows as you'd wish them to be.'

Ma Gables sat back and adjusted herself, as if there was no hurry in the request and Anna thought a little, gazing into the hearth, not really her own, just as this wasn't truly her home.

'I'd most like my days to be spent in Heartbourne but –' she hesitated.

'No obstacles, ignore them Anna, just paint the picture you most desire.'

'Well then, that's easy,' she smiled broadly at the vision in her mind, 'I'd like to be back in Heartbourne, with Will at my side, and the boys playing in our old garden with Ivor, while Will and I tie back the roses on the trellis, for it's summer again, Ma Gables, and the cloud that descended on our happiness has rained its day, and has distilled on the breeze of forgiveness. That's what I most desire in the world.'

175

'Are you sure, Anna? Be careful, my dear, for believe me,' she spoke carefully, 'no husband ever married the woman he loved, thinking he would one day smother her in jealousy.'

'But why, Will's not about to make my wrong his by smothering me!'

'Are you sure, my dear Anna? Are you sure you can forgive him? Trust him not to succumb to such uncontrolled and jealous rage again? Under such circumstances, Anna, some husbands and wives do live apart.'

'Under such circumstances? A separation? Why? To what do you refer?' Anna shook her head, shocked and confused.

'Why? I'll tell you why, Anna; because if divorce were a cheaper business, there's many an apothecary and an undertaker who'd be complaining about his loss of trade, believe me. And, may I add,' she leant forward on her stick staring seriously at Anna, 'plenty of judges who'd have less call for use of their black caps at the quarterly assizes.'

'But I protest, Ma Gables! Whatever's got into your mind? Neither Will nor I are about to smother, or bludgeon, or poison each other! Where does this begin?'

'It begins with a raised hand, Anna, a raised hand to an innocent wife! Anna, you could come back to Heartbourne and live peaceably among friends, your Creator would forgive you for avoiding your own demise!'

Meanwhile, in the parlour, a parallel conversation was taking place.

'I want you to create a scenario, Will, if you please, to draw a sketch of the future. What do you see?'

'I'd find it testing to see the future, as matters stand, Abraham. You see, the 'good Christian wife' you see in Anna, isn't how she appears to me.'

'And how does she appear to you, Will?'

'I'm not sure I'm obliged to speak about my marriage before anyone but the priest or my Maker, Abraham.'

'I could take you to the priest from hereabouts, if you prefer, but I'm afraid, under the circumstances, that kind and loving friends have become concerned for your wife, and thus, yes, you are obliged to speak about your marriage to someone, Will. I am merely offering to be that someone. Take your choice.'

'Under the circumstances? Under the circumstances? What do you know about my marriage already? Is there no end to my wife's affairs that are better known to others than to me?'

The speed of Will's rising anger was not lost on Abraham. He lowered his head and gazed into the grate, lit by Anna's hand.

He spoke quietly, without looking at Will, 'Sit back down, if you please.'

Will squarely glared at Abraham, as he descended back into his chair, 'What 'circumstances' do you speak of?'

'Do you deny that you raised your voice to your wife, three nights ago now, for surely you remember the occasion, unless of course, this is a commonplace occurrence in his house?'

'No, it is not, even under the duress of a wife with an eye and a mind for another man, I ordinarily hold my tongue. This is not sufficient reason for your meddling in our union before God, such as it is.'

'Do you deny then, that you abused her roundly, calling her foul names as if she were a prostitute of gross repute?'

Will looked down for a moment and closed his eyes before returning them back up to meet his challenger's, 'No, I don't deny it. I'm not proud of my opinion of my wife, but I'm not to blame for it, believe me.'

'Do you deny that you then raised your hand and struck your wife across her face?'

'Is this what she says?' Will rose up in anger, 'Does she add false witness to her sins as she goes on? I'll not stand for it!'

Will strode from the room, kicking a child's stool from his path, resistant to Abraham's calls for calmness and reason.

Alerted to his coming by his roar, Anna and Ma Gables stood before the hearth as he entered, 'Is this the report you give of me now? And it's me they talk of taking to the priest to ask for forgiveness! What parody of justice have we here? Anna, I command you to tell them it isn't true, I laid no hand upon you!'

177

The four of them stood square, as if posed for a quadrille. Anna remained strangely still and took her time, as Will's heavy breaths laboured on, the only sound in the room.

'The cheek he slapped was his own. It wasn't a pretty act, as he questioned my reasons for wishing to return to Heartbourne, questioned why he'd married me, but the cheek was his own. He'd asked, if there was more he didn't know of in my past, and questioned, if my access to all homes about the village, was not a convenient cover for a whore of lewd acts. He'd asked, if he had any guarantee, my morals were not more in keeping with the likes of Penny Mires, than those that a husband might expect, having married his priest's only daughter. Then, he slapped himself soundly across the cheek, as if in reprimand for his own stupidity, in trusting me, in making me his wife.'

As the four adults stood in assembled silence, the sobbing of a small child reached their ears. The voice of an elder brother comforted the infant, with broken confidence, in fits and starts, telling him, that all would be well.

Anna withdrew, to go to her boys.

'What's happened here?' asked Will, a little, but not much more calmly, as Anna could be heard escorting their weeping sons upstairs.

Emmaline sought the eye of her husband and he nodded to her twice, gently.

'What's happened here is something, and nothing, and then a great deal of harm. If I may explain simply, it all amounts to folly and fallibility, and nothing as yet, as irreparable as Abraham and I feared.

'If you recall, it was I, and not you, that was living with Anna full time, during the period the alleged wrongdoing took place. For all your accusations are just that, and nothing more. Anna's head was turned for a moment, just a moment, by a pretty face and do you know just what she did? She turned her head straight back to you. She didn't hold her eyes on Raphael De Vine, she fixed them on you.

'When a wife becomes a mother, her attention is diverted, split; some women think you cannot be a perfect mother and a perfect wife, most women choose. More fortunate women don't have to, more fortunate women have husbands who choose to become fathers, to the extent that their attention is split also, and they don't so much mind not being the only bright stars shining in their wives' eyes, they are more generous than that, with their hearts. Such a man Anna found beside her, when her attention was drawn back to you. Such a man, she found, when she looked at you that spring, that you rose in ascendancy far beyond the reach of a flower with a pretty face, Will. So much, did her heart swell when she looked on you, that she left behind her friends and father, and followed you here to Frampton, to be with you, Will, where she chose to be.

She paused for a moment and silence breathed in the room.

'Moreover, when I asked her tonight, yes, tonight, what future she wished for, in spite of your harsh unkindness towards her, the answer was still to be by your side, only with the dark cloud between you, 'distilled by forgiveness'.'

'Were those her words, Emmaline?' asked Abraham.

'Yes, they were, and she still meant your forgiveness of her, Will, for what amounts to very little wrong, in this life.'

'My wife is very gentle in her reprimand to you, William Godstone, but I'm afraid I'll not be so, for as I see the case right now, the forgiveness that is owed is in the opposite direction. Imagine, if Anna had a mother still living, William. Do you think you'd have managed to keep the two of them apart so long, to torment and abuse your good wife with gross wrongs, of which she is not guilty? What if her father were to know of your betrayal of his trust, in bringing her here, only to doubt and humiliate her? How many times, Will, have you spoken to your wife in the terms I overheard on Wednesday night? How long have you kept her in isolation of comfort from the truth and forgiveness? Women are placed on this earth at the mercy of their husbands, and with that responsibility goes God's trust in man! She was guilty of folly, for a moment, but your fallibility of judgement, your casting asunder of her from your heart and your pity, of that now you, William Godstone, stand accused!'

179

Without uttering a word, Will made for the front door and yanking it open wide, threw himself out, into the night.

Through the darkness, Abraham and Emmaline waited with Anna. The boys were in bed, although Anna doubted if poor Theo slept. When the hearth's warmth diminished, the small party adjourned to the parlour, where Anna tended and kept the fire burning, all night.

At some weary hour, not out of a lack of love or duty, but merely as the result of human frailty, all three, severally, fell to sleep.

Abraham and Emmaline awoke to the rather frank enquiries of Samuel, as to why they were still here, and why did they still have their clothes on in the night-time? Theo steered his younger brother away from such awkward interactions, telling him not to mind about that, but to fetch his manners, and to come and help Mother with their unexpected guests' breakfast.

Abraham and Emmaline stretched out their stiffened joints and followed the boys through to Anna's kitchen.

It was a trialsome meal, with Theo attempting to fend off Samuel's repeated enquiries as to where his father was. Anna was thankful that Sam appeared not to remember the raised voices, which had caused his own sorrow the night before. Theo, his face a little gaunt, she was more concerned about.

Her own thoughts were fragmented by fear and anxiety: fear that harm may've come to Will; fear that he mayn't have seen his way clear to the truth and forgiveness; anxiety that, if that was the case, maybe separation rather than further decay was the only, pitiful answer. Better that, than tramping forward to the future Emmaline had predicted, the one any maid or porter could read about luridly in the *Sussex Advertiser*, each and every quarter. The vision of her name on a wanted poster (or was it Will's?) span through her imagination. The black silk. The gloves. The assizes. The judge. It all pictured itself before her as a bedevilled dream rendered incarnate, it seemed impossible even to think it could come true, but then, so a while ago, would've Will's raised voice and his cruel words and his raised hand above her, just for a moment, this time.

Theo reluctantly accepted that he must go to school. Anna would've preferred to keep him with them, but she was too uncertain as to how or where they would find Will, or what might ensue when they did, to succour her maternal instinct in the matter.

After a prayer led by Abraham, to bless their endeavour and the course of events that might follow, he stepped out with Samuel, his old walking partner from Sunday mornings. Emmaline took Anna's arm but before they'd reached the gate, a messenger came running with a note in his hand. While Abraham sought out a coin, Anna read the rather cramped writing. Will had been found unharmed but apparently drunk and sleeping it off, under a piece of tarpaulin, in no less unsuitably Holy a place than plumb square at the base of the unfinished spire.

'Go back inside with Samuel,' said Abraham, with a cautious look on his face, 'in drink but in church? It's difficult to know. I'll return as soon as I'm able.'

Anna and Emmaline had no choice but to wait once more. At least he'd not come to any grievous physical harm, thought Anna, the first prayer answered; she scarcely dared hope for the rest.

Three hours later, Will came home accompanied by Abraham. Will, with an ashen face, asked to speak to Anna alone.

Chapter Twenty Seven

'What was said in that kitchen, while Abraham and Emmaline walked about Anna's garden with Sam, will only ever be fully known to Anna and Will, God bless their souls. That the grace that God had already dispensed to them both, they extended to each other in forgiveness, that much, we do know. That tears were shed and love restored, is a blessing all of us around this table should be humbly grateful for.'

'And, why is that?' asked Catherine quietly, still not wishing to disturb the sleeping Freddie.

'Because we are their future, the one they chose to build; we all owe our existence to their mutual forgiveness,' whispered Elise smiling, 'all of us, along with Susannah, on that step outside with your father.'

Susannah got up and walked in, 'How come, Grandma?'

Her father followed to listen.

'Because, as a result of that forgiveness of each other's human fallibility, love was re-found, and eight years later, a daughter born to Will and Anna, whom they called Elise.'

'But, that's your name, Grandma,' Freddie spoke without opening his eyes, 'was the baby you?'

'Yes, it was, my child.'

'Well, I'm glad that you were born, Grandma, but you still haven't told us about the two front doors.'

'Well, if your mother doesn't need me to help serve?'

'No, Grandma, you carry on.' Catherine placed her hand on her grandmother's shoulder as she arose.

'We'll do it together, Mother?' Susannah tentatively enquired, 'Grandma, what happened with Retty's baby?'

'Well, if you and your father don't mind laying,' said Elizabeth, 'Catherine and I'll serve. Mother, was it really as much as eight years later that you were born?'

'Yes, there was a considerable age between my brothers and me, that's why I used to love listening to them telling stories about my father, when I was still a girl.'

'Only stories?' asked Catherine, 'I don't understand, you said they forgave each other. What, did he desert her after all that time?'

'Not exactly, no. It was all very heart-breaking though. It makes me feel sorrowful, even now.

'Let's see, the happiest and saddest moments of the history. Let's start with the best of it, then. I'm very pleased to tell you, that Henrietta was delivered of a living son, with hearty lungs, and that Anna was correct in her predictions, to a degree. Abraham was persuaded that the senior Gables' permanent home should be re-established in Heartbourne, that he might once more enjoy the comforts and company of life as a married man, while his wife might be allowed to relish the role of a grandmother. Five nights of the week he resided in Heartbourne, coming up to Frampton for two nights and three days each week, to continue supervision of his very successful business dealings. During this time, he stopped as a lodger with Will and Anna, there being noticeably no further additions to the family, and therefore no further pressure on rooms in their modest cottage.

'The grand extensions to St Mark's were completed on schedule, about seven years before my birth. The spire was considered to be as lofty, grand and worthy an offering of praise, as any cathedral possessed in the land. The townsfolk of Frampton were exceedingly proud of the new spire which rose over two hundred and seventy feet from the ground, high above the original Norman building. The spire could be viewed from any direction for over forty miles around, or so it was bragged, and was only surpassed in altitude, so it was told, by two other spires in the kingdom. The Pipingford Masonry Gang was held in the highest esteem for the quality of the work and fine carving. Indeed, people for a hundred miles or more around felt quite compelled to come and view the new spectacle.

'That was, for the first eight years, for unbeknown to the Pipingford masons, the architects and the subscribers of Frampton, their fine new construction lay squarely on top of an underground lake, not too deep beneath the footsteps of worshippers, craftsmen and clergymen alike. Also unknown to all but our Creator, was the fatal development of fissures in the soft strata beneath St Mark's. Fault lines had developed, as a direct result of the great excavation of stone in the nearby quarry, stone which now exerted a formidable weight down upon the ancient wooden cores of the piers, which rested no longer just in stone, but in rising water, got in between the widening cracks in the soft rock below them.

'The core of the piers began to rot, the first anyone knowing of it being alarming settlements and displacements. Necessary repairs were immediately embarked upon; everyone was incredulous that such fine, strong work should be in danger. For the Pipingford Gang, there was also the matter of their pride at stake and Will, was a particularly proud man. Strong framings of timber were placed under the each of the four arches of the tower beneath the spire. These held, and showed no sign of weakness whatsoever, until the spire's last moments.

'The week before the catastrophe, there was a slight yielding in parts of the new stone and mortar work in the north-east pier. A slight movement was observed in the south-east pier and certain fissures from the original work could be seen creeping, like witches' fingers, into the new supports. The fissures were seen but the rather complacent opinion taken, that when enough time had passed to allow the new work to solidify, work which had been constructed using much stronger mortar than that available to their Norman predecessors, the fissures would be unimportant. The underground water in the soft rock and the burgeoning fissures and cracks below earth, were not known about.

'One Sunday morning, as the good townsfolk of Frampton filed in to prayer, it was noticed that the fissures in the easterly piers had become cracks. Immediately following the service, screens were erected and a flurry of anxious activity to support, prop up and rescue the proud spire was begun. Day and night without ceasing the Pipingford Gang toiled, desperate to resurrect their reputations and shore up the spire. Their task was to sustain on each pier, an enormous weight of unimaginable tons. They toiled and strained but when masonry was held up in one place by props, the restraint caused it to issue forth on the nearby surfaces faster than it was humanly possible to apply adjoining support. Sixty workmen strove for success and finally, on Wednesday, at half past three after midnight, they stood back from their achievements with cautious content and left the building.

'When they returned, however, a mere three hours later, they were dismayed; braces had buckled and twisted under tremendous strain and in places, fine streams of powder poured forth like stone purls, polluting the air with dry mists of dust. The cores of the piers were plainly crushed. Their efforts had proved futile.

'Most of the men were for abandonment, but Will, full of the spirit of pride and hope, unable or unwilling to believe the good Lord would allow such an event to take place, spurred several of the sixty back to work, shouting encouragement and demanding action, as he climbed the strong timber framing of the north east arch and drew down a pulley seat for men to join him. Without warning, there came a sudden shaking all around them and a quaking from below. The timber frames shook and the church walls separated from the structure of the tower, with an enormous creaking and a monumental, thundering shudder. The men scattered outwards, they cried for Will to follow but as he started out for God's firm earth, heavy stones burst out and fell around him. The third of them struck him on the head with such force, he was seen to sway and then fall insensible onto the stone flooring, some twenty feet below. The ground shifting palpably beneath their feet, rumblings in the very walls around them, even his most faithful of friends could do nothing but think of their own souls and scramble for safety.

'The Lord will not blame them, I'm sure, for as the coroner believed, Will was most certainly already with his Creator, as the tower around him separated at its base. The gap between stone upon stone widened outwards and the top of the spire was seen to sink a little to the east, like a candle softly falling in its socket, so was told, from afar. The base of the tower parted further and further from itself, the split following up into the spire before the top piece and cap stone descended centrally, intact. It landed almost slowly, reverberating, complete, a section of about twenty feet over Will's poor dead body, as if a readymade mausoleum sent from above.

Chapter Twenty Eight

'Anna was for weeks, inconsolable. Emmaline Gables moved back up to tend to the boys and my infant self. For days on end, Anna sat insensible or drifted in speech through the times of her marriage at random, between the good and the bad, forever seemingly blaming herself for the difficulties they had suffered, with no memory of Will's own wrong.

'Abraham and Emmaline began to fear for Anna's mind, when a letter arrived from Millie with news on three fronts.

Dear Ma Gables,

For I do hope you don't mind me addressing you as such, but such has become your role in our lives, that I'm sure I don't know how else to write it on this paper. Forgive me, if I offend, for I write with news that needs must be imparted to you, and to Anna, but that others fear to impart, for reasons various which will become apparent, I am sure.

First, Henrietta is too considerate of Anna's pitiful condition to write of it herself, but she is, most visibly now, expecting once more. The two mishaps she's suffered, since Henry's quick birth, have strained on her nerves and I find her fretful, Ma'am, at the least imaginings and anxious beyond calming, for the safety of her unborn infant, that I fear her very anxiety and the physical manifestation of it shall bring the child harm. Oh, what am I to do? For I have not the greatness of your presence to bring that peace to her, that I know your command and your kind, loving hand would bring! Is there no persuading of Anna to return to us, here in Heartbourne, that you might tend to them both in one place, while 'tis necessary?

Second, also pertinent to Anna's longed for, sought for return; her father is unwell, once more. Ma Gables please hide this letter from her safely and only relay its contents as you see fit, for I fear for her father; he has that kind of transparent look, like alabaster you can almost see through. Dr Snelling has enquired twice now, as to Anna's state and whether she is fit enough for travel. I know we do hope and pray that the good Lord would not press upon her such a grief, so close to that of losing Will, but He is, as we all know, inscrutable in the matter of who he chooses to take, or when he chooses to take them. Who on earth would have thought, when Anna and I both wed so young, that both our marriages would have been so short? I don't pretend to know a great deal in this life, but about this, I know more than most and even Millie Price might be of some comfort, if we could but persuade dear Anna to come home.

My third (I almost quake to mention his name in a letter that'll be carried to Will Godstone's house) concerns Raphael De Vine. As all Heartbourne knows, his marriage was a less harmonious affair than any man would desire, with his wife seemingly addicted to acts indecorous, infuriating, unlawful or all three. Well, the alliance does seem, quite finally, to have come to an end. In short, Violet De Vine has relieved Heartbourne of her presence but unfortunately not without cruel damage to her husband. Word has it, although I'll not be accused of gossip (but how else is word supposed to come to folk who ought to know it?) that she was responsible for the accident herself. Anyhow, an accident there was, about the same time, I do believe, as the spire on St Mark's was falling.

Raphael was engaged in a less ambitious task than Will, fixing the weathervane on the roof of Whyly, that'd been blown crooked in the storm the night before. Well, along came Violet, shouting up about some squabble or another of such trifling import that no one even seems to know its nature. Raphael, according to farm hand witnesses, continued with his task as though she, and her scolding voice, were not present. Well, the farm lads sensed some sport and sauntered over to the house, close by where Raphael was working, passing comment on the angle of the vane as if to assist Will in his repositioning of it, all the time imagining that Violet, and her rancorous remarks, weren't present. Raphael joined in, quite naturally finding amusement and camaraderie and a sudden intense concern, that Whyly's weathervane should be restored to the exact perpendicular.

Violet De Vine took the bait, as a fat carp takes a tiny maggot. She became enraged as the conversation continued without her and she rattled the ladder at its base, where she was standing, in her wrath. Well, the extent of her culpability will never be known, was it her anger or the faulty positioning of the ladder that caused it to fall? Was Raphael distracted? Did he lose his balance and cause it to slip himself? Probably the first, but the outcome is the same; the ladder suddenly became unstuck and slid sideways across the guttering, heading straight for the farm hands below. They scampered out of the way and nothing was left but the harsh earth for Raphael's back to break on. The crunch of bones, they say, did cause their stomachs to roil.

For a while, Violet stayed and made some kind of shabby attempt to nurse him. It lasted about three weeks, before she packed a bag and got on a coach to Portsmouth with her hair dishevelled, stinking of liquor. She hasn't been seen or heard of since, although I do believe that Christopher Coates is making some discreet enquiries with relatives his has in that county.

Raphael is honourably wrestling with his pride, attempting to refuse the charity of the parish but pitifully struggling to fulfil from a seat, any small carpentry task that does not require more of his body than he is able to use. Dr Snelling says than some slow, modest improvement may follow, but that any kind of major recovery is not to be expected at this stage. It is not envisaged that he will walk again. The parish has, at the bidding of your father and unbeknown to Raphael himself, raised funds to purchase for him a new-fangled 'Bath Chair', which looks a little like an upholstered tub on wheels, would you believe, which may be pulled around by a man or beast to enable such an invalid to be transported about from place to place. We await its arrival with anticipation. Whether or not Raphael's pride will be prevailed upon to use such a contraption, is unknown to anyone.

In the meantime, he has consented to the necessary attendance of a so called 'nurse', who comes twice daily to raise and descend him. She is portly enough for the task, but appears to be mainly in drink and should be dismissed, in favour of the good matrons of the village fulfilling the task, if you ask me. The trouble is, though, would it be seen as honest? Most of us have been seen or heard to utter a sentimental sigh in his masculine presence, and he is, still in God's law, a married man.

Anyhow, I leave it to your judgement, how best to convey all this to Anna. You know, Ma Gables, how Retty and I still do miss her. Her father's condition must surely prick her conscience, with the needle of a daughter's duty? And, she is unlikely to be accosted by Raphael out and about at any time soon; the Bath Chair is likely to take three months or more to arrive, it still being in manufacture. Oh, could she not come home, even for a while? Henrietta would be most grateful.

Please accept my humble prayers for your continued good health and that of Mr Gables.

Your sincere servant,

Mrs Millicent Price

Mrs Gables reflected that her first opinion of a person was rarely faulty and that she'd been correct; Millie Price was a good friend indeed. The difficulty, now, was in how to convey these necessary points to Anna. If it were anyone else, she could've just idly left the letter lying around; eyes would glance, a name would jump out, the information would be imparted. Most people weren't saints about these things, she thought. Trouble was, this was Anna, née Porter.

That evening, after Anna had turned in for the night, Emmaline read Millie's letter to Abraham and sought his advice.

'My dear Emmaline,' he said kindly, looking over his reading glasses at her, 'What, may I ask, is the sum of the intelligence you wish to convey to Anna?'

'Why, all that's in this letter,' she said, holding it by its sides.

'Then, my suggestion is, that you give her the letter to read for herself. She is a God fearing, kind and sensitive woman, Emmaline. First, I ask you this, would Anna want you to be with Henrietta, at this time?'

'But of course, if she knew...'

'Second, would she be devastated, if she let her father down? If he slipped away, without her knowing, because so called friends kept her away from him by not imparting the truth about his condition?'

'Why, she's been away from him far too much of latter years already.'

'Third, I ask you, what would she prefer, a conversation with you in broad daylight regarding Raphael's poor state? Or the privacy of discovering it alone, from a letter, where her response might remain between the good Lord and herself?'

Emmaline chewed on her cheek a little, 'Abraham Gables, if I tell you once in every ten years, is it enough, that God blessed me indeed, when he gave you to me as a husband?'

'Once in every ten, as you say,' he shook his newspaper and returning to it, smiled a little, 'for any more, for some folk, might be considered to be a trifle sentimental, don't you know?'

Chapter Twenty Nine

'Anna put the letter down on the bed beside her. She drew herself up and sighed deeply. It was no good, this state of desolation. She walked to the open window and listened to the birds and the sounds of her family. Theo, now eighteen, was playing with little Elise, making her laugh boisterously as he swung her around. Samuel, at the far more serious age of eleven, was deep in conversation with Abraham, while helping him to string up the poles on which this year's peas and beans would grow and flourish. The sight of Abraham with her son put her in mind of her own father, when she was Samuel's age. He used to read to her more than help in the garden, though. She thought of her father, in his sick bed, reading alone, and of Retty, in her state of nervous anxiety. She watched her children and then saw Ma Gables come out beneath her, to pick some rosemary for the beef stew she could smell cooking in her kitchen below. The people who loved her, needed her to return to them. She needed to come back.

Anna got dressed and went down into the garden. It was the first time she'd been outside for eight weeks. Mr and Mrs Gables looked at each other a little anxiously and then back to Anna. Anna asked, if she might borrow Theo, for around an hour. The request was readily assented to and she then asked Theo if he wouldn't mind putting on his Sunday clothes and accompanying her for a while.

When he was ready, he walked alongside her a little anxiously, as she trod the path he suspected she would, to St Mark's. As they walked in through the grand arch of the west tower one or two of the gang, on recognising Anna, stopped working and stood still, out of respect. A soft ripple of whispers travelled around the still-standing arches of the church. One man put down his adze and bent his head, another, working on the breach between outside and in, removed his cap. The sound of chipping chisels slowly came to a halt. Anna walked sombrely down the aisle to the screen which hid the spot where Will had fallen. Will's master builder,

Benjamin Fry, seeming to understand, pulled the screen to one side. He announced to one and all that it was time for a short, early luncheon and the workmen departed, many of them known to Anna muttering their condolences as they left, several of them squeezing Theo's shoulder as he stood at her side.

Anna walked to the spot, the place, she thought, where he'd been found, when he chose to forgive her and return to her. The tiles had been cleaned but she could still see Will's blood, where the grout had been irrevocably stained a dark, red-brown between the neat black and white squares. She knelt down, to make her peace with the Lord.

After around twenty minutes, she stood up, thanked Benjamin and took Theo's offered arm, as support in her journey back.

That evening, after a meal prepared by Anna and Emmaline together, everything was settled. Theo was to be given leave from his post as a clerk in Abraham's firm (where he'd been for two years by then) to accompany his mother and siblings back to Heartbourne. They were to stay for at least a week. Anna was firm and then mute in her resistance towards the idea of a permanent removal, offering the settled lives of her sons as reason for remaining in Frampton. Raphael's name was not mentioned before them. Fierce loyalty to Will hunkered down in Anna's heart.

As she was bringing back to the kitchen the last of the crockery for the day, Anna distinctly heard Ma Gables whispering as she entered the room. Coming in backwards, with her load upon a tray, she then heard a rustling sound and Theo's whisper, also. As she turned, she discerned that Emmaline was secreting something up her sleeve as the two of them stood up, scraping their chairs simultaneously and looking at her expectantly, for no obvious reason.

Anna laughed gently, 'And what are you two about, to be looking so guilty like?'

'Why nothing, Mother,' said Theo, crossing to her and kissing her on the forehead, while relieving her of the tray.

'Now, I ought to turn in, for I'll need to give notes to a colleague in the morning before we can depart, and Abraham, I know, is anxious for your return to Heartbourne Vicarage.'

It was late morning when the wheels of Will's cart, now driven by Abraham, rolled into the sightline of a row of slender poplars. The tips of the splendid trees bowed down to greet her and Anna's heart leapt, with unchecked delight, at the familiar sight. Anna's emotions fluctuated but her misgivings were tempered with strong, warm welcome breezes. Not least of these breathed upon her, when their humble transport drew to a halt outside her childhood home.

Once they were installed, Anna went in to her father and read to him for over an hour. After that they drank tea, talked of the past and recalled their favourite passages from texts they'd read, when Anna was still a girl of sixteen. Anna looked at his sallow skin as he dozed. The plumpness was gone from him now, from his face, his shoulders, his hands and arms. He seemed diminished. A tear traced its way to her chin and dropped down onto her fichu.

She came away, leaving her father to sleep and wandered around the rooms of the first home she'd ever known, the one that'd also seen the death of a spouse, and yet held such happy memories for her, the child of that cut short marriage. She inhaled the familiar scents; the books of her father's study, the herbs of her mother's kitchen, even the mud and polish mixture of the garden boot room.

Her own children's laughter took her out into the first garden she'd ever tended and she stood with her hands on her hips, at the sight of the untidy spring boarders.

Mrs Gables came out and stood behind her, 'It'll take more than a week to set these in order to your standards, Mrs Godstone, by my reckoning.'

'Hmm, we'll have to see about that, Mrs Gables,' she said, with humorous emphasis, pulling up a dead chrysanthemum, 'and don't think I don't know what you're up to, because I do.'

'Up to! Why, I don't know what you mean, Anna Godstone, a plain speaking woman of my years 'up to' anything?'

193

Anna nudged Ma Gables' elbow with her own and they giggled like school girls. It was the first time Anna had felt anything like light-hearted in spirit, since Will's fall. She breathed in the air of Heartbourne, as she took the offered crook of Emmaline's arm. They walked together, while the children played unfettered by care, in the damp but mild spring warmth of April.

The next day, Anna was summoned by a note from Ma Gables, delivered by George Jenner, to attend luncheon at Retty's, where Millie was also to be present. Anna sent one back, requesting that they come to the vicarage instead, to be waited on by her but a puce George Jenner brought a second note, in which Ma Gables stated peremptorily, that preparations had already been made and that she was expected.

Close to the appointed hour, Anna had just left her father's room and was descending the staircase to organise the children, when a gentle tapping came upon the vicarage door.

A hand, which had not turned that polished brass knob for many a year, slowly opened the door. A voice called out, 'Yoo hoo! It's only me!'

Anna ran down the remainder of the flight and the two friends clasped each other in somewhat irregular and noisy pleasure, Millie shrieking with such delight and calling out, 'It's Anna Godstone, Anna Godstone,' so many times that Anna had to quiet her, for the Reverend Thomas Porter's sake.

'I've been sent to fetch you by her majesty herself, I ask you, Anna, she doesn't change, imperious as ever. Anyhow, we're commanded to set out early to allow the extra time for folk (and she is right on this point, Anna, you must admit) are bound to want to be saying hello and what not and greeting you back.

'Now, where are the children, for I've not yet met Elise?'

Millie was enchanted with my former self and holding each of my small plump hands, she pronounced me, 'The most beautiful child in the kingdom. Anna, Elise has your dark amber eyes.'

When the party finally arrived at Buttsfield Lane, after many a welcome home and congratulation on such a pretty babe (much to Theo's amusement and Samuel's disgust) Anna was equally in admiration of the long, blonde curly locks and the emerald green eyes of the eight year old Henry Gables, who was really, 'Quite tall for his age,' as Ma Gables kept informing them. No one smirked or giggled behind their tea cup, no one at all, as she pronounced this fact proudly, for about the seventh time, least of all Retty. Indeed, Retty seemed much, much more relaxed than she'd been spoken of in Millie's letter, now that Emmaline was home.

Anna soon found herself laying a second clean cup on the table each day, as she cleared away her family's breakfast crockery: Millie became a daily morning visitor at the vicarage and she and Anna found a solace in the recollection of all things past, with boisterous laughter at most, mixed in with the occasional tear, in a shared understanding of bereavement. Anna understood how, after over a decade, Millie still missed her lost husband.

Anna allowed herself to be bowled along by the affection she was shown by the people of Heartbourne and one week turned into two and then three. Under her tendering care and with the added stimulation of her company, her father took a turn for the better and he unexpectedly began to recuperate. Anna worried about how sustained or not his improvement would be, should she remove once more to Frampton. As she pulled out yet another unwanted weed from the border she was working on, and tossed it into the trug beside her, she sat back on her heels. Surely, Will would understand her staying for a while, for the sake of her father? And she hadn't, as Millie had predicted in her letter, so much as caught a glimpse of Raphael in her travels about the village. Maybe, she could stay, at least until the new-fangled transportation for him had arrived. It couldn't be disrespectful or disloyal to her husband's memory, if there were no chance of her encountering him, could it?

Thus, Anna reasoned with herself, and soon arrangements were made for Theo to return to his post, hosting his mentor in the trade for a few days each week, as Anna had done before him. Anna, meanwhile, grew accustomed to the easy warmth and familiarity of village life once more. Samuel attended lessons with Mr Crouch (while Anna drank tea and listened to news of how his poor wife had died, some said through suicide, would you believe?) and occasionally Mr Turner (widowed also, but then, his wife had always been a sickly thing and his mother-in-law had made his life wretched with her incessant scolding, by all accounts). Anna pruned her father's camellias and tidied his shrubs, while hearing how eleven grains of arsenic, no less, and a larger fatal dose, had been found in the innards of Charles French in February and how his wife Mary was to be up before the judge in the Lewes quarterly sessions for the 'Onion Pie Murder', as it'd been commonly referred to about all Sussex that spring. Anna shuddered at the thought of it and asked Millie not to dwell on such a terrible history.

Anna delighted in Millie's sometimes incorrigible company. She considered each moment she spent in very different conversation with her father, as a timely gift. She was thankful to the Lord for time to grieve, and yet somehow, feel restored, with blessings renewed in Heartbourne.

She was particularly amused at the sheer amount of time Retty and Ma Gables spent in each other's company and the quick wry wit which passed between them, almost causing Abraham to frown on one or two occasions, if he could but have suppressed his own smile, for, as he stated, shaking his head, 'When the innocent foible of a chatterer is taken up by you two, there's no mercy to be had.'

May strolled on as a small Elise Godstone tottered about the brick pathways of the vicarage garden. June was glorious and, as they sat for a short while by the village pond, Millie commented how she couldn't believe it was only a few months since the hoar frost in Heartbourne had been so severe, that the ice had cracked underfoot for five full weeks, before the cold snap broke.

'Such contrasts life brings,' observed Anna.

'We have no choice but to accept them,' said Millie. 'You do know, Anna, don't you?'

Anna gulped and blinked, as her eyes smarted a little, 'I know, I do know, I just don't want to, that's all.'

The Reverend Thomas Porter's funeral was a dignified and sombre event. Mr Porter had ministered to the people of the village his entire adult life, never moving from the place where he'd spent his married life. For two weeks, a subdued atmosphere hovered about the village, at least, wherever Anna was present.

The mourning was broken by the arrival of a gift of the priest's own instigation; the collaborative efforts of the people of Heartbourne to provide Raphael De Vine with a brand new 'Bath Chair'. The makers, in their quest to promote and advertise such contraptions, had the chair delivered festooned with ribbons on the rear of a wagon with a man following behind with cymbals, no less, and another halloing and calling and distributing fliers in the wake of the vehicle's progress.

Anna bowed her head and walked past the spectacle home, so she thought, to the vicarage. When she arrived, however, she was greeted with the sight of a rather measly looking man with scraped back hair, sitting on his own suitcase. He was dressed in black and wore a clerical collar.

Chapter Thirty

'Anna had been prevailed upon to remain in Heartbourne for over three months now, but with her father's death, and the family (most folk said with unseemly haste) ousted from their home at the vicarage by its new incumbent, the Reverend John Fuller, Anna had, she mused, excuse enough fit for public consumption to return to Frampton. And yet, she stayed on.

Millie and Retty saw her, each time Raphael passed by in his Bath Chair, drop her eyes to the ground in an attempt to walk by unnoticed. The dark crimson of her cheeks, when she raised her sight once more, told even Millie Price not to pass comment.

Anna wrestled with her conscience and avoided the parts of village where she knew Raphael might be, for fortunately the Gables' house (where she was put up for a while) was as near far distant as you could get from the carpentry.

Mr and Mrs Gables had an extensive garden which stretched down to the mews behind, on Old Wood Lane. There, at the bottom of his land, Abraham had decided to build a cottage to provide a rental income, for he was inclining towards playing a less active role in business affairs as his age increased. As Anna watched the work in progress from her bedroom window, one warm morning, she decided to take little Elise down for a walk to view the project more closely.

We ambled down through the garden and across the field beyond, before coming to the half built house. Anna could see from the work that it was to be quite a sizable property, larger than she'd realised from the distance and she wandered around to the front, in an attempt to gauge how many bedrooms there were to be. Coming around the corner, her sight was directed downwards, as she guided me across the uneven, disordered terrain. She was quite within two feet of Raphael, when she looked up and saw him and there was no avoiding speaking to him, if good form were to be maintained in front of his workmen.

Raphael spoke first, 'Good morning, Anna,' he looked at her directly and her heart thumped as if clapping at the lungs within her chest. 'Can you give me just a moment?' he asked, encouraged by the involuntary return of her gaze.

His Bath Chair was hard up against a trestle table and he was directing two men on some technicality, the language of, which meant nothing to Anna. The tone of his voice, his knowledge and authority, as he carefully explained some point to the men and drew a sketch to help them understand, that, she couldn't help but be sensible to. Even seated, the sight of his still well-toned, hirsute arms, still affected her. She trembled a little, at the return of such strength of emotion, but there was no dignified exit to be had.

Raphael was again the first to recover, 'Have you come to view the work on your new home, Anna?' he asked proudly, as the men went off out of earshot.

'My new home?' she said, genuinely and visibly taken aback.

'Oh, oh no,' said Raphael, realising his mistake too late. 'You didn't know? A surprise and now I've spoiled it!' he placed his face in his hands, desperate that his opening gambit, after eleven years of waiting, should be such a gaffe.

Anna could see his distress and was called by her very nature to relieve it, 'I didn't know, no, I must admit and I find myself overwhelmed by Abraham and Emmaline's kindness, not for the first time in my life but we needn't let them know of such a small blunder, Raphael. Indeed, you've done me a kindness, in truth, as I think on it, for I hadn't planned to stay in Heartbourne and at least I may now prepare for their disappointment.'

'Their disappointment. I see. Or you could consider, instead, just not creating it?' He rubbed the back of his well tanned neck, aware that he was manipulating her and on one level regretting it. On another level, though, as he looked at her, Anna, he was humanly unequal to resisting the temptation of the only chance likely to present itself of persuading her to stay. He was quite well aware that she'd been conscientiously avoiding him since her return.

'I'm afraid that that's simply impossible, Mr De Vine.'

He was stung by her distant formality, 'Why impossible? For it seems almost churlish to turn away from such benevolence, such love.'

'I have my family to consider.' She looked down at her child, unable to control from rising to her face the swell of confused emotions she felt: indignation at his presumption in passing comment; rashness in her desire to fly to any branch of a reason to stay and roost here forever.

'Not sure what folk'll make of it.'

'If it's a secret, and I decline it, then people are not to know. And, anyhow, what's the place of 'the opinion of folk', next to doing what's right, Raphael?'

His Christian name, the return of her sight again, he tried not to smile at the conquest, as he actually admired her rising spirit.

He stayed her gaze, 'Just saying,' he said, almost appearing to back away from public confrontation before adding, 'right for whom, though?'

Anna glared at him, angry, indignant, passionate and yet by no means any less the priest's daughter she'd always been, so she told herself; she was not going to row publically with this man, who was in the eyes of God, even if abandoned, still a married man.

'Good day to you, Mr De Vine,' her chilly manner externally composed, she led her little Elise away.

Raphael wanted to call after her, to add more to his heartfelt attempt to provoke her to stay, but he feared he may've been too clumsy fisted already. He'd tried, that's all he could content himself, which was one hundred per cent more than he'd had the chance of when he got up that morning, he did realise.

All afternoon, Anna was preoccupied, but without her own home for the moment, it was hard to break away and gain the time she needed to think. At moments, when she and Ma Gables were alone together in the kitchen, she started to notice Ma Gables' humming. Humming, she thought, the usual sign of a happy secret. Raphael's words came back to her. Would it be churlish to turn away from such kindness? To take away Ma and Pa Gables' joy in the act of giving so freely? And yet, was such thought merely an excuse to succumb to her deep desire to dwell in Heartbourne forever, among such love and friends? Or, was the truth that, turning away was a turning away from a different kind of love, and Raphael well knew it. His familiarity in using her first name and asking her to wait. The directness of his gaze. His deliberate challenge to the notion of her leaving. Those marbled blue eyes.

Ma Gables was wrapped up in her own musings, as she hummed away, and with preparations for Abraham's birthday supper in hand, Anna had no opportunity to escape to Millie's either.

The evening's supper was such a mellow, pleasant celebration and after their guests had left, Ma and Pa Gables, Anna and Theo sat around the fire in contented reflection, with a little tot of Nantz each as a night cap. Anna looked around the room and felt at peace with her decision; Heartbourne was her home, these people were her family, she had only encountered Raphael once in nearly four months and the cottage; such thoughtfulness, such love. She must stay.

Chapter Thirty One

'Two weeks later, Anna stepped from the driver's seat of Will's cart. She hesitated for a moment, before lifting the latch on the white picket gate that led to their simple brick cottage in Frampton. She looked across to the much grander residence next door, remembering how she and Will, half in humour, half in earnest, had once referred to it as 'Verity's prison'. As her gaze rested where it'd fallen, she remembered the unity created by the shared understandings which develop between a husband and wife over time. Her attention was drawn back to the present, however, as she caught a distinct movement in the curtain behind an un-shuttered window. Much to her surprise, for the house had been shut up, abandoned almost, for many years now, she saw a man's face appear behind the glass, just for a second, before removing itself promptly upon meeting her gaze. How odd, she thought. Should he be there or not? A caretaker, maybe? He looked almost a little familiar but then, she'd only caught sight of him for a mere moment.

Little Elise, my former self, was fretting and Theo, unaware of why Anna had stopped, was waiting with a heavy sack to come by, 'Oh sorry, Theo,' she said, stepping out of his way and, distracted by the mundane, the significant sighting went unheeded.

Once inside, Anna set about reordering her kitchen, which administered only by two men for several months, was not as any woman would have it. As she prepared a meal for her children in their own cottage once more, she attempted to be grateful in spirit. When little Elise kept asking where Grandma and Grandpa Gables were, she resisted the temptation to be tetchy and just sighed. The family meal was also somewhat subdued, with Samuel in a great sulk about returning to town. At the end of it, Theo quietly put his hand upon her shoulder and kissed her head.

At least the nightmares will now stop, thought Anna, as she lay alone in bed that night, surely, they must do now? The nightmares were what had prompted her return to Frampton after all. It seemed as though that first interaction with Raphael had let out the Genie of Passion into her soul once more. Having not seen Raphael for many years, she had quelled all sense of fascination and yearning for him. When he was first abroad in his chair, she'd averted her sight from him but after Abraham's birthday, it was as if he, Raphael, was everywhere and anywhere she went.

During the day time, she controlled and supervised her thoughts with strict adherence to her wish to honour Will's memory and do nothing that would anger him in heaven, or would have done so here on earth. At night, however, her dreams, with their nebulous sensuality, allowed the Genie to roam free of its lamp. But it didn't stop there, that was the trouble, at some point, with some trigger, she knew not what, the dream would turn dark and become a nightmare where Will was stalking towards her with his hand in the air, raised as it had been that night, when Abraham had stood at the door.

Anna lay awake for a while, afraid to close her eyes, fearful, questioning; what if the strategy of removal didn't work? What if only turgid time would toil against the urgent desire and break the spell? She felt unsure, unwilling to discover.

Restless, she got up and went downstairs to fetch a glass of water. Treading quietly, she thought she heard a movement come from Theo's room, but it wasn't all that late for a young man and he did sometimes sit up and read, she knew. She continued on but as she reached the inner lobby way that led into the kitchen, she trod on something, sharp as ice. Not wanting to wake or distress her children, she winced and drew in quick air but avoided crying out. She lowered her candle to view the flagstones and saw broken glass. The open shelf next to where she stood being the place where plain glasses were kept, she presumed that one of them had fallen or been knocked off. It was a warm, still summer's night and no breeze came or fluctuation from the temperature outside, to tell her her mistake; that the glass had in fact fallen from the broken pane of the casement beside her, the small pane just below the window's latch.

Anna crept on into the kitchen, placing her candle down on the table and crossing to fetch the dustpan and brush from their cupboard. Crouched down, with her head in the cupboard, wondering at what age we start having the sense not to keep things so low down, she was grasped from behind unawares and held up against an unpleasantly warm, robust and malodorous body, pressed up behind her own.

'Don't even think of yelling for no help,' with one arm across her middle and another, crooked up holding a knife to her neck, his spittle hit her earlobe and she winced, but offered no sound, 'or your little'un will be not only motherless, but dead to boot.'

The face at Verity's window, how could she have been so heedless, so careless? But then, they'd all stopped fearing, stopped watching, over the passage of time, for Nathan Lunsford. That was the familiarity she'd half recognised. Although altered, as he flung her into a chair, she could see the resemblance to the likeness drawn up for those, 'Wanted' posters, ordered by John Carroll, over ten years ago.

'Now, I tell you what you're going to do for me, missy...' he leaned over her as he half whispered, half hissed, 'What? Did you think I'd live out the rest of my life as an outlaw, hiding and clawing and rummaging about in the undergrowth for victuals and some kind of life? Did you think,' he leant back in closely with the glinting blade not an inch from Anna's exposed throat, 'that you'd condemn me and escape my vengeance for your meddling, Anna Godstone?'

Anna remained still, Lunsford's words about Elise uppermost in her mind, she silently prayed.

'I'll tell you what you'll do, you'll write a letter, on this here piece of note paper,' he fetched out a somewhat battered sheet from his coat, 'telling of how you was so tired of this life and of widowhood, and how without your dear, dead husband, you could bear to live no more.'

'Why, Sir,' she placed as much derision into the term as she dared muster, more than a little of Ma Gables having rubbed off on her over the years, 'if you have the temerity to tell me you intend to kill me, why should I do anything you bid me at all?'

'Wh-hy-hy!' Lunsford growled lowly and banged his fist on the table in anger. It wasn't much but Anna hoped it was enough. It was, after all, a small cottage.

He stood up, his belly protruding out between his shirt and his waistband, his grubby brown braces rubbing the unsightly dark curled hair, 'Why I don't mean to kill ye, just give the pain of it to those who love you. I don't intend to release to you. Oh no, not after all these years you've obliged me to live in brackish water. You can do me service for what you've done to me,' he leant back over her, leering at her with his glare, 'in more ways than one.' He glanced down her loose cotton nightgown to her bare breasts and lifted a finger to a nipple. With his mouth open, he closed his eyes and inhaled her.

Watching from the crack of the doorway, with no knife of his own, Theo was incensed with wrath at this affront to his mother. He lunged at Lunsford's unguarded moment and rushed into the room with such fervour and speed that he knocked Lunsford to the ground with one strike of such force, that the villain fell flat and lay on the stone floor moaning insensibly and bleeding from the head.

Samuel, following thick upon Theo's arrival, saw Lunsford's knife with its menacing gleam, cartwheeling its way across the kitchen floor. He ran forward and arrested its spinning with his heel.

'The rope, the spare rope,' Anna regained herself as Sam handed Theo the knife, 'in the rear lobby.'

By the time Lunsford had regained full consciousness, he found himself with a bloodied head, bound and gagged and with the constable called for.

Chapter Thirty Two

'Following the next Tunbridge Wells' quarterly sessions, Nathan Lunsford's public hanging saw one of the greatest attendances the county had ever known. Theo read an account of it to his mother that evening from the *Sussex Advertiser*, as they sat before the parlour fire together. Anna shivered and pulled her shawl around herself more tightly, as if an internal chill were created at the very echo of Lunsford's name in the room. Theo looked at his mother rather concernedly, as she gazed, horrified, into the hot flames. She was afraid, she'd said (remembering Ruth) that in spite of everything, they'd sent him to his damnation, rather than prompted his redemption.

Theo had always felt protective of his mother, never more so than now; his father was dead and he'd already needed to save her from the outstretched grasp of Lunsford and a fate of unspeakable shame, for a virtuous widow such as Anna, who'd only ever known her poor dead husband.

'May I ask you a question, Ma?'

'You can ask, though I won't promise to answer,' she said, moving out of her seat to stoke the fire.

'May I ask what was in that letter from your Uncle Christopher, this morning, that so disturbed you?'

'It contained news, that's all, news of the death of a woman about the same age as me.'

'A woman. I see.' He paused, before going on. 'Why stay on, here in Frampton, Ma? Why don't you go back to Heartbourne, for good? The new cottage is all but finished now, and I know Abraham is just looking for the right moment to ask you again, if you'll come home. From the outside, Ma, it makes no sense.'

'Well, from the inside, it does to me,' she said, sitting back down and regarding him.

'Penny for them,' he said nudging her foot playfully with his own.

'You're still my son,' she said archly, but then smiled. She fell silent, as she contemplated the options. She supposed that he'd always been blessed with a wisdom beyond his years and that if she didn't explain, a distance might grow between them, which she'd truly regret. Still, he was her son, her son and Will's, would it be seemly, to bare all? She started to lose her thoughts again in contemplation of the flickering flames; after all, with Violet's death, things were now altered, if only a little.

Theo broached the difficulty as gently as he was able, 'Would it be out of turn to mention the name of Raphael De Vine?'

'And how or what do you know about that?' She sat up, somewhat defensively.

'Ma, I was nine when he nearly hit you, Ma, don't defend it, Pa nearly hit you. There, now it's been said. Grown-ups don't think to keep their voices down when they argue, Ma, and for a good while you and Pa weren't happy, you have to admit it.'

Anna chose not to respond but also, he noted, not to silence him.

'Grandma and Grandpa Gables came one night and threatened to take you away from him. I'd heard him say cruel things to you but never mention a name. Grandma Gables stated his name, and yet defended your honour, Ma. Ma, they both said you'd done no wrong. Pa was jealous, that's all, only his jealousy was turning into a rage against you.'

Anna held her hands to the sides of her head, pushing her hair backwards, 'Oh, Theo, you were a child, seeing and hearing through the eyes and ears of a child: I can't go back on my word to your father that I'd never make him jealous again. I promised him, Theo.'

Anna was weeping at the memory of the sorrow caused, but nevertheless, Theo continued to tread forward gently, 'Bear with me, Ma. You promised never to make him jealous again, were those your exact words?'

'To me, it was and is akin to a vow, Theo. What if he's looking down from above and sees me returning to Heartbourne, spending time in the company of Raphael? How should I be able to greet him before my Maker, if I did such a thing?'

'Why, Mother! We're told at the resurrection, we'll be there as angels, not as husbands and wives, or brothers and sisters, you know that...'

'I promised never to make him jealous again.'

'Nor can you, Mother, not any more, for I'm sure you'll agree Pa's in heaven, God willing, as we speak.'

'God willing, I'm sure, for I do hope no fault of mine has caused him to fall from Grace.'

Will sighed at her continued self-flagellation and pressed on, 'Ma, he'd want you to be happy, to have the comfort of a good and loving man by your side while you live, for jealousy's a human emotion that simply doesn't exist in heaven, that's what the good Lord meant. You can't break your vow, if Pa is beyond all jealousy, above all understanding of it, as an angel up above.'

Anna sat, silent and still. The whole basis of her decision making had been tapped, ever so lightly, by the chisel of Theo's words and had crumbled, like flawed stone, to dust.

'Have you been reading my mail, Theo Godstone?'

'No, not really, Ma. Well, if you leave a thing on the table and a name jumps out at a soul...'

'Theodore Godstone!' she shook her head at him.

'Ma, there is no jealousy in heaven and you need comfort on this earth, God knows that.'

Anna pursed her lips and put aside her indignation in preference for deep thought. Theo took up his book and after glancing at her, settled down to read.

The evening wore on and once or twice he looked across at his mother as she shifted in her chair and frowned deeply. Once or twice, he caught her eye, and raised his brow as if in silent question to her.

'I am thinking, Theo, but it is a leap for me, from where I was. Your father's not been dead a year, young man, remember that now, please.'

At about their usual hour of retiring, Theo closed his book and placed it back on his father's table beside him.

Anna stirred, 'At the end of the day, I suppose it could only ever be a friendship, given his condition, I mean. It's not as if we would marry, or anything of that nature. We would just be friends, companions maybe; there would be no sin, however you regarded it, if you take what you say about jealousy into account. On my part, I would still die your father's wife, both in body and soul.'

'If that's the agreement with yourself that'd allow you to live in peace, in Heartbourne, it sounds reasoned, Christian and compassionate to me, Ma.'

'Compassionate, to whom?'

'Why, to yourself, Ma, it is allowed, you know.'

She nudged his foot, with her own.

Chapter Thirty Three

'Now, you're finally getting there, Grandma!' said Freddie, triumphantly. 'This is Old Wood Lane, isn't it? Where we live, where you grew up? Did Raphael carve the roses, Grandma, above the doors? Because, that's the kind of carpentry job you could do sitting down, you know.'

'Of course we know, Freddie, but I bet they're not roses, are they, Grandma?'

'Well spotted, Catherine, and you're right, Freddie, they were carved by Raphael De Vine, carved out of love for Anna, as are many of the elements, as I look around this house, even now. Most anything that didn't require heavy work was finished to perfection by his hand, with love sprung from the heart. The flowers, however, are in fact...' she paused, and looked around the meal table as the four women spoke as one, '...camellias.'

'Anna first saw them immediately upon her return to Heartbourne, that September. As soon as Theo drew up the pathway, Abraham insisted the women stop their fussing and waving them aside with his 'kerchief, he proudly took Anna upon his own arm, proprietorially. He led her down the garden in ceremony, with Emmaline and Elise, Millie and Retty, Theo and Sam, and Henry with his tiny brother, Archie, all following in duos, as Ivor raced across the field. As Anna came into view of the tender, initial stages garden, that had been created for her by friends, she struggled not to cry with joy and humility at such love.

'We cleared, and planted, and pegged out fences, all in the mere hope that you would return to us, even me, Anna!' Millie told her proudly.

Abraham took her around to the front entrance and there he pointed out the camellias, above what is now your front door. He mentioned that Raphael had carved them and then strode on, in a rather transparent attempt to seem oblivious to the significance of the information he'd just imparted.

'There are four bedrooms upstairs and three reception rooms below, so I suppose one of those could be used as a bedroom also, if required.'

Abraham revelled in showing Anna around his finished opus and she duly became tenant to the Gables, at a peppercorn rent. Without exception, everyone was delighted with the new arrangements in Heartbourne.

'This door, Freddie, and this room in which we're sitting, did not yet exist.'

'How come, Grandma?'

'Well, Anna and her chattels were installed in Camellia Cottage (as this house was known, before it became the vicarage, when your parents married, Freddie). Sam resumed school, Theo travelled back and forth from Frampton each weekend, and I, as a small child, could regularly be seen leading Millie Price around the garden, following my mother about her work. Some of my earliest memories are of attempting, rather poorly I fear, to help my mother, while Millie chatted on.

'Anna was more content than she'd been at any time since she'd discovered she was expecting her third child. Sightings of Raphael, being pulled along in his Bath Chair, were occasional but nothing more. Christmas, with roast beef and a good suet pudding surrounding it, was shared and blessed with a company of nearly twenty, once the entire Gables family had been welcomed, in addition to Millie. I remember the Pickens fetching round their own stick chairs, while I myself quite enjoyed the added height of being perched on a laundry basket for the celebratory meal.

'February was the father of many a chilblain that year, as the passing feet of villagers pressed down snow into layer, upon layer, upon layer of treacherous ice. Anna was picking her footfalls carefully, very early one morning, going past the carpentry. It was not a way she would usually traverse but she was on her way to visit old widow Durrant, who was something of a cause of concern at her years, in such weather. A raised voice and a vicious cackle caused her to stop.

'It was followed by Raphael's voice, raised also but more dignified in tone, 'Would you control yourself, please! God knows, you remind me of my wife!'

'Your wife! Your wife!' shrieked a female voice, 'Would you slur me with such a comparison, eh? I'll learn you, young snake!'

Anna, instead of continuing on, slipped her path sideways into the mews, not in sight of the street but from where she could see the double-door entrance of the carpentry, where Raphael now resided downstairs. She watched, as the doors shuddered open with a rattle and as one of them was pushed erratically, by Raphael's nurse, using her posterior to persuade it over the fresh snowfall. The nurse stopped, once or twice, to swig from a flask as she went.

'Nell! Nellie! Whatever in...It's frozen...Nell, now no, don't, for pity's sake!'

Raphael's two apprentices, called by the commotion, had now come to the upper workroom window which they opened to witness the spectacle of Raphael being wheeled, hauled out over the crunching snow, on public display to them and the blacksmith's opposite, in nothing but his nightshirt.

'Nell! Nellie!'

'See how particular you feel about aught, now!' squawked Nell, swaying sideward, before making her way back through the snow, in staggered paces, to Raphael's rooms.

The two apprentices were plainly much amused by these proceedings and their hilarity leaked out, echoing around the mews. The workmen and stable hands around and about the blacksmith's merely shook their heads. They were no strangers to commotion opposite, but, Anna overheard them muttering, this was a little in the extreme, in such a climate.

Anna strode into the fray, 'Young gentlemen,' she addressed herself to the two apprentices above, 'if that is what you are, I demand your presence down this staircase at once!'

The two straightened up, glanced at each other, looking abashed, and in common with most human beings when commanded by a figure of seemingly robust authority, did what they were told. They came careering down the wooden outside staircase and stood before Anna, adjusting their caps.

'You look like slowcoach choir boys caught out on your time,' she considered, 'only not so pretty.'

Raphael's smile broadened like dawn light across his face and he later reported that he no longer felt the cold.

Anna crossed over and took a spare blanket from a pile by the blacksmith's boy, 'May I?' she asked and the boy nodded fiercely, in fear of his soul. She walked over and gave it to Raphael, 'You may be needing this,' she said, and smiled gently. They looked at each other for a moment. She then addressed herself to the apprentices once more, 'Take hold of the bar and follow me, if you please.'

One of them shrugged, the other said, 'Larks!' as if there was to be no missing out on such an opportunity; they promptly complied with Anna's request.

As the lads took hold of the chair's pulling bar, Nellie came running out of the carpentry, shouting and gesticulating, 'Oi! Oi! Where d'you think you're going with 'im?'

Anna walked over to her regally, and said, 'Nellie Pains, your services, such as they were, are no longer required. Please pack up your belongings and vacate the premises before this afternoon, or I shall call upon officers of the law, to bring you to account for your conduct this morning. A crippled man, in his nightshirt, in the snow? Public account, Nellie?'

Nellie screwed up her face and muttered in ill temper before tramping back off inside, in defeat.

So, Raphael was delivered to Camellia Cottage in the snow, having been paraded through the village, hauled along in his Bath Chair by his apprentices, loosely covered by no more than a nightshirt and a borrowed, plaid horse blanket. Anna had inadvertently taken her decision, to take him under the protection of her own roof, very publically indeed.

By breakfast time, the whole village was very well informed that Raphael De Vine was now lodging at Camellia Cottage. A widow and a widower together; how fitting, it was agreed. Although, had the particulars of Mrs De Vine's death ever been properly ascertained? They didn't know. And both such handsome figures in the village, although they could rest content, of course, there could be no question of any 'goings on', given Raphael's unfortunate condition. Sighs were exhaled and heads shaken in sadness.

By lunch time, the arrangement was generally quite approved of by the maids and matrons of Heartbourne alike; comfort and company for each of them, without the worry of damnation through immorality or sin.

The morning had passed pleasantly, with the apprentices joining in and adding to the spirit of the fun, ferrying Raphael's bed and his mattress and other sundry possessions, back and forth in a cart. They came and went, telling tales of Nell Pains' progress and abuse each time they removed more articles. Samuel, ever proud to be the man of the house, whenever Theo was away, assisted Raphael's dressing and generally, through his piping chatter, helped to lessen the pressure of intimacy Anna and Raphael might have felt, had they been left alone together in their new arrangement, quite so soon.

Raphael was established in the hitherto unused third room downstairs, another nod to respectability approved of around the village, when it was heard of by about two o'clock of the afternoon. Everyone was thought to be content. Everyone was, with one exception: the new priest, Mr Fuller.

I was still an infant and had been put down for my afternoon nap. Samuel was outside, feeding Anna's chickens. Anna and Raphael were sharing their first domestic moment in private.

'Well, I must say I'm amazed, Anna.'

'I know, it's a very handsome cottage, we are blessed.'

'No, not at that, although the handiwork is, as you say, to be admired.'

'Modesty, as well as good looks, is it?'

He ignored her teasing, 'Amazed at the fortitude of your friends, I must admit, in such a village for idle chatter as ever there was and on such an occasion for it, yet not a peek from Millie or Retty.'

'I see, Raphael; you're amazed that the courtesy of my friends rises above their curiosity on such an occasion? How impudent, I must say.'

He caught the mischief in her eyes as she glanced at him, 'Impudence? Impudence? Coming from the brazen woman, who just this morning, carted me across the village in the snow to her abode, without my request or my consent?'

Anna smiled broadly and crossed over to the window, 'Sam?' she called out of it, 'Would you mind strolling over to ask Grandma Gables if she and the others would like to come over for a cup of tea?'

Just as she caught Sam's assent, there came a smart rap upon the cottage door. It was Mr Fuller. She greeted him and welcomed him in, noticing as she did, Nell Pains, skulking on the ice, across the other side of the lane.

The Reverend John Fuller sat upright on Anna's Windsor chair, opposite Raphael, with his hands placed one on the other on top of his silver capped, ebony cane. He sombrely explained his objection to the arrangements, namely, the fact that Raphael was known to be married but was no more officially a widower than by rumour and, dare he say it, rumour, perhaps based on common desire, rather than fact.

Raphael was adamant he'd evidence from correspondence telling of her death, but admitted he'd not been informed of, or heard report of, a funeral. He explained that Violet hadn't lived a regular life and that, at such a distance from Portsmouth, without travelling there, which it'd be very difficult for him to do, it'd be hard for him to verify facts he'd simply taken at face value.

Anna pitched in, pointing out that the new arrangements were merely those of lodger and householder, not husband and wife, but at inspection of Raphael's downstairs room and sight of his old marital bed within it, Mr Fuller declared that it simply wouldn't do.

At that very moment, Ma Gables and her followers descended upon Camellia Cottage bearing cake and warm biscuits, halloing and expecting their tea to be something of a celebration. Imagine their disappointment when Anna explained the news. Everyone quietened down and looked to Ma Gables for a riposte, a sturdy rebuttal of the priest's objections but Ma Gables simply chewed on her left cheek and sucked in her lips, unable to refute the case.

'Well, if that's all there is to be said,' said Mr Fuller slowly, 'shall I send for the apprentices, to remove the bed once more?'

'No, Mr Fuller,' thundered Ma Gables, rising on her stick, 'you shall not. We apparently, have no firm proof, merely word of Violet's death. The fact that you'll not take the word of Anna's Uncle, the brother to the wife of our former, and much loved priest, the Reverend Thomas Porter in this correspondence, is most unappreciated. However, word can be sent that evidence is required, for the sake of harmony in the village and I have no doubt that such word will be quick in forthcoming: Christopher Coates is not a grade of man to make error in his communication on a point of such gravity.'

'In the meantime,' the priest was puce with pomposity at this challenge to his authority, 'I cannot sanction the morality of the current arrangements; I say, send for the bed to be taken away.'

'You will do no such thing, Anna Godstone, for I'll not see that drunken travesty of a nurse out there, satisfied with triumph in her snowbound malignity. Raphael De Vine, you're to come and lodge with me until this matter is resolved to everyone's satisfaction. That is, if the good priest does not question my own capacity to refrain from acts immoral, while my husband is abroad? For if 'tis so, we could always ground Grandfather Gables to ensure that Grandmother Gables does not cause the moral disintegration of the village!'

The Reverend John Fuller picked up his hat from the table, 'That,' he paused and glared at Emmaline, 'Mrs Gables,' he paused again, aware of the ridiculousness of the suggestion, 'will not be necessary.' And with that he left Camellia Cottage, trudging away through the snow, in a positive huff.

Raphael was the first to break, unable to contain an almighty great snigger and like water released from a dam, once the merriment was loosed, there was no containing it. Within seconds, everyone was roaring and gasping with laughter, even Anna and Ma Gables, who'd at first attempted to damp it down a little, still respectful of the priest's position, not wishing him to hear it, but at length, even they, could not stop the laughter from exploding from their bellies.

Chapter Thirty Four

'Uncle Christopher responded to their letters promptly, reassuring them that Violet's untimely leaving of this world was undisputed, cold, stone fact. He had, however, for the time being, travelled back down to Wessex, as his poor beloved Ruth was quite unwell. He apologised profusely for being unable to relieve their distress immediately, but feared that he was obliged to crave their patience in the matter, for a while.

The villagers of Heartbourne were unanimous in their view, that the ministry of Mr John Fuller was nothing akin to the Christ-like benevolence they'd been accustomed to in the hands of the Reverend Thomas Porter all their lives. There were murmurs and mutterings that they disliked the change.

On the evening that they'd received their own letter from the kindly Christopher Coates, Abraham and Emmaline sat down to discuss the matter and came up with a rather subversive plan of their own. They went into Raphael's own little study and ran the idea past him. He immediately, willingly, came on board.

The next morning, Anna was busy about her usual round of tasks and had just handed Millie a set of clean sheets and was turning around to find the matching pillow slips, when a great rumbling reached their ears from outside, not unlike timbers descending to the ground.

Millie handed Anna back the linen, 'Why, whatever was that?' she asked herself, crossing to the window and opening it to try to ascertain. She called down to the assembled men, 'Abraham, Henry, Raphael, what's going on?'

'Oh, just a small delivery, my dear,' said Abraham, 'there may be a little disturbance through the day, if you would please apologise to Anna for it in advance, I would be most grateful.'

Millie strained around a little, in an attempt to gain sight of the area the men's attention was focused on but even though this house is built in the old style, with the eaves above overhanging the ground floor, she was still unable to see.

Anna had come over, 'Did you catch all that?' Millie asked, and Anna nodded. 'Now, why would Abraham Gables come over all enigmatic, all of a sudden?' she folded her arms.

'That, Millie Price,' said Anna, leaning out of the window herself, just in time to see Henry pulling Raphael out of their sight line, glancing up at the two women as he did so, 'is a very good question.'

Millie shrugged her shoulders and giggled, 'Only one thing for it then!'

Millie ran off down the staircase like a young maid after her lover, leaving Anna to scoop me up, and follow down in a more seemly fashion (for she was keenly aware that Raphael was among the company below).

When Anna got outside, she was amazed, for gathered there were over twenty workmen, all people she knew from the village, all at work on or around the plot of land directly beside her cottage. Several of them were digging, or should I say hacking, to begin with, through the snow and thick ice, making a start on what appeared to be foundation trenches.

Anna looked at Abraham and asked, 'What's this?'

Millie's approach was, as usual, more direct, 'I mean, whoever starts on a building project in this weather, with ice as thick as bricks to contend with?'

'I'll tell you who,' Raphael's soft tones made Anna close her eyes for a moment as a thrill ran through her; she opened them and returned his look, 'a man who has a point to make, particularly one,' and he turned meaningfully to Abraham, 'on behalf of his much admired wife.'

Abraham chuckled, 'Perceptive, I see young man, as well as an able carpenter. I only pray that you too, one day, may be as fortunate in marriage as I have been with Emmaline; then, only then, Raphael, will you truly understand.'

Millie Price swore, for the rest of her years, that both Anna and Raphael blushed to a depth that outbid the blooms of the crimson camellias Anna so loved to grow.

'Now, was that the piping of your kettle I heard, Anna?' Abraham asked, taking Anna's arm in a fatherly fashion, 'These young men might be able to keep themselves warm in this white stuff but an old chap like me needs a little sustenance to keep himself going, I do declare.'

Work on Raphael's cottage, built to adjoin Anna's own, was carried out at such a pace that the whole was completed within a month. Everyone and anyone from the village pitched in, whenever, wherever and however they were able, in spite of the persistent snow. The talk, and hence the universal message, went not unnoticed by Mr Fuller.

The final act of defiance was the disassembling and reassembling of Raphael's bed next door. The Reverend Mr Fuller was called for, as he had so forcefully assumed authority over the situation, to approve the new arrangements. So many folk from the village had contributed to the construction of the new cottage, that a veritable crowd had assembled to witness the verdict of their new priest. He was shown around the premises with due decorum and gravitas by Abraham Gables. He then reappeared outside and walked across to the other side of the lane ceremonially. He leant on his smart, ebony cane, assessing the now, terrace of two, opposite. His attention was caught by the fine, detailed carving above each front door. Two houses, he thought. Who could complain?

'Oh, very well,' he said, with good grace, 'have it your own way!' and he waved his cane in the direction of the cottages.

The roar of approval which went up from the villagers, really quite surprised him and the warmth and enthusiasm of the hugs and the slaps of camaraderie were not a thing he was accustomed to, but apart from being near knocked off the perpendicular by the strength of the strapping Henry Gables, he was quite sensible, having gained the disapproval of these people, of how equally genuine and wholehearted their new approval seemed to be. He was beginning to understand the people of Heartbourne, he thought, maybe a little.

Chapter Thirty Five

'Three weeks later, Anna received a letter from her Uncle Christopher.

My dearest Anna,

I was, I admit, nothing short of delighted to read of the outcome of your united little foray into the territory of controversy with a priest. How delightful to relish the frisson of such audacity; I must admit I might even go as so far as to consider, from this moment on, Abraham and Emmaline Gables to be nothing short of much valued friends. I will tonight convey to them as much, in a separate letter of thanks. In short, praise be to God for true and faithful friends in difficulty, Anna!

On the matter of proof regarding Violet's death, I am currently in pursuit of this. I am as I write, en route to Portsmouth, regarding another matter appertaining to this event and with your acceptance of me as a guest in your new dwelling, expect to be with you very soon. I am, however, due to the delicacy of negotiations on a certain point, unable to furnish you with the convenience of an exact date of arrival, for which I apologise but can do no more at present.

I shall write again, I do hope, within two days.

Yours in servitude,

Christopher Coates Esq

Anna didn't know quite what to make of such oblique reference to she knew not what. She satisfied herself that the main point was confirmed, that Raphael was indeed a widower and therefore, in holding him in her heart, even if she were never to hold him in her arms, she was committing no sin. She busied herself with the delight of caring for him and waited for further news from her uncle. Anna continued under the illusion that although they were plainly in love, their relationship was to remain platonic.

Raphael, meanwhile, girded his desires for the future with no such iron bar restrictions. He trod carefully in his banter, keenly aware that Anna might possibly be labouring under the same misconception as many about a man unable to walk; an extended presumption, in his case untrue. He was aware also, from sensitive and mature intimations from Theo, that following Will's death, Anna was not yet ready to contemplate a new marital union and that there were lingering feelings of guilt surrounding the events of the spring when they'd first met. For now, he was content. Maybe the enforced separation was a good thing that would allow Anna to take her time. Meanwhile, he loved the way she cared for him with understated kindness and concern for his needs. She seemed to anticipate his every difficulty and go ahead to meet it and so there was no fuss, no bother and no embarrassment. After marriage to Violet, it was like bathing in tranquil waters in the shade of soft, green ferns. To him, at present, it was as if she made love to him with every touch of her hand and the warmth of every broad smile she cast upon him, whenever their eyes met.

It was March and the snowdrops were late that year, having been held back by the lengthy duration of the frozen weather. Two days later, the bright spring sunshine seemed to leap in through the windows and after such a long winter-tide, Anna relished the thought of whole days of pleasure, to be spent in her new garden. She was surprised, however, when she went to the post office, that there was no further word from Uncle Christopher. Curious, she thought, but she supposed there was no hurry, now that the new cottage had been built, although it seemed so strange, of an evening, to be so close to one another and yet sitting by separate firesides.

It was Friday and already dark by the time Theo drew up outside. Anna went out to assist him with a lantern. As they were relieving the pony of Will's cart for the day, they both heard a second set of hooves, clip clopping down the lane. They came out of Abraham's hay barn as Uncle Christopher drew his vehicle to a halt. They both went to call out, halloo in welcome, but Uncle Christopher waved from his driving seat and indicated gently with a fingertip across his lips, for them to be silent.

Mystified, they drew closer, as Anna's now aging uncle descended, rather awkwardly, plainly carrying a rather cumbersome bundle under his fantastical cloak.

'Go and fetch Raphael please, Theo,' whispered Uncle Christopher, 'I need to speak to you all together, as a family.'

'I'll see to the horse,' Anna fell in with the whispering also, like a fellow smuggler not wishing to be heard and taken up, 'you go on in, I'll not be a minute.'

'When Anna returned, she was amazed, for as she came through the camellia doorway, that lands you straight into the sitting room, as you say, Freddie, there was a homely scene that quite stole her heart. Raphael was in his Bath Chair, surrounded by Uncle Christopher, Theo, Samuel and even my small self, holding a young infant in his arms.

'Anna,' he said, as a single tear fell down his face, 'I have a son.'

After an initial kerfuffle of delight, everyone sat down to listen to Uncle Christopher tell the tale of Pip's birth, the story of Violet's last days. I remember seeking out my mother's lap, from where I still had good sight of the baby.

'Well, I'm afraid the tale was nearly a very sorry one indeed for poor young Pip here, my dears, hmm...let me begin. It seems that Violet left Heartbourne, not simply because she was too shallow of soul to care for an invalid husband, but because she'd realised she was in fact, with child by him.

'She travelled to Portsmouth, where she sought out a woman she'd once known, who would rid a woman of her unborn child for a fee of a guinea. Unable to muster the full amount, having spent a deal on loose living along the way, the woman set Violet to work for her, to earn the shortfall, before she'd agree to carry out the procedure.

'During this time, however, the child quickened and faced with daily experience of the grim nature of what she'd proposed, Violet found herself unable to go through with her first intention.

'In drink, Violet argued with the old woman over money, wishing to be paid for her services, which, she was told, had not been the bargain. The old woman, being a soul bereft of pity, violently threw Violet out onto the pavement, without a single coin in her pocket.

'In her condition and with no husband beside her, she was in no fit state to be taken on as a servant in any respectable household. It was summer, however, and the weather being mild, rather than submit to the strictures of life upon the parish, Violet took to the life of a vagabond, stealing her sustenance where she could and sleeping under sundry shelters or sea defences, anywhere she came to know she'd go unnoticed, so long as she didn't stay too long, in any one place.

'My searches for her returned news to me, for even in such a place as Spice Island, the figure of Violet De Vine had not gone completely without notice. Unbeknown to her, I came and arranged for her to be taken into what I hoped would be a place of safety, for the child to be delivered.

Uncle Christopher turned his sight upon the infant, 'Forgive me, young man, if I robbed you of a mother, for I acted, so I thought, to save your life. Anyhow, I know not why or the particulars of it, or if it was neglect in her hour of travail, but Violet did not survive the birth. Perhaps it was due to her own neglect of herself in the months leading up to the delivery. Maybe, I only seek to comfort myself with the absence of blame for my part. I find it hard, but I will never know the truth of it. It was difficult enough, to bring this happy scene I see before me to pass, I can tell you.'

Anna crossed the room and taking out a bottle, poured Uncle Christopher a small glass of orange shrub, which he gladly drained, to the health of the baby.

Raphael spoke first, 'No one, not even the Lord would blame you, Christopher; Violet was not a controllable creature.'

'Well, self-pity will not do, maybe regret, remorse, that things were no better in how they turned out, will have to do.

'I found myself unable to travel and lay claim to the child immediately, my dear Ruth being unwell, so I continued to send money and request regular reports on the young chap's progress.

'Well, imagine my dismay and fright when upon my indication that I was intending to travel to Portsmouth, to collect the infant, and was in need of proof of Violet's death; all communication ceased completely. Ruth bade me go and quickly, and I left her in the safe and loving hands of Amelia and Verity.

'When I arrived at the house, my spirits sank, for it was all shut up and I could gain no reply to my knocking. I stood for some time, Fear grasping and straining at my sinews with her monstrous talons. A neighbour must have seen me, taken pity, so I thought, for she came to the door and opening it just ajar, drew my attention with a hiss. She looked at me but remained silent. Looking down, I realised her hand was outstretched. I fumbled and furnished it with a coin.

'I presume you're looking for the bairn? Are you the father?'

'No, no, a friend, you might say, his benefactor.'

'Of course,' she sneered in disbelief but I found I cared not. 'They sold him, for coins, to a sweep whose wife reckons they'll have him working come two rounds of a season.'

'Naively, I asked how I'd find him; out came the hand protruding from the door again. She slipped me a piece of paper, I noticed already prepared, with an address upon it. I breathed in the cold, damp, salt air and went to bid her good night but she was gone. I was faced with a blank door but I had the necessary information in my hand.

'The next morning, I sought out the doctor in those parts and was in more luck; he had indeed attended Violet, only to find that he'd been called too late. He confirmed there appeared to be no foul play, that she'd undoubtedly died of infection, either from herself or those, if any, who'd attended her. He furnished me with a letter for Mr Fuller, Raphael, I'm afraid in the absence of friends, she lies in an unmarked pauper's grave. I'm truly sorry.'

'Without wishing to sound unchristian, I'm afraid I'm much of the view that she chose her own fate, Christopher, whereas this young chap...'

'Ah, yes, well that was a simple, tawdry transaction in Southsea, to save his soul from misery and an early meeting with his Maker, judging from the five year old I left behind, whose eyes still haunt me.

'Anyhow,' he said raising his glass and waving it in Anna's direction, 'I'm delighted to see him safely in his father's arms for Violet, as you know, was a third cousin of mine and therefore, however distantly, this young chap is a cousin of ours also.' He raised his refill, 'To your health, young Philip De Vine.'

Anna handed to Raphael and Theo a glass each, and even took a small toast in fortification herself.

Chapter Thirty Six

'That night, as I often did at the age of two, I crept into my mother's bed and slept the night in her arms. I remember awaking to her humming to Pip, as she kissed me on the head and gently rocked his cradle with her free arm. I propped myself up, I think content, that I was not to be usurped and looked down at Pip. Lisping in accompaniment to my dear mother, I joined in a tune she'd always sung, as she'd rocked me.

That morning, we all attended church, as our village priest might have expected but what Mr Fuller hadn't foreseen, was the materialisation of young Pip. As we all filed out in turn to shake hands and depart, the new priest bent and whispered most intently to Raphael. He then beckoned to Anna and took her into their private conversation.

Quite rightly, for a man in charge of all our immortal souls, upon hearing the details of the case, he was painfully concerned that young Pip, at the age of six months, had not yet been (so far as we could presume) baptised into the church. Almost as in fear that Pip should die that very day, he beseeched us to return at two o'clock.

The ceremony was, it has to be said, very respectably attended for such short notice, with many a Gables and Millie and half a dozen other well-wishers besides. Theo, Millie and Retty were all, for the first time in their lives, appointed as proud and respected godparents.

As one and all began to drift away, Mr Fuller led Anna and Raphael into his vestry. Quite what was said, we simply don't know, but the blush on Anna's cheek was still evident when they emerged.

Anna began falteringly, 'He says, that the way that we look on each other, would indicate that we're not merely friends.'

A ripple of laughter waved around the pillars of the church, while Emmaline and Abraham just pursed their lips and smiled.

'In short,' Raphael took Anna's hand, 'in order to protect, what I believe, Ma Gables, you recently referred to as the, 'moral fabric of the village'...' he looked to Anna to continue.

'We are to be married on Saturday next.'

A cheer went up and with a feeling that all was set right in the world, the assembled company congratulated the pair with hugs and proud slaps and, Samuel and Abraham noticed in mild, mutual disapproval, some handkerchief business.

Anna and Raphael's wedding was one that was talked of in Heartbourne, until the facts gave way to much legend and fable. The fact that the whole village was invited and indeed turned up, was much to the bride and groom's honour and delight.   The fact that every scrap of bunting the village possessed festooned Anna's garden, was also true. That the guests were so numerous, the harvest supper tables and benches had to be fetched and the field between the Gables and the De Vines used as an impromptu extension to their breakfast party, was a testament to the regard in which the village held these two dear souls of their number. That the bones of the spit roast pigs, provided by Abraham, fell into the flames bare, and the fiddlers played and the villagers danced, until the evening braziers burned low, was a memory that Anna and Raphael held dear in their hearts, all their lives.

The notion that Rob Pickens had risen from the table, taken a great mallet and beaten the first blow to knock down the wall between the two cottages and that such was his industry, that the job was finished by supper time, was maybe a little fantastical. So too, perhaps, was the Heartbourne belief, that from that day forward, if a bride of the village found herself still barren, if she could but catch hold of Christopher Coates' black cloak, her crib would be filled within a twelve month. Unless, of course, it's true what they say, about belief being the true father of prophecy.

Anna felt herself to be blessed, as she laid young Pip into his crib that night. When the new priest had taken them into the vestry, she'd agreed, there was no other sensible way forward for Pip's sake, than for their two households to become one.

She imagined Will as a truly divine angel, who wouldn't mind, under the circumstances. In short, she'd learnt to love with compassion both for herself and others, not with fear. She was a little surprised, when she entered her wedding bed that night and then really rather delighted. It was unexpected, but as they were now man and wife, what could she do? So she prayed and continued to love what the Lord had sent her, without worrying.'

'You see, I was right,' said Freddie sitting up straight, 'we do live in a house with two front doors.'

'Yes, Freddie, that's exactly what I'm saying, nothing more at all.'

'Oh, I think we all know,' said the current priest, also named Thomas, 'that's not true.'

'So, Father?' asked Susannah, very softly.

Thomas looked at Elizabeth in question, 'Well, do we agree with your mother?'

Elizabeth smiled and nodded, 'Would we ever dare do anything else?'

'Why, I don't know what you mean, I'm sure!' said Elise, shaking her head.

'Then, Susannah, you may consider yourself engaged to be married, to young Joseph Adam.'

Susannah threw her arms about her father as her mother smiled and her grandmother sighed in approval.

All wrapped up once more, against the winter chill, Elise stepped out into the snow. Instead of minding, however, she relished each crunch as she trod her way over to the opposite side of the lane. She turned and faced the Camellia Cottage of her childhood. Her eyes roved over the beautiful carving above the two front doors. She smiled, as the snow began to collect in the folds of her cloak.

At length, she spoke as if to the heavens, 'And so, my dear Archie, you'll be pleased to hear; the dance begins again.'

With that, she leant her weight upon her stick, clicked her heels twice sharply and chuckling, stepped her way forward, home.

4605370R00128

Printed in Great Britain
by Amazon.co.uk, Ltd.,
Marston Gate.